THE LANGUAGE
OF BODIES

THE
LANGUAGE
OF
BODIES

SUZANNE DEWITT HALL

Woodhall Press
Norwalk, CT

woodhall press

Woodhall Press, 81 Old Saugatuck Road, Norwalk, CT 06855
WoodhallPress.com

Cover design: Jessica Dionne Wright
Layout artist: Amie McCracken

Library of Congress Cataloging-in-Publication Data available

ISBN 978-1-954907-46-1 (paper: alk paper)
ISBN 978-1-954907-47-8 (electronic)

First Edition
Distributed by Independent Publishers Group
(800) 888-4741

Printed in the United States of America

PROLOGUE

I liked wearing sunglasses. Behind them, I could hide.

They needed to be dark though, the darker the better, so when people looked at me it was as if I didn't have eyes at all, just black holes where the vision used to be.

Sunglasses were useful in making people believe I was blind. They were part of the costume. I could convince them even without the specs, but it was tiring to hold my eyes in a way which projected blankness. It's hard not registering emotion as images are carried through from retina to brain. Shades made all that effort unnecessary. It also saved time. When visitors to the museum saw me sitting behind the counter with dark glasses on, they understood more quickly what I wanted them to think. I didn't have to say anything, just had to hold my shoulders a certain way, tip my head as if listening carefully, and they got it.

They came to the place for all sorts of reasons. It was positioned on a deserted stretch of highway, so some stopped hoping to find a bathroom. Others were exploring Route 66 and the roadside oddity was one destination among many. Only a few were aficionados who came to the Wild West Wax Museum to study the stories of outlaws who miraculously outwitted death. Some just hoped to touch their guns.

I welcomed them all from my position behind the ticket desk. Sometimes I was the real me, my pale eyes naked and available to meet their gaze. Other times I wore the glasses and played the role of blind woman, the better to assess them as they walked around the gift shop, picking up snow globes, and asking how far it was to Uranus, MO. I decided which way to play it as I watched them get out of their cars and approach the door, choosing by how they walked and interacted with each other.

Sometimes I wished I really *was* sightless, as sightless as the dead, a soul with no eyes to see my own face, or the faces of parents jerking the arms of their kids, or the faces of the good ole boys who came in to scan me up and down. I could feel their assessment from behind my black lenses: their eyes running across the front of my shirt and then up to the furrows around my mouth. They didn't know what to make of me. Sometimes they shrugged their shoulders as if their confusion was so deep it had to be released physically.

I felt sorry for the women who came in with those avaricious men; sorry they didn't want more for themselves than what the guys offered. Some of the women watched it happening. They knew what the men were doing, but just rolled their eyes and turned away. A few nudged them, or pulled them toward one of the shelves. Most didn't. I wished the women would walk out without them and drive off in their cars and pickup trucks, leaving a rising cloud of dust as they sped away. If they did, the dudes would be left behind with me, and as hungry as I was for vengeance, I might have killed them.

But they weren't the man I wanted to destroy. So I bided my time, watching them from the superiority of my disguise, and plotting my revenge.

TRANSCRIPT

Tape-recorded Interview

Christopher David Jackson/Detective Andrew Young and Detective Richard Davis

Davis: This is detective Richard Davis with the Peytonsville Missouri Police Department. The time is 9:54 A.M. This will be a taped conversation with last name Jackson, first name Christopher, middle name David. Date of birth February 14, 1971. Christopher, I've turned on a tape recorder so I can record our conversation.

Jackson: Okay.

Davis: Detective Young and I advised you of your rights when we talked earlier today, is that correct?

Jackson: That's correct.

Davis: Are you employed?

Jackson: Yes.

Davis: Place of employment?

Jackson: I work out at Fisher's Lime and Quarry. I'm a production scheduler. Or I used to be. Not sure if they'll take me back after this.

Young: Do you know why you're here, Christopher?

Jackson: Yes.

Davis: Why are you here?

Jackson: Because I killed her.

Young: Who'd you kill?

Jackson: That tranny newscaster.

Davis: Do you know her name?

Jackson: Mitchell. Charlotte Mitchell.

Chapter 1

Everyone told me not to do anything drastic for a year. I wasn't supposed to sell our house, though I wanted to run away every single day, or quit my job though I could barely get out of bed in the morning. I wasn't supposed to shave my head and mortify my flesh though I wanted my exterior to match the ugliness of my interior. Big decisions were to be avoided because people in mourning apparently experience logic paralysis for a year, after which some miracle of chronology permits them to make wise choices again. Intellectually, I recognized it made sense. Not only was I worn out from simply continuing to live, I was encased in a grief-induced cocoon of stupidity.

I let phone calls go to voicemail. Mail piled up on the kitchen table. The grass grew so long I'm surprised the neighbors didn't report it to the village powers-that-be. Eventually someone started cutting it for me. I never saw who did it, never bothered turning toward the mower's rumble or the green scent wafting through windows I'd left open for weeks, barely noticing the change of temperature as the months marched from that horrible November to spring.

I wasn't capable of rational thinking, but not in the ways the holders of traditional wisdom assumed. I would have sold my house, shaved my head, and gotten a "GUILTY" tattoo on my forehead if I'd been able to function well enough to do any of them.

But I wasn't functioning.

Eventually the mail started sliding off the table. The paper avalanche compelled me to start sorting it, throwing circulars and junk mail into the recycle bin, and setting important-looking or personal stuff to the side. I debated about throwing the huge stack of condolence cards away, but didn't. It wasn't the senders' fault I couldn't handle it, and eventually I might be able to manage going through them. Normal people would send thank-you notes in response. It was my responsibility to pretend normalcy. Eventually.

I hadn't been sorting very long when a business-sized envelope from our insurance agent caught my attention. It didn't look like a bill, and it was addressed to me rather than Char, who'd taken care of stuff like insurance and utility payments. The letter inside explained that the agent had been trying to reach me to find out how I wanted Char's life insurance distribution handled. It was the kind of thing that triggered a mental spiral into darkness, and I sat spinning for a few minutes, but decided to call the damned office and get the conversation over with. I needed the money. Funerals are expensive, and my leave of absence hit our savings hard.

I punched in the number on the letterhead. A young male voice answered. "Is Manny available?" I asked.

"He is! Hold on for just a minute and I'll connect you." I was surprised he hadn't asked for my name. Surprised, and relieved. The phone clicked into canned music but I didn't have to listen long.

"This is Manny Ocampo."

"Hey, Manny, it's Maddie Wells."

"Maddie! How are you doing?"

"I'm okay." I didn't bother to drag out my response. I'd learned that the shorter my answers, the fewer questions they asked. I heard his hesitation, and could tell he was trying to figure out whether to probe. Finally, he spoke again.

"Good, good. I guess that's all that can be expected."

"Yes."

"I'm glad you called. It took a while to get the proper processes followed for your distribution, given…" Manny paused, his discomfort traveling through the phone's tiny speaker. "…the circumstances of Charlotte's death. But we're all set now and the bureaucrats are happy!" He followed the statement with an uncomfortable chuckle, then cleared his throat. He was a super nice guy, and I felt sorry he had to have this conversation with someone who was doing so little to help it along. "So now that's all cleared up, I just need your instructions about how you want Charlotte's benefit distributed to you."

"Isn't that usually done with a check?"

"It often is, yes, but with such a large amount, we like to give people the option of depositing the funds electronically. If you prefer a check, you can of course come pick one up. But it's not something we'd want to send through the mail, as you can imagine."

It was hard to remember the last time Shimmy and I talked about life insurance. Maybe five years ago? Back then we'd agreed on $100,000 each, figuring it would be enough to cover funeral expenses plus a little extra so we wouldn't have to worry about finances while grieving. But it had been hard to pay real attention; the idea of death had been so far-fetched.

"I guess a hundred grand *is* a lot to send through the mail," I said.

"A hundred grand? Maddie, do you know how much Charlotte was insured for?"

Obviously, it wasn't for $100,000 as we'd discussed. "Apparently not." I hadn't thought about the insurance money actively, but knowing it was coming had allowed me to ignore the financial impact of being on grief leave. My stomach clenched. "Just tell me what we're looking at."

"Well I think you'll be pleasantly surprised." He stated a staggering sum, and my brain checked out for a moment while it processed what he'd said. "Maddie?" he asked.

I forced myself to respond. "That can't be right."

"Oh, it is. I remember when she came in to talk to me about it," he said.

I could run away forever with that kind of money. Go to Nepal. Morocco. Kazakhstan. Somewhere I didn't know the language and life was alien for a reason unrelated to Char.

"She hoped you'd never get it, but I'm wondering if she had the second sight or something."

"What do you mean?" Madagascar. South Korea.

"It's like she must have known. She came in and talked about the mortality rate for trans women of color."

"That's why she insured herself for so much?" My throat closed at the thought of Char wanting to take care of me so abundantly.

"Apparently. I mentioned some of this stuff in my voicemail messages. I take it you haven't listened to them?"

"No. I've been... busy."

"Charlotte thought if something happened to her, you could use the money coupled with her name to try to make a difference for other trans people."

My dreams of escape halted.

"You still there?"

"Yes." My voice sounded tight, which wasn't surprising, given that my whole body was rigid.

"Like a foundation or something. That's what she was hoping when she increased her coverage."

"Why didn't she ever tell *me* that?" I asked.

"I have no idea."

"No one else knows, right?"

"I would never disclose that kind of information."

"Good. I don't want word getting around." I had visions of people hounding me about places the money should go, and I wasn't ready to deal with any of it.

"I understand. Do you still want a check?"

"No, I guess not. You'd better transfer the funds."

"That works. I'll just need your banking information."

"I'll have to get back to you with all that. I'll call tomorrow."

"That's fine. I hope the money will end up helping you, Maddie. I know Charlotte thought it could make a difference."

I said goodbye and got off the phone as quickly as I could. It felt like a punch in the face. I hated paperwork and avoided charity events like the plague. Being stuffed into a space with so many people was overwhelming. I saw right through the phony sucking up of vultures who wanted to see what they could get out of Char. When I was forced to go to one, I'd pull her away from the carnivores into a circle of real friends as fast as possible. It annoyed her when I did it, because she thought she didn't need protection.

If I created a charity like she wanted, *I'd* be the target of all that avarice. There was no way I could set up a foundation right now. She should have understood that. Instead of helping me run somewhere foreign and disconnected from my pain, she wanted me to connect deeper.

The next day I got Manny details for the funds transfer, and decided to pretend the money wasn't there. But someone from the bank called and said it was too much to keep in an account connected to my debit card. She lectured me about being fiscally responsible and pressured me into talking to an investment specialist. Money turned out to be hard to ignore. I had a massive responsibility I never wanted to take on, as if Char had left a baby in a basket on the doorstep which I was supposed to care for, direct, and grow without her help.

I didn't like it.

I didn't like it one little bit.

Chapter 2

Char loved diners, and that made me love them too. Our favorite was a shining metal dining car in Ipswich, populated with codgers whose wives had died or who preferred the diner's pie to theirs. The pie alone was worth the trip; we sometimes drove down after supper to split a piece.

I headed to the place a few nights later, when the house felt more than usually empty and my stomach couldn't stop grumbling about meatloaf and coconut cream. It had been a long time since I'd eaten in a restaurant. Hopefully something there would be comforting. Maybe while watching people and listening in on their chats the way I had with Char, I'd re-experience the delight in her eyes, and feel the burst of warmth in my chest which erupted every time I saw that light. It was risky though. The whole thing might be torture without her; a reminder of what no longer was and never would be again. Most days I wouldn't take the risk, but on that day it felt worth it.

The weather was a vile mix of rain and sleet, so I rushed through the door and pulled back the wet fabric of my hood as the combination of scents hit, coffee, garlic, and cinnamon intermixing in a way that was weirdly appetizing. The counter was full, but we preferred the red vinyl booths anyway. Nothing had changed since the last time we were there. It all felt familiar and comfortable, which triggered guilt. I pushed the guilt down and picked up a laminated menu. Weekly specials were attached to the front on a small rectangle of paper.

"I'm Lee, and I'll be serving you tonight," a voice said, pulling me away from the menu. The waitress was tall and willowy, with a long, copper ponytail. She smiled at me, and her green eyes were friendly. "Can I get you something to drink? Something to warm you up, maybe?"

"Black coffee would be great." I smiled back, not remembering the woman from previous visits. "I really want it for my pie, but could use some now."

"Coffee it is, and I'll bring a fresh cup when dessert comes."

"Sounds like a plan."

"Be right back with it." She smiled again and turned away.

I reviewed menu options even though I knew what I was having. Lee came right back and placed a steaming mug and water glass in front of me. "How's the meatloaf tonight?" I asked. It was always the same, always fantastic, but I wanted to hear her voice again.

"The boys seem to like it!" she gestured at the line of elderly men sitting on the revolving stools at the counter. "Haven't heard a single complaint, and trust me, I'd hear it if they had one." Lee grinned.

"I'll bet you would." I took a final look at the menu. "I guess I'll go with that, then." She held her hand out to take it, and I complied, wishing she'd leave it behind for use as cover and distraction in case it was needed.

"Do you want it as listed?" She leaned closer and dropped her volume. "I'd swap broccoli for the green beans. Unless you like them camo-colored."

In my view, over-cooked green beans were a necessary part of the diner experience, but I took her advice for the sake of my colon's health. "Sounds like wisdom. Let's do that."

"You've got it! It will only take a minute."

"Thanks, Lee." There was in no rush. Returning to the diner had been easier than I expected, and I was content to hang out for a while. Crooked streams of water drizzled down the window, blurring my view of the packed parking lot. I let my mind rest, listening to silverware clinking against heavy stoneware plates, and the voices of people mixing together in all their separate conversations. The combination of warmth, streaming water, and chatting was soporific. I blinked myself awake when Lee returned with my food.

"Here you go." She must have seen my sleepiness. "Warm in here, isn't it?" She set the heaped plate in front of me, and plopped down a small bowl of brown gravy. "I didn't ask if you wanted any, but most people like it with the mashed potatoes. And it doesn't come automatically."

"That's great." Normally I liked the contrast of creamy, buttery potatoes with the acidic sweetness of the meatloaf's tomatoey glaze. But there was something about this girl that made me want her to feel helpful.

"Need anything else?"

The plate looked complete, and my stomach grumbled. "I'm good. Thanks!"

"You're welcome. I'll check back in a few minutes to see how you're doing."

The coffee was strong and delicious, just as I'd remembered it. The meatloaf was full of flavor, and the broccoli was green and resisted my fork, just as she'd reported. I should have stuck with the green beans.

I returned to listening, but this time allowed the sound to separate into different conversations, zooming in and back out again if they weren't interesting. Char would have loved being there, elegantly eating her fried clams and chowder. She had a metabolism like a furnace and never had to worry about calories. I was glad for her, particularly in the business she was in, but sometimes it was irritating. On me, extra calories settled right at my stomach, making me look like a pregnant middle-schooler. She would have eavesdropped too, and she was better at it. She'd catch a few phrases and then fill me in, telling me which group to listen to.

I ate, and listened, and tried not to feel guilty for enjoying it without her. And then I heard her name: "Charlotte Mitchell." The voice was male. It came from the counter of old men.

I looked up and tuned in, checking out the body language of the geezers assembled there. One guy was leaning toward the man next to him. The short salt-and-pepper whiskers on his cheeks looked scratchy beneath his worn cap.

"Isn't that her?" he asked. His companion glanced over his shoulder toward me, then turned back with a nod, not caring that I was watching.

"Ayuh. Looks like her. She's just a scrap of a thing, isn't she?" They were both surprisingly loud. A woman I worked with complained about how hard-of-hearing her husband had gotten. She said they arrived at church late one Sunday, and everything was quiet when he suddenly farted behind her as they walked in. People in the pews turned to look at her with giggles or glares, and she was mortified. Meanwhile, he didn't realize it was audible. These guys must be like that. Losing their judgment along with their hearing.

"Can't say I understand anything about those transvestites." The first guy was speaking again. "Not sure what the good Lord almighty makes of them."

Char used to say trans people proved the male and femaleness of God. If there *was* an infinite being keeping watch over the universe, they had to adore her, because being with Char was the closest thing to divinity I'd ever experienced.

The guy was still talking. "Even so, that Mitchell was good at what he did. Made the news interesting."

The tips of my ears started to burn.

"Sure had the right voice for it."

"Body too, though I don't like to admit it." The two men chortled. If they said another word about Char's body I would go over there and slam their heads together.

"I know what you mean, and I won't tell anybody you said it."

"But here's what I don't get." His voice dropped slightly, and he leaned even closer, like he didn't want to be overheard. But he was plenty loud enough that I could make out his words. "Why didn't the wife go with him?"

Her, I thought.

"Good question."

"If your wife, husband, whatever the hell they called each other, was winning some big award, wouldn't you want to be there?" I swear my heart stopped beating when he said it. "Jan always came to my awards, back when I was police chief. That's what you do when you love someone. Am I right?"

"'Course you're right."

I no longer wanted to listen, no longer wanted the food which was turning to stone in my gut. I dug in my pocket and pulled out a twenty, then grabbed my coat and slid out of the booth. I threw the bill on the table just as Lee approached, her face transforming into concern.

"Is everything okay?" She looked at my nearly full plate, then back up at my face. "No pie after all?"

"No. No pie. Thanks." I didn't want to be rude but had to get out of there. I pushed past her, hurrying to get out the door before I started screaming. "Sorry."

"Have… have a nice evening," she called after me, her voice faltering at the end as if realizing my evening wasn't going to be very nice.

I ran through the drizzle and climbed in my car.

That's what you do when you love someone.

The words echoed in my brain, not that it was anything new, it was just in a different voice, a man's voice, rather than my own. Now there were two voices accusing me in the same words, in different words, in a thousand words.

If I'd really loved her, I would have gone with her. If I'd really loved her, I would have saved her.

I hadn't gone with Char, hadn't saved her, and couldn't save her now. It was too late.

But I was starting to realize I had to do *something*, and it needed to be a hell of a lot more drastic than starting a charity.

Chapter 3

The old men who'd talked about Char in the diner uncovered a pool of rage I hadn't realized existed, and it wasn't just directed at Christopher Jackson. I was mad that Char put me in the position to have to deal with all that money without being able to spend it stupidly, and that I now had to honor what was essentially a death wish. Mad that she put herself in the spotlight so she became a target. Mad that she never got in touch while she was away so I could know whether or not she forgave me. Mad that she'd pressured me so hard to go on the trip with her, because I desperately wished I'd gone.

There were a million reasons to be mad, and the anger felt good. Guilt made me feel like the air was filled with iron particles and Earth's gravity had been amped up a notch. Being mad distracted me from the guilt the men in the diner refueled, and made me feel lighter.

I stewed in the fury for a day or two, watching it, encouraging it, and finding ways to feed it. There was plenty of fuel. Shimmy was everywhere; her spirit saturated each piece of furniture we'd picked out together and the books still sitting on her bedside table. I'd glance at a title and remember what she'd said about it as she read before turning out the light. She didn't realize it, but she made faces while reading and I sometimes watched her, following what was happening just by the way she cocked an eyebrow or curled her lips. Ordinary items she'd picked up and sat back down again were now imbued with invisible magic, and those objects were everywhere.

The house was also filled with religious objects, and one day I'd had enough. Crucifixes graced the walls of all the rooms, and if you've never experienced Christ on the cross hovering over you while you sit on the toilet, you're missing out. A rosary hung from the lamp on Shimmy's bedside table. A long-handled rawhide rattle rested on the top of her dresser, with the sacred bundle lying behind it. Their surfaces bore a coat of dust, and when I picked up the rattle in my rage, the dark outline of a balloon-headed snake was left behind. I broke its long handle over my knee, then slammed the round head against the floor hoping it would fly off. It didn't, so I stomped on it until it flattened with a crunch. I picked up the bundle next, ready to rip it open and tear everything to bits, but then I remembered how she created it when her grandmother died.

Char worked at the kitchen table where we drank coffee in the morning, and where the mail had grown into a tower of Babel after she died. Char adored her grandmother, and referred to her using the Potawatomi term "Nokmes." Once I got to know her, I also called her Nokmes; my grandmother. She'd brought a few things from Nokmes' house right after her grandmother's death; things which seemed odd at the time, though I didn't question her because Char's grief was so profound.

"Do you need help?" I asked.

"No," she said. "This is something I need to do myself."

"Okay." I stayed close by while she worked, feeling Shimmy's grief and something beneath it, something deep and stony. Char unfolded the flannel nightgown which had been Nokmes' favorite. She picked up a pair of scissors and cut a large rectangle from the fabric, then neatly folded the remainder. Next, she took a piece of birch bark and wrote Nokmes' name on it using a Sharpie. She placed it in the center of the square of flowered flannel. Char's beautiful hands moved again and I saw her pick up something long, soft, and glimmering in the light.

"What's that?" I asked.

"It's a lock of her hair."

I thought back to when we'd been with her, after her death, and didn't remember Char's mom giving it to her.

"When did you get it?"

"During the viewing. At the end of the first night, while everyone was leaving."

The casket had been open during the viewing hours and the funeral, and Nokmes' hair was loose and flowing around her shoulders. I'd been in charge of seeing people out, because Char and her mother were lost in their grieving. She must have done it then.

"You took scissors with you?"

"Yes. I knew I had to make a sacred bundle." Char explained that bundles were kept by Potawatomi clans to collect their hallowed stories, and wanted to make one for the story of her grandmother. "It isn't how the people would do it, but it's how I am doing it." She pulled the silky lock of hair through her palm a final time, and laid it on top of the birch bark on the fabric. She added her grandmother's rosary to the pile, then rolled up the flannel, tucking in the ends like a burrito.

"Is that it?"

"For now." She picked up an old ribbon. "Nokmes had this tucked in her Bible. She told me she was wearing it in her braid when she graduated from the residential school. If it were me, I would have burned it, given the horrors that occurred at so many of them. But she kept it, so I'm keeping it." Shimmy's connection to Catholicism and Potawatomi spirituality was a complex dynamic, but it reflected the essential bothness of her being. She was masculine and feminine; public and private; smart and sensitive; African American and Native American.

Char tied the bundle up with the ribbon, then set it down on the table and rested her hands on it. She was quiet, and I assumed she was praying. After a few moments, she nodded her head, picked the bundle up, and took it to our bedroom. It had been on the center of her dresser ever since.

The rattle was still on the floor, squashed and broken. I obviously couldn't destroy the bundle, instead, I tore around the house, pulling crucifixes off the small nails I'd hammered in where Char directed. I threw them all in the trash, along with the gilded icons she'd positioned on her desk. My anger pumped and my feet pounded through the house, as if daring Char's ancestors or saints to try and stop me.

The last thing I did was yank open the drawer I called her voodoo cupboard, with its collection of blessed salt, holy water vials, and smudge sticks. The Catholic crap went straight into a garbage bag. I grabbed the sage clusters and tore them into pieces, throwing handfuls of the herb at the mirror in which Char used to gaze as she decided whether a pair of earrings went with her outfit. I screamed with rage because she wasn't reflected beside me. I yelled that her faith was stupid and hadn't saved her. I threw the sage, and it rained down on the sacred bundle like a shower of tears.

Like fistfuls of dirt falling on a casket.

My rage was lessened, but not spent. It needed a new target.

Chapter 4

It took a while to get back into the groove at work, which shouldn't have been surprising given I'd been gone for a year. By the end of my first month in the small museum near home, however, the routine of identifying new acquisitions, cross-referencing various collections, and doing restoration tasks like cleaning and sewing offered a guilty sense of normalcy. I'd returned to work at the end of November, and the annual holiday party was coming up. I'd probably drown in all the forced Christmas cheer, but figured it was best to make an appearance, which meant I needed to find a gag gift.

Good Goods was tucked between a florist and a dog groomer on one of the cozy side streets splitting off from Merrivliet's main drag. Char and I passed the shop frequently on walks around our beloved town, giggling over the store's name and pronouncing it with exaggerated British accents. The display windows were filled with a mishmash of furniture, Christmas decorations, and knick-knacks.

I wished we'd stopped in together while she was alive. My days were interwoven with thoughts about all the things we should have done.

Things I should have done.

Things I shouldn't have done.

Things which still needed to be done.

A bell on the door jingled when I entered, and a large ginger cat raised its head to blink at me from where it lay in a puddle of late afternoon sun streaming in from the front window. It burbled a greeting as I stomped snow from my feet, then laid its head back down and closed its eyes.

"Buonasera!" a woman's voice said from the back of the shop. "What a lovely thing to have a visitor so close to when I am closing."

I peered into the dimness trying to make out who was speaking. "Am I too late?" I asked. "I can come back another time."

"No, no! Do not be silly. I was saying what a pleasure it is to see you. Come in. Tell me who you are."

What an odd way to greet a customer, I thought as I walked toward her. The place smelled like dust, church incense, and cleaning products. She was old and well-padded, planted on a tall stool behind a glass display case. On the counter was a heap of lacy linens; primarily handkerchiefs from the mid-20th century.

"I am sorting to see what should be done with these. Some women like to collect the old hankies, especially if they are fancy with flowers and lace crotcheted in." I puzzled for a moment about what "crotcheted" might mean and decided she must have meant crocheted. I was about to tell her I was a textile and costume conservator, but she spoke again before I could answer. "I think it is because of this verde movement. People are trying to not be making so many things to throw away. But handkerchiefs seem to be silly economies. Throw away the tissues filled with all your nose contents, and stop buying so many new clothes and electric things you stare at until your eyes fall out of your head." She looked up again from her sorting. "Don't you think so?" My mind was still a blur from trying to follow what she'd said, so I gave it a little shake. "What is your name, pretty lady?" she asked.

"It's Maddie."

"Maddie?" she asked. "How does a girl get called such a thing? You do not look like an angry person."

"It's a nickname," I said. "It's short for Madelaine."

"Ah! Now *that* is a name! It comes from Magdala, and means something like 'high tower.' This is a good omen for your life. You could be like the Lady Magdalene, who loved Gesù so magnificamente."

I thought about that for a moment, wondering what Mary Magdalene's life had been like after the death of the one she loved so much, and wishing

Shimmy would appear to me as Jesus had after *he'd* been brutalized by hate. If Mary hadn't seen him, maybe she would have been consumed by a hunger for revenge, like I was. The woman was still staring at me.

"She was given much opportunity, and much trial." She peered intently over the top of her small glasses. When I didn't respond, she tipped her gray curls to the side and continued. "I think you have had much trial as well. Some faces cannot hide it." I ducked my head. The strange woman was kind, but it felt like if she looked at me too closely, she'd see all the way in, and I wasn't prepared for that kind of nakedness. "Wait!" she said, startling me into looking back up. "I just realized who you are. I saw you last year, when it happened. On the television."

I don't want to talk about it.

"You are the wife of the one who was murdered," she continued. "The beautiful one, the caster of news. I am so very sorry. Your pain must be terrible." I nodded, hoping that might be enough. "Of course, this explains your face." She shook her head, her expression dolorous, the wrinkles beneath her eyes deepening as her dark brows drew together. My throat tightened. "Humanity can be so very inumano. I sometimes do not know what Dio was thinking when he made us all. We blame it on that snake in the garden, but I cannot help but blame God too. You did not deserve this, and of course your bella Charlotte did not either."

I wondered if she knew Shimmy was trans. Would an elderly Italian woman be so kind if she knew?

"Of course, people are also good. We are a bag of mixes, humanity. *You* are good, I can tell this."

Obviously, her powers of observation were flawed, so I didn't need to worry about her gazing into my eyes. She interpreted my expression of disbelief properly, however.

"You *are* good, Madelaina! It is as obvious as your nose. In some people you can see the goodness shining. You are one of those."

"If you say so," I said, trying to shrug the conversation elsewhere.

After a long gaze while I looked everywhere other than at her, she took pity on me. "So, what is it you are needing to come here? Why have you blessed me on this night, when I was feeling like a lonely old vecchia who is not useful for anything?"

"I'm looking for a gag gift." It was a relief to talk about something else. "We always do a Yankee swap at the office holiday party, and I thought I might find something here." I paused for a moment. "But what should I call you? Mrs….?"

"My name is Maria, and so you may call me Maria."

"It is a pleasure to meet you," I said.

She leaned toward me and bowed her head, gracefully sweeping her arms out as if she was curtseying despite being perched on the stool. "The pleasure is mine. Now. Do you have something in mind for this gagging gift?" Maria placed her age-spotted hands on the counter, bracing herself as she shifted to plant one foot safely on the ground. "We have many fine things, as you can see. And all at such wonderful prices." She pulled her plump behind the rest of the way off the stool and worked her way around the counter to meet me. She walked with an odd rolling gait, as if one leg was shorter than the other. I turned with her to look around the shop's strange collection of wares. The cat stood up sleepily and began to stretch. "Have you met Mr. Clyde yet?" Maria asked.

"Sort of, on my way in. He's a handsome fellow."

"Si, and he knows it. 'Pride cometh before a fall,' even for a gatto, signore," she said. The cat extended a paw toward her, as if wanting to make a truce.

I walked around to see what might work for the party, and Maria examined objects with me. We considered a velvet clown painting and a chipped duck decoy which had been turned into a planter. Nothing seemed quite right. I wandered toward a wall of bookshelves.

"Maybe a book?" I said.

"There is something for everyone in books. You look. I will sit. My hip is barking." Maria wobbled her way back to her seat behind the counter, and resumed poking through the pile of linens. She started humming, but I didn't recognize the tune.

The shelves contained old best sellers intermixed with crumbling volumes of classics. I wondered if there were any books on revenge, but didn't see anything. One section was filled with cookbooks. My co-workers included a number of foodies, so I browsed the titles, looking for something funny. I found a yellowing paperback with a picture of a guy holding a baguette on the cover, surrounded by curvaceous bathing beauties. It was ridiculous and perfect; we could voice our outrage about the sexist claptrap the world couldn't seem to leave behind.

I placed the relic on a nearby table, and thumbed through some of the other old cookbooks. Hand-written recipe cards and newspaper clips were tucked into several. One had comments scribbled in the margins about how much the owner had liked a particular recipe. I'm not sure how long I stood there with Maria's humming as background music. But I wasn't really thinking for a change; lulled by the charm of old illustrations and the simple comfort of food preparation spelled out across the pages.

I took several tomes back with me to the counter. Maria had completed her sorting and was scanning a list of numbers in a ledger. "You are finished? I think you were having a fine time, in the books."

"I was, actually."

"You are taking all these, then? Did you find one for your Yankee switch?"

"Yes. And a few for myself."

"Good! I can see that they were terapeutico." She pulled out a bag and slid my small collection into it. "That will be $5.00."

"That's all?"

"Si! I told you I have wonderful prices. Were you thinking I was a liar?" Her chin lifted but her eyes twinkled behind the thick lenses.

"Of course not," I said, but I decided to tease her back. "I don't know you well enough to come to that kind of conclusion." I handed her the money, and she laughed out loud.

"She is a quick one, Mr. Clyde! And feisty. We will be glad now to have Madelaina as our friend."

I smiled and took my bag. "Thank you for your help. It was a real pleasure meeting you," I said.

"You will visit us again? Soon? Next time, I will have cookies for you. Amaretti, I think."

"I'd love to. But how will you know I'm coming?"

"Oh, I will know. I always know. I felt you coming tonight, but thought you would be someone else. Good night, little one."

I left the store, puzzling at her oddness, but somehow believing she would, in fact, know. I went home and spent the rest of the evening with a glass of wine and the cookbooks. It was the first night of peace I'd experienced since Char's death.

In the weeks which followed, I went a little crazy and bought a *lot* of cookbooks. Volumes from the sixties and seventies were my favorite. Pictures of happy families gathering to taste a gelatin wiener mold or chili and corn chip casserole were relentlessly cheerful, but in a good way. I tried making a few recipes, and took a few dishes in to share with my co-workers at Preservation New England.

On bad nights I'd read through several books. Char had been gone a little over a year, and life had become a closed space in which I huddled, tight and hiding, like a wounded animal waiting to die. It may sound odd, but I think the cookbooks saved me. They brought me just enough comfort to survive so I could carry out the plan which was slowly gestating.

Chapter 5

Beams from the streetlight shone through the bedroom window so I could see the gleaming smoothness of her calf, an impossibly bright sheen of light glowing against the darkness of her flesh, sleekness I could never achieve on my own legs, no matter how much I slathered them with lotion or oil.

Char didn't care. She said she loved my bumps and the scars I'd accumulated from all my years of stumbling and bumbling with razors.

My hand glowed white against that impossibly dark smoothness as it slid up from ankle to knee, lifting her calf to meet my lips. Her scent reached my nostrils, then filled my chest, and I was suddenly starving; starved for her, starved to be one again. I didn't know which way to satisfy her, wasn't sure what she wanted, only knew the heat was rising hot and fast and that I needed to take action—for her or for me—and so I shifted to look at her face, feeling the pulsing between my legs increasing and demanding, needing to read her eyes, to ask what it was she wanted. I pulled back and looked at her face, sought her eyes, because the heat in my center had built to the point of raging, and knew it was about to boil over. I called out her name as my center convulsed. I called out her name as I sought her face, wanting to look in her eyes as I came.

But they weren't there. She lay there, suddenly still, with no eyes at all.

I tore myself awake, and sat up, the brightness from the streetlight enough to see that the bed was empty and I was alone, gasping and crying at the emptiness while my body finished its horrendous spasms. My stomach spasmed too, and I fought the urge to vomit. I wanted to go back to sleep, to return to the place and time before I'd looked up, when Shimmy was warm and whole and I was plotting how best to please her. When the light from the window shone on her, and her skin shone from within, and my hand glowed against her impossible smoothness. I wanted to go back to when that scene had been real.

But there was no going back, there was only the final spasming of my body which I tried to hate, but couldn't because it wasn't my flesh's fault. It had a language of its own which was disconnected from my bad decisions, and completely deaf to my brain's repetition that perpetual hunger was its new reality. It couldn't hear and didn't care and insisted on its own self-soothing even if I wouldn't cooperate.

It wasn't the first time I'd had the dream. I didn't want them to stop, not even the part where she became the dead Shimmy. I loved the first part, before I saw and knew. It was the only time I got to be with her again.

And I deserved the second part, where I was forced to remember.

Chapter 6

The bustle of Boston felt bizarre when I finally traveled to the main office. It was like being in a film where the world isn't quite as you expect and something strange and potentially horrifying lurks around the corner.

Preservation New England Headquarters looked the same as when I left. The people whose desks I scuttled past offered hellos coupled with small smiles, their furrowed brows indicating sympathy. I plunged through the sea of faces and waved palms, offering my own tight smile to each person who greeted me. By the time I reached my cubicle, I was exhausted, and plunged straight into paperwork.

The most recent newsletter from the American Association of Museums popped into my email mid-afternoon. I scrolled through it quickly to see if they had any articles on textiles. A crudely designed graphic screamed for attention in the job postings section. It read:

Help maintain history! Historic Route 66! Offers a great deal of independence. Free room and comfortable stipend. Management experience a must.
Wild West Wax Museum, Larimer, MO

Missouri. Reading the word in the ad destroyed the easy relaxation that working had created.

I mapped the wax museum's address and discovered it was only half an hour from the place Char was murdered. It was hard to think of the guy who did it as a human bearing a name rather than an evil monster that I wanted to destroy. But he did have a name: Christopher Jackson.

He had a name, and he had a home, and that home was a town called Peytonsville, MO. The map reported Peytonsville as just nine minutes away from the Wild West Wax Museum.

Jackson probably had family in the area. I knew he had a wife named Sarah. I wasn't sure if they had kids. Hopefully not, because with a father like that, they were fucked. I tipped back in my squeaky office chair and took a few sips of my coffee.

Sarah Jackson probably still lived there. Nine minutes away from the museum.

I leaned forward to my laptop again, and checked the distance from Peytonsville to Potosi Correctional Center, where the bastard was currently rotting. I hoped someone would murder him while he was incarcerated, but given that it was in rural Missouri, there was a good chance he'd been crowned prison hero. The institution was 51 minutes away from his hometown. 51 minutes for little wifey to drive to see him.

I sat, and thought, and sipped.

I wondered if the monster ever worried about her, living there in that small town.

He would be right to worry.

TRANSCRIPT

Davis: How did you meet Charlotte Mitchell?

Jackson: I heard she was going to be in St. Louis. The guys were talking about it at work. Said there was a big conference or some shit. Turns out it was tranny memorial day. Who knew?

Davis: It's called the Transgender Day of Remembrance.

Jackson: That's it. I decided to check it out. Figured it would be kind of like going to the circus. The whole schedule was on a website, if you can believe it. Didn't even try to hide what they were doing.

Young: Did you know Ms. Mitchell would be there?

Jackson: I didn't know she existed until those bozos were talking. Turned out she was some kind of headliner though. Do I call her she, or he?

Young: She.

Jackson: She. I thought so, but it's fucking confusing.

Young: You're doing fine.

Jackson: They had pictures of her on the website and everything. Thought it might be interesting to meet her.

Davis: Did you know you were going to kill her when you went?

Jackson: Of course not! I was just going to go check it out. See some freaks, go back home.

Young: Why'd the plan change?

Jackson: Well, that's a long story. Once I saw her, I just wanted to meet her. There was something about her. She was powerful, you know? Had that kind of energy you can't stop looking at. Like a magnetic force. Ever meet somebody like that?

Young: So, you went up to the conference. What day was that?

Jackson: Saturday. I went up Saturday morning. Told my wife I was going hunting, and drove up. Traffic was a bitch, even though it was a weekend. I don't know why anyone would want to live in the city.

Davis: Did you go straight to the hotel where the conference took place? The Downtown Sojourner?

Jackson: Yeah.

Davis: What did you do then?

Jackson: I just kind of hung out. Walked around. Listened to a few speakers.

Young: There was no record of you registering.

Jackson: Why would I register?

Young: According to the organizers, if you wanted to attend any of the events you needed a nametag. They had pretty tight security.

Jackson: I saw a cop in the lobby. Didn't realize that's why he was there.

Young: That's why.

Jackson: Guess their security wasn't all that tight because they never approached me. I looked around. Checked out the information tables. Stayed in the back of the room when talks were going on. It was kind of boring. Apparently the cop didn't think I was a threat. Do I look like a threat?

Davis: How did you encounter Charlotte Mitchell?

Jackson: I was on the lookout for her all morning, but never saw her. Schedule said she'd be at this garden thing at 1:00, so I left about noon to grab a sandwich on the Hill, and then drove to the garden.

Young: What's the name of the place where you got the sandwich?

Jackson: Bon Jovi's or some shit. Johnovies? Can't really remember.

Young: Giovani's? On Shaw Ave?

Jackson: I have no idea. I just drove around and stopped at a place that looked good. There's a million of them there in Guidoville. You know the area?

Young: Used to work up there.

Jackson: Those Italians know how to make a sub. Meat must have been an inch thick.

Davis: Did you eat it there?

Jackson: No. I drove over to the garden. Ate it while I was driving. Pretty messy, but worth it. I was starving. Wanted to get there early so I could watch, because I wasn't sure what kind of crowd there'd be.

Davis: So, you drove to the garden. About what time did you get there?

Jackson: Maybe 12:30? 12:40? I had plenty of time. Watched her car pull up. She got out and boy, she looked beautiful. Wore a blue coat, that color all the news ladies and female politicians wear. Like it's a uniform.

Davis: Did you stay in your car?

Jackson: No, I got out after the crowd started forming.

Young: What did you do then?

Jackson: Just sort of stood there. She was talking to people. Shaking hands. There were lots of those trans people there. Both kinds. Made me nervous.

Young: Why'd it make you nervous?

Jackson: I don't know. It's just… what are they exactly? Know what I mean?

Davis: So, you stood around, watching Charlotte Mitchell.

Jackson: Yeah. She seemed different from all the rest of them. Better looking, for sure. She was gorgeous, right? Even for a tranny?

Davis: How did it make you feel, watching her?

Jackson: I don't know. Confused, I guess? She was so pretty. Prettier than everyone, even the normal people. I didn't know what to think.

Young: How long did you stay there?

Jackson: To the end of her talk.

Davis: Then what did you do?

Jackson: Watched her chit chat with everyone and then take off. She got back in the same car and left. Once she was gone, I took a drive around the city. I don't get up there much. Thought about going to the zoo, because I had some time to kill before the banquet thing at night.

Davis: Charlotte Mitchell spoke at that event, is that correct?

Jackson: Yep. I figured I'd head back that way to do some more tranny watching, and then listen to her speech during the dinner.

Young: What time did you return to the hotel?

Jackson: Must have been about 5:30? There weren't many of the conference people around when I got there. Just a few in the bar, so I went in there, had a drink.

Davis: How long did you stay in the bar?

Jackson: The banquet started at 6:00 so I waited until most of the people headed in. Then I went in and sat at an empty seat.

Young: No one asked you why you weren't wearing a conference badge?

Jackson: I had a badge by then. Found one with a broken lanyard in the parking garage! How's that for luck?

Davis: It was your lucky day, you think?

Jackson: Maybe not so lucky. You got a point there.

Chapter 7

I decided to call the Wild West Wax Museum. A woman picked up on the third ring, and I jumped right in. "Hi, I'm calling about the job opening."

"Oh, that's just wonderful. Can you hold on for a moment? My husband Gerald will want to talk to you." Her voice sounded weathered but cheerful.

"That shouldn't be necessary! I just have a few questions."

"Well, he's the one with *all* the answers. Give me just a second." Her voice grew muffled. "Gerry! Someone's calling about the job!"

A man's gravelly voice came on the line a moment later. "Hello there. You interested in the job?"

"I might be." I said. "I thought maybe you could tell me about it so I can decide."

"Sure, sure! Have you visited the museum before?"

"No, I haven't. I'm calling from Massachusetts. I've never been to Missouri."

"Massachusetts? And you want to move down here and work for us?"

I chuckled awkwardly, trying to dissolve the suspicion leaking around his words. "I thought it might be time to see another part of the country. Learn more about our great nation." My words were a play to the stereotype I'd assumed for Gerry. I felt guilty about it for a minute.

"I've lived here my whole life. Worked in the museum for the last chunk of it. We just love it, but it's time to move on."

"Can you tell me a little about the museum, Mr....?"

"Last name's Harris. But call me Gerry."

"All right, Gerry." I started picking at the skin around the base of my thumbnail.

"A friend of my dad's opened it in 1962. I took over running it 25 years ago, and have been darned proud to do so, with my wife Doris at my side." Presumably Doris had answered the phone.

"Sounds like it's become an institution in your area," I said. Jackson probably visited the place.

"It is indeed, and we're mighty protective of it." The caution in his voice had receded as he'd talked, but was surfacing again. "Not going to hire just anyone."

"That's understandable," I said. Shimmy tried to stop me from messing with my cuticles when I was nervous, warning that my fingernails would form ridges. She was right; my nails were bumpy. I moved from my thumb to the pointer finger. "Your father was a friend of Mr. Turilli?" I'd learned the name while doing background research.

"Sure was."

"Mr. Turilli discovered J. Frank Dalton, right? The elderly man who claimed he was Jesse James?"

"He didn't just claim it, he was the real deal."

"But Jesse was killed in 1882. Shot in the back by one of his own gang."

"That's what Jesse *wanted* you to think. But it wasn't really him."

"It wasn't?"

"Nope. He faked the whole thing, so he wouldn't end up in jail."

"Really!" I longed to lecture him about historical method but kept my mouth shut because the job could pave the way to getting back at Jackson. I tugged on a hangnail instead.

"There's all kinds of proof. Mr. Turilli managed the Meramec Caverns. You can see them if you come down. He moved Jesse into a cabin at the caverns as a tourist attraction, and Jesse stayed there until he died in 1951." I'd read most of these details, but let him keep talking. "Mr. Turilli was convinced, and spent 20 years collecting evidence."

The research I'd done didn't agree with Turilli's assessment, but I'd used Preservation New England's database, which didn't tend to support fringe theories. I *did* find out that Jesse had granular eyelids which caused him to blink a lot. His eyes were large and crystal blue, reportedly his strongest feature. My eyes were blue, but not large. Char's eyes were large but not blue. Hers were gorgeous: long-lashed and green.

I often wondered where Char's eyes went. I obsessed over it, even. I wanted to find them. Maybe if I really did go down there, I *could* find them. But meanwhile, I needed to participate in the conversation on the phone.

Gerry was still rattling along about the other outlaws featured in the museum. "Then there's Brushy Bill Roberts, who was really Billy the Kid. He corroborated Dalton's story. And of course, Captain John Calhoun Brown, who was really Bill Longley. They tried to hang him in 1875, but he finagled himself some sort of harness and didn't die. Lived for 43 more years after that. You just couldn't keep these guys down, and that's the truth."

"Truth can be such a slippery thing, can't it?" I said, tuning my thoughts back to what he was telling me.

"We get a lot of skeptics coming in." An edge of defensiveness crept into Gerry's voice. "But listen up: Dalton was really Jesse James. Roberts was Billy the Kid. Brown was Longley. Believe it, or hang up."

I had to figure out a way to bite my tongue while still talking to him. "I'll do some more reading. These stories are new to me, but it's fascinating."

Gerry made a small noncommittal grunt.

The hangnail ripped, shooting a sharp barb of pain down my finger. "Can you tell me more about the exhibits?"

He took the bait. "We've got a film which tells the stories, and wax figures set in tableaus for the different outlaws, and all sorts of artifacts." Gerry rambled on for a moment about the museum's trove of guilty treasures. "There's also a collection of guns, if you're an enthusiast?"

"Not so much, really."

"Guess you wouldn't be, coming from Boston. Bean Town, don't they call it? Always wanted to go there."

"Some do call it that, yes. But I live on the North Shore."

"What kind of experience do you have? Have you worked with wax figures before? How did you hear about the job?" His questions came rapid-fire.

"I'm a textile conservator, and I support the collections of a number of historic buildings around Massachusetts. I've been working with museums for eleven years." My voice sounded overly eager and obsequious.

"Our figures' costumes could probably use some attention. We aren't exactly specialists in that arena."

"I would take good care of them. How soon do you want someone to start?"

"Pretty quickly. Doris and I are moving to Florida to be near the great-grandkids and the good weather."

The woman's voice chimed in the background, saying "She doesn't care about all that, Gerry. Just stick to business!"

He heeded her advice and got back to the topic. "We need to hire someone fast, and you never know when a body might walk in the door and be the perfect candidate!"

"That's true," I said. There were probably unaccounted for bodies all over the region.

"Want to send your resume?"

"I have some thinking to do. It's a pretty big move."

"We want someone who's as passionate about the truth as we are. There's so much fake news around. So, think hard."

I did feel passionately, but not in the way he hoped. "Thank you for your time, and for all the information," I offered.

"You are welcome. Miss…?"

I thought about giving him a false name so I couldn't be associated with Char's death, but decided not to add any more complexity to the whole thing. Besides, since Char and I didn't have the same last name, it seemed unlikely anyone would have heard of me, even that close to ground zero. "Wells," I finally said. "Maddie Wells. But please call me Maddie."

"You'll need to act fast, like I said, but I'm picky. This place is special."

"Got it. Have a great day," I said, disgusted by my continued fatuousness. We disconnected the call.

It seemed ridiculous to take a job at a roadside oddity given the professional credibility I'd worked so hard to cultivate. But it would provide a cover for being in the place Jackson's loved ones dwelled. I could walk among them, camouflaged. That is *if* Harris would even hire me.

I sucked the blood which oozed from the torn hangnail, trying to remember when I'd last updated my resume.

Chapter 8

Good Goods smelled like coffee and lemon when I went in, and Clyde pushed through a beaded curtain to greet me. "Hello?" I called. I'd returned to the shop a few times since that first visit, and it felt like Maria had adopted me. She came out a moment later.

"Buonasera, Madelaina! How did you know I needed you to abracadabra to me tonight?"

The truth was I'd come to the shop because one way or another, I'd be leaving town soon. The call to the museum made that obvious. I was really going to do something. It felt like I was misleading her, because she thought I was a good person, but I couldn't see a way around it because her warmth drew me like a magnet. "I guess we just needed each other, and poof, here I am."

"Is it too late for you to be drinking coffee? I just made myself an espresso, because my eyes have been heavy all day, and I must stay awake until at least 9:00 when my news lady comes on."

The phrase "news lady" twanged my grief strings, but I just swallowed hard, and replied. "I've already had too much caffeine, but thank you."

"Today I made lemon meatballs and so you will need a drink. A sip of something between bites, and it's like you never tasted them before, all over again." She gestured toward the beaded curtain. "Come with me." I followed her through the clicking beads and into a workroom. It was dimly lit, with two high slits for windows, and smelled a bit like Char's sage. A table on one wall was fitted with an electric kettle and supplies, and Maria headed there to assemble a cup of herbal tea for me.

"How have you been?" I asked.

"Oh, my hip it is aching but I am not surprised. The winds blow and the clouds are heavy like my eyeballs, which always means my bones will swell and start their howling. But I am blessed, grazie Dio, especially now that you have come to see me." Maria placed the cup in front of me, along with a tin of vibrant yellow cookies, topped with icing.

I thanked her, took a cookie, and bit into it. The cookie was dense, giving, and aromatically lemony. "Yum!" I said.

Maria nodded as if acknowledging the obvious. "How was your work today?" she asked. "Did you discover the fabric of the universe yet?"

"Still searching," I replied.

"I am convinced it is the cloth of Madre Maria's mantella. Perhaps one day you will open an old trunk, put your hand in to touch, and suddenly you will be looking into another time." Maria imagined my job to be a better paid version of hers, with both of us pawing through boxes of history's castoffs, just from different sources. In many ways, she was right. "Maybe you will be looking at your Char," she continued.

A barb of unreasonable hope pierced my heart at the idea of such magic. "If I found a time-travel trunk I'd climb in and never come back out again," I said.

"It would not be the trunk that is magic, mia bambina. It would be the Madre's blue cloak." She said it as if exasperated by my slowness.

"My mistake." I pulled my punctured heart away from the unreasonable craving for a mystical relativity robe. "Did any new cookbooks come in?" I asked, hoping to redirect her.

"New new, or new old?"

"New old," I laughed. I finished the first cookie, and helped myself to a second. "These are amazing."

"No new old books yet, though there may be some in the boxes from today." Maria pointed to a collection of containers on the floor against the back wall.

"I'll check back later this week, once you've sorted them."

"How are you doing with the other things? The loss and the griefing?"

I still hadn't mastered the language of mourning or learned how to mutter the right phrases to make people shut up and go away. Of course, I didn't want Maria to either shut up *or* go away, because she was wonderful, and a welcome distraction.

"I'm not sure how to answer that. I'm really lonely. And I'm angry." I didn't mention the guilt because I didn't want to talk about it. "There's nothing I can do about any of it." *Except move to Missouri and pluck out the eyes of Char's murderer's wife.* "I'm wondering if I might need to make a change of scenery for a while." Going to prison for mutilating someone would definitely provide alternate scenery.

Maria nodded. "That could be wise. Get away from all the memories. Blow the dust of pain from your soul. You should go stay in a house of light. At the ocean."

"A lighthouse?"

"Sì! I have heard there are places you can rent in these houses. Where you are right on the sea itself. You should go there. God will speak to you in such a place."

"I'll give it some thought." It sounded wonderful, really, but I had a mission to accomplish. Maybe I'd stay in a lighthouse after I was released from prison. As a celebration.

"I have something for you." Maria brushed sunshine-colored crumbs from her lap and stood to reach into the pocket of her worn floral apron. She pulled out a small, colorful card and handed it to me. On the front was a gilded picture of a woman sitting on a throne, with a miniature human on her lap. Glowing coronas circled both their heads. Given Char's fascination with Catholic objects, I knew it was an image of Mary and the baby Jesus. Mary glittered with jewels. She also wore a crown. I turned the card over to read the text on the back, but Maria began explaining the image.

"She is Mamma Schiavona, a black Madonna, the one they call the Serving Mother. There are many black Madonnas all over the world. But Mamma Schiavona is in Italia."

"She's striking. Strong. Watchful."

"Sì. I remember her from my childhood. I don't know why it took me so long to think of her, but Dio woke me from sleeping and told me to give this to you."

"Why would God do that?"

"There is a connection," she said. "Have you heard of the femminiello?"

"I don't think so."

"In the area of Napoli, there are many people like your Carlotta. The people who are both. Maschile and femminile."

"Masculine and feminine?" Obviously, Maria *did* know Char was trans.

"Yes. They are called the femminiello, and they go each year to make a festival for Mamma Schiavona."

"Why do they do that?"

"Hundreds of years ago, two men were traveling to her church when someone saw them holding hands and perhaps exchanging a kiss. The gossip spread and many people became angry. They took the men's clothes and tied them to a tree so they would freeze to death or be eaten by wolves. But Mamma Schiovona, she sees how much the men love each other, and she says 'NO!'" Maria threw her hands in the air with the passion of the retelling. "The chains come flying off, and the men are free! From that day they lived together in the town so people could see proof that Mamma did such a miracle."

"Impressive!"

Maria seemed to think I was buying the whole thing, and she kept going. "Yes, yes," she said, nodding her head so that the soft skin of her chins jounced. "So the femminiello have adopted her as their own Mamma, and they go each year up the steep mountain to her sanctuary in Montevergine. They go at the end of Christmas, when it is time for the candle blessing. They hold a festival to honor her. And I think, to celebrate themselves. That they can be there. That they have a Mother who loves them."

"How lovely." It *was* lovely, even though the original story seemed sketchy.

She looked at me again, suddenly serious and searching. "They call her the Madonna of Transformation," she said. "Do you see?"

"The Madonna of Transformation," I said, imagining a line of trans women winding up a mountainside, candles lighting their faces as they walked. "I wish Charlotte would have known about her." I turned the holy card back to the picture side, thinking about how much Shimmy would have loved knowing there was a special saint—a manifestation of Mary, no less—who was especially devoted to transgender people.

"You must keep her close by your side. Lift up your questions and prayers to her. She will ask her Son to help you."

Maria was so sincere and intense that I didn't want to laugh off the idea. "I'll keep it in my pocket. How's that?"

"Bene." Maria nodded. "Molto bene. She will help you. I am certain of it. Now, I must kick you to the door. I promised Clyde a bath, and he is not patient."

"Clyde lets you give him *baths*?"

"Lets me? He loves them! Clyde is not the average of cats."

"He sure isn't." I got up to leave, tucking the card in my back pocket, as promised. "Thanks again for the card. And for the cookies! They were fantastic."

"You are welcome, Madelaina."

"See you later, Clyde." I walked to the workroom door and stepped through the waterfall of beads to go back out to the shop. Maria followed me, praising Clyde for having waited until their tea time was finished. She locked the door behind me and stood watching while I headed to my car.

As I climbed in, a tall, elegant redhead walked up to the store. Her expression broke into delight as she saw Maria. She waved, and I realized it was the girl who'd waited on me at the diner that day. Lee. I heard the door jingle as Maria re-opened it for her.

"Lelita! What are you doing here? Come and help me bathe Clyde. He stinks like a hyena." I laughed and started the car, glad they were friends.

That night I took a glass of wine and an old cookbook and settled in the stiff wingback chair I'd been using since Char's death. She and I usually sat at either end of our slouchy couch, shifting toward center when we wanted to touch or be touched. Sometimes one of us would recline with our head in the other's lap, our fingers smoothing down the other's hair, listening to the soft coos of pleasure the other issued at the touch. I hadn't sat on the couch since I got the news. I figured I should just get rid of it, and hope someone else could feel loving and loved on it as we had. The wingback looked better than it felt, but it was a gentle form of penance.

The wine was cheap and rather sour, perfectly fine for my needs. The cookbook was from the 1940s and focused on cookies. I checked the index for the delicious lemon meatball cookies Maria made, but there was nothing like them in it.

It was funny; even though I was alone in the lonely house, with Char's memory and my guilt shifting around just outside my field of concentration, looking at the book calmed my spirit. It brought me the same kind of relaxed peace that spending time with Maria did. It didn't change the direction I was headed, but it was a nice moment of rest before rushing into the storm.

Chapter 9

I decided to put the museum decision in the hands of fate and applied for the job, figuring if I got it, I'd know I was supposed to follow in Jesse James' footsteps and dole out vengeance. It wouldn't bring Charlotte back. Nothing could. But it would make me feel better for a little while.

Doris was thrilled when I called back, my morning coffee still in hand. She put her husband on the phone immediately, just as she had during our first call.

"What do you look like?" Gerry asked right away. It was an odd question for a job interview, probably even illegal. "I like to put a face to a name."

I wondered if he was trying to find out if I was physically disabled without violating any laws, or maybe some race he didn't trust. I decided to answer despite the inappropriateness of the question. "I'm short and thin, with blue eyes and curly blond hair. People tell me I look like a doll." I sounded like one of those female protagonists in a novel who complains her eyes are too big and her mouth is too wide, and you're supposed to realize she's drop-dead gorgeous. "I'm sort of pasty, and weird-looking," I corrected. "Full disclosure."

"Well, we can't control what we look like, can we? Tell me more about your job at Preservation New England. Do they have any wax figures?"

"No, they don't." I hoped he'd overlook the lack. "Most of my work takes place in antique homes and other buildings which have been preserved and are open to the public for viewing. There are farms, and custom houses, places like that. I travel around making sure textiles are properly cared for so they'll still be here for people to appreciate in hundreds of years."

"Your resume is impressive. Best candidate we've received so far."

"I'm glad to hear it."

"But it still seems odd that you'd want to come here to work."

I looked at the skin which was trying to heal at the base of one finger-nail, battling the urge to blurt out that I didn't *want* to work there, but needed to. "The stories intrigue me," I said, which was true, though not in a way Gerry would appreciate. "The outlaws you highlight are so iconic, and the survival claims have significant impact for how scholarship should approach questions like this when they arise." I'd practiced my answer, but the words still sounded like bullshit. "Plus, my dad was a big fan of Westerns." Another lie. "Taking the job would honor those memories."

Gerry mercifully traveled down that thought skein, sharing a few of his own memories and peppering in facts about the museum. He eventually asked about my education and the kinds of things I did each day. The conversation went on for about fifteen minutes.

"Do you have any questions for me?" he finally asked.

"Yes. Your ad mentioned management experience is required. How many employees are we talking about?" Hopefully there wouldn't be a big team of eyes watching me.

"Management isn't always about employees. You'd be running the whole thing. You won't be managing people so much as details, like keeping the shelves of the gift shop stocked, doing the bookkeeping, stuff like that."

"I see," I said, relieved. "That all sounds fine. I'm used to managing budgets and tracking expenses. I'm sure I could handle your books. What software do you use?"

"Doris has ledgers to keep track of everything. If we hire you, she'll show you how they work." Maria used an old ledger book for Good Goods. She'd probably get along fabulously with the Harrises. "Responsibility and reli-ability are critical. You'd be in control of the till and could run away with all the cash if you wanted. And you'd be responsible for cutting yourself a paycheck. So we have to trust you. How do I know you're trustworthy?"

"That's a good question." I wasn't trustworthy. I wanted the job for the sole purpose of committing nefarious deeds. But none of those deeds involved stealing a week's worth of customer receipts. "I can give you references," I said. "You can talk to them."

"Ever been to jail?" Gerry asked.

"Not yet."

"Me either. Still time though, eh?" We chuckled together, but my humor was darker than he realized. "I'll need those references then," he said.

"Can I call Doris back in the morning with them?"

"Sure, sure. And don't give me the names of your sister or your boyfriend or some nonsense like that. I'll find out. You can't fool an old codger like me."

"I don't have a sister *or* a boyfriend, so we should be good."

"You get me those references, and I'll call them straight away." With that, the interview was done.

The job was a kind of surreal madness; a museum filled with wax bodies arriving at my door like a horse-shaped gift offered by the gods of darkness.

I was nervous about references. If anyone put two and two together, they'd realize how close the museum was to where Char was killed, and I didn't need people gossiping about that. I'd have to list people from my previous job, and Gerry could figure that out in just a question or two.

My third cup of coffee was bitter and burnt, but it suited my frame of mind. If I was a decent human being, I'd get a T-shirt made with "burned and bitter" emblazoned on the front, so people would know what they'd encounter if they got too close. Maybe I'd do that once all of it was over.

But not yet. I didn't want to forewarn anyone.

Chapter 10

"Gently. You're pushing so hard you'll get down into the white part where life is bitter." Maria took the lemon and grater out of my hands. "Gently, gently, like so." She demonstrated how to do it correctly, and a tiny shower of yellow zest fell to the plate below. "Do you see now? Not so much pushing! You'll give yourself the carpaccio tunnel, and the cookies will taste like regret."

"Okay, I think I've got it." I took back the lemon and tried it myself. "Better?" The scent was clean and delicious.

"Sì," Maria said, returning to her bowl where she added sugar to the shortening and began beating it with a wooden spoon. "One and il quarto cups sugar. Then you stir until it is all creamy."

"You're the one who's going to get carpal tunnel at that rate! I didn't know your arm could move that fast."

"When you have many things to do, you learn to do them quickly. Did you write that down? One and il quarto."

"Got it." I updated my notes and finished zesting. Maria was teaching me how to make the lemon meatball cookies she'd fed me. "What's next?"

"I need you to crack four eggs in this, while I keep stirring. Unless they are giants, and then you can use three. But mostly you will need four."

The wax museum job offer had come quickly, despite the outdated references. I'd been working up the courage to tell Maria the news. I told myself I couldn't wait to escape from the house Char and I lived in together, and the cobble-stoned town we walked, and the television screen that no longer showed her picture, live and glowing with energy. I tried to believe I needed to see what kind of place would incubate enough hate to destroy such a shining star. I *did* want to hurt someone back. That much was genuine. I picked up an egg and decided to jump into the subject. "So, it looks like I'll be moving," I said, cracking the egg and watching it drop into her bowl.

Maria stopped stirring. "What do you mean, moving?"

"I got a new job." I cracked another egg. "It's out of state." She resumed stirring while looking straight at me. "In Missouri," I said.

She stopped stirring again. "Missouri," she said.

"Yes." The third egg plopped in and settled against her spoon.

"Missouri." Maria shook her head and began beating furiously. The soft skin at her jawline quivered with the movement. "A new job."

"Yes," I said. This was getting uncomfortable. The last egg dropped in, and I gathered up the shells. I threw them away, then walked to the sink, rinsed my hands, and grabbed a paper towel to wipe down the table.

"I am supposed to believe that out of the center of nothingness you get a new job in the place where your Shimmy was murdered." She looked at me over her glasses, shaking her head as her mouth curved into a frown. "Add the sour cream we measured. And the lemon zest you almost ruined. Then vanilla. Only one teaspoon." I moved to comply, and she kept stirring. "Do you think I am stupido? Or maybe born off the turnip wagon just yesterday?"

"Of course not!" I grabbed a spatula and scraped the sour cream out of the measuring cup. "You're very smart."

"Also wise. I ask for God to grant me wisdom, like Salomone. I am too wise to believe this is some coincidence, Madelaina."

"I just thought maybe it would help to go down there."

"Help?" Her eyes blazed incredulity.

"Maybe I can feel some closure," I said. The word sounded stupid even in my own ear. "Is there anything else I should be doing?" I was flustered, and needed to vent my nerves through action.

"Get the baking sheets out from the bottom of the stove." Maria flicked her head toward the oven. "Closure," she said, dumping flour into the bowl and stirring again, this time more slowly. "I used to work in the underpants factory, long ago. Did I tell you?"

I shook my head. "I don't think so." The change of subject was odd.

"The panty shanty, they called it in our town. At the panty shanty there was closure, and it was the buttons on men's underwear. So that's what I think of your closure." She put the bowl down and rested her fists on her hips. "Give me the pans."

I handed them over. "I'd be where it happened," I said. "Maybe it will make it seem more real."

Maria began forming quarter-sized balls of dough and placing them on a cookie sheet. "It seems to me your life is filled with this reality. You are lonely. You are sad. You feel guilty."

How did she know I felt guilty?

"Becoming real is not the purpose of your insanity."

"Maybe I just want to escape all this. Our house. This town. All the memories." Maria just kept rolling balls of dough and glaring. "Can I help?" I finally asked.

"Sì," Maria sighed.

I walked closer and plucked up some dough. I couldn't very well tell her I was going to go down there and maybe kill someone, even though researching Jesse James and the other outlaws taught me that sometimes good guys wear black hats and even white hats are smudged with dirt. I wasn't sure what color my hat was and I didn't really care. The morality of what I was going to do would be up to history to decide.

"So you don't want to tell me what it is you are up to. Okay. I cannot force you." She glanced at the first ball I placed next to her neat rows. "That one is too small. They must be mostly the same size. If they are too small, they dry out in the middle."

I picked the ball back up and added a dab more dough.

"Bene," she said, satisfied with the replacement. We continued working in silence for a few minutes, filling the cookie sheets and popping the first two in the oven. "We should drink some water. It is good to be rehydrated." She carried the mixing bowl to the sink, then filled two glasses with water. "Drink," she ordered.

I drank. It felt like a reprieve: while drinking, I wasn't expected to talk.

Maria sat down at the table and sighed again, gazing mournfully at me. Clyde appeared, and I hoped he'd be another distraction. I set the glass down and bent to pet him. "Hey, Clydesdale! Where've you been all this time? You usually show up right away when I'm here."

"He's been sleepy today. Stayed up too late last night, complaining because I have him on a diet. So of course he kept me up too, but I would rather make cookies with you than sleep, because you are my friend."

Her tone was clear; I should feel guilty for not explaining what was going on. "I'm sorry! I'm not sure I even understand it myself." I knew more than I was willing to let on, but lots of parts were still foggy.

"Hmmph." Maria's expression was skeptical. It felt like her gaze saw a lot more than was comfortable. I moved to the sink to wash the mixing bowl and get away from her eyes. "Hmmph," she said again. I didn't respond, just ran hot water and picked up the sponge.

"You never told me what happened," she said. "Maybe it would help you to tell me." I stood stock still, frozen by her words. A woman turned waxwork. "Maybe if you spoke it, you wouldn't need to move down to the middle of the country, away from the ocean which can blow away heartache. Away from me so I cannot take care of you." Maria's voice went from scolding to soft and concerned.

The idea of speaking it all was both horrifying and tantalizing. I couldn't imagine trying to explain what I'd seen and done, and what it would feel like to go through it all again. But part of me wanted to pour it out, to vomit out the truth so that maybe the emotional nausea would stop and I could start to feel better.

I decided to tell her, even though it wouldn't make anything better. It certainly wouldn't change my mind about what I was going down there to do.

"All right," I said in defeat, and plunged back into the memories.

Chapter 11

"Honey, I want you there. This is a big day for me." Char looked hurt.

"I know it's important, Shimmy," I said. I was experimenting with West Indian food and the scent of curry and coconut milk was rich in the air. The spices made my eyes water and my stomach rumble. I wished the conversation would drift and disappear with the steam rising from the pots in front of me, but I could tell that wasn't going to happen.

Char was being honored for her work in promoting transgender awareness. The journey hadn't been easy; it was unheard of for a television station to have her on camera at all. But she was persistent. When she'd held the news anchor position long enough to gain a following, Char convinced the powers at CXBY in Boston to offer a memorial each time a trans person was murdered. They took some flack initially, but once the station began to be viewed as pioneers, Char's passion for the cause was recognized as useful, and the memorials were another step on the station's path to becoming industry vanguards.

She deserved the honor. She really did. But I had a fear of flying, and didn't enjoy hovering at the edge of the limelight she warranted. I'd be happier staying home, with evenings devoted to reading and a few glasses of red.

"Maybe you could take a train? A bus?" She didn't seem to realize flying wasn't the only problem. Or she *did* realize it, but she wanted it to be different.

"I'd be traveling for days, Char!" She'd told me St. Louis was the most progressive city in the region, but all I could picture were rebel flags and trucks with gun racks. I didn't understand why she'd want to go somewhere people would treat her like a freak, but if she insisted on it, I didn't have to be a witness.

"Maddie…"

"It's not like I won't see you get the award. Someone must be livestreaming it."

"But I want you *there*. It's not just about you watching."

I tipped my head back and looked at the ceiling, as if the tiny cracks in the plaster held the answer to her unreasonableness. The silence unfolded between us. I heard the hum of the refrigerator and a dog barking down the street. Our stillness stretched longer than usual, but finally, she broke it.

"Okay. I give up." Her eyes were irritated rather than hurt when she said it, the resignation in her voice obvious.

I sighed; long and loud. "*Damn* it, Char." I slammed the spoon down on the counter. She just gazed back at me, her soft beauty calcifying into granite. Silence spun between us again, but this time she was in control of the spin. "All right!" I finally said. "I'll go."

The joy transforming her face was something I knew I'd never forget. She morphed from a gleaming statue of fury into a beaming six-year-old at Christmas. "You will?" she said.

"Yes."

She came to me then, cupping my face to gaze into me, deep. Her eyes shone as if she were about to cry. "Thank you, Maddie. I adore you."

I smiled back into her, back through those liquid eyes which let her heart pour out so easily. "I don't know how, but I'll do it," I said. "I love you too."

"We'll call the doctor. She can prescribe something. Xanax, or whatever."

The spices no longer smelled good. My stomach lurched, and my heart began to thump. She felt it right away.

"Shh," she said. "Don't think about it now. I'll take care of all the details. You'll just need to show up, pop a pill, and follow my directions."

I took a few deep breaths, concentrating on calming my heart. I struggled with anxiety periodically, but flying was the one thing guaranteed to bring on a full-blown panic attack. Just the thought of it made me feel like passing out. I kept breathing, stayed upright, and served dinner. Char chattered away about the things we'd do while we were in St. Louis, and I tried to act enthusiastic.

The next morning Shimmy booked my ticket, called the doctor, and picked up my script. When the departure day came, I made it through check in and even got through security. The panic didn't start until we were waiting at the gate.

"Now boarding AirSouth Exclusive Advantage members. If you are an Exclusive Advantage member, you are free to board." The announcement kicked people into motion, pulling their carry-ons closer and adjusting their jackets. My breathing picked up pace.

"Maddie?" Char said.

I shook my head, trying to breathe more slowly. A gaggle of people disappeared through the maw of the bridge.

"We are now boarding our First Class passengers only," a second announcement rang out. "First Class ticket holders are free to board."

My heart began to patter, a thing I thought was made up in romance novels. It pattered at a fast, uneven pace though I wasn't feeling love, or lust, or anything remotely associated with hope. My breathing picked up speed, and I could feel sweat forming on my forehead.

The first-class boarders were mostly business people looking bored, but one teenager with tattoos and purple hair walked among them; a skull-blazoned backpack strapped to her back. She paused in front of me on her way to the gate, looking concerned. "Dude," she said.

Sweat beaded my upper lip and I wondered if I looked as green as I felt. I tried my old trick of silently reciting poetry to calm down, clicking clumsily through the words of Frost's "Road Not Taken," probably inspired by the idea of being a traveler. The teenager headed to the doorway.

"Maddie." Char sounded concerned but also firm, like she was about to control whatever was raging inside me despite the Xanax I'd dutifully swallowed 45 minutes before.

"I'm... I'll... I'll be okay." I stammered.

But I wasn't okay.

The boarding announcements continued, and my panic grew each time the attendant spoke. "Just breathe, sweetheart. It will pass," Char said. As a newscaster she'd been trained not to let emotion show, no matter how horrifying, heartbreaking, or hilarious a story might be. She employed this technique now, but I knew her too well. I saw concern about me, confusion about what to do, impatience, and anger.

"I... I think I need to lie down. Just for a minute." I seriously considered curling up on the floor in front of the seats where we were sitting.

"You can't just lie down on the floor of an airport, Maddie."

The waiting area was empty except for us. The attendant who'd made the boarding announcements kept looking at me. I could tell she was about to call medical or security.

"This is your last call for flight 3289 to St. Louis. Final boarding for St. Louis." She stared straight at us as she said it.

I looked up at Char. Her expression was pleading, but as she searched my face, it hardened into resignation. The cinching around my chest instantly loosened a notch and a sense of guilty relief made my heart pound in a new pattern that felt like "Thank God, thank God, thank God."

Char saw the shift in my own face. She turned, grabbed the handle of her rolling suitcase, and walked away.

"I'm sorry Char," I called to her. "I'll be watching."

She didn't look back.

"I love you!" I called out again.

She disappeared through the bridge doorway without replying.

"I'm sorry," I said.

My path was chosen, and it made all the difference.

Chapter 12

Shimmy looked beautiful standing in the weak November sunlight, surrounded by local politicians and members of transgender advocacy groups. The organizers had set up a small, raised stage with a podium at the wide end of the triangular Transgender Memorial Garden. She was framed by the spindly fingers of winter-barren young trees. The garden must have been a pretty sight in spring. Now it was stark, and Char was a splash of color in contrast; wearing the tailored royal blue coat she'd purchased for the occasion.

Char's body language on television fascinated me. She was naturally graceful and elegant, her motion hypnotically fluid and utterly feminine. At home she was also feminine—how could she not be—but her movement became more athletic and less balletic when she was tired. I liked that she could be unguarded with me, knowing her femininity wouldn't be questioned. She knew I knew who she was and loved her regardless of whether her knees were pressed together demurely or sprawled wide at the end of a long day. The looseness of her body language was an unspoken gift of intimacy. Something no one else got to experience. I loved that.

As she delivered her speech, Shimmy spoke words of inspiration, hope, and subtle insurgency, and her eyes glowed with the passion of her message. She was chilled, though. It showed in the tightness of her jaw muscles. Char was prone to cold, and the coat was more for show than for warmth. We hadn't thought she'd need the one she wore to handle New England wind and snow, but St. Louis obviously got plenty cold. I'd heard the essential message many times before, so I let the sound of her voice flow around me and watched the language of her face and hands. She was in her element, and her body radiated confidence.

The important moment for me would be at the end, when she'd give the signal. She gave it at the conclusion of every broadcast; lifting a hand to her heart while smiling into the camera. Throughout the years, people asked me what the gesture meant, guessing it was a message of love for all the viewers. But Char said it was just for me, and I received it that way, every time I saw it. That was a gift Char had; she made everyone feel like the only person who mattered. But the signal, the gesture, *that* was mine alone.

I waited for her to wrap up her speech and send me the love sign, drifting in and out but tuning back in shortly before she said the words she always spoke in memorials to slain transgender people: "Rest in power, beloved children of God, now that you are free to be." She bent her head for a moment, as if in prayer, then turned, and walked off the stage. A commentator began to speak, listing the names and roles of the people who followed her toward the cars lining the adjacent street.

She hadn't given me the love sign.

I sat, stunned for a moment, not understanding what had just happened. Was she distracted by the audience? Had the event moved her so much that it left her scatterbrained? Neither of these things made sense. Shimmy was a consummate professional. She didn't get shaken by anything, which was why newscasting was such a great fit for her.

She must have done it intentionally.

I clicked off the TV and threw the remote so it bounced off the couch, then barrel-rolled across the age-marred floor boards. I'd disappointed her by not going, but it wasn't by choice. Char knew the panic attack was real, and that I hadn't *meant* for it to happen. In contrast, not making the love sign was a deliberate action to show me she was angry. She chose to withhold it from me.

I wobbled between my own anger and worry that I'd finally pushed her over the edge. Maybe she'd had enough of my neuroses and my lack of ability to do the hard stuff.

She didn't answer her phone, which was probably a good thing. I paced around the house, killing time until the evening keynote address. The Boston station wasn't covering it, so I'd planned to livestream it. I was sure she'd have calmed down enough by then because she rarely harbored resentments for long. Shimmy was slow to anger and quick to forgive, which was convenient because I'm irritating. At a few minutes before 8:00 I went to the website of the Transgender Advocacy Network which was hosting the conference, but the conference page said events wouldn't be streamed, because there were too many attendees who weren't able to live their gender publicly. Broadcasting video would out them.

I couldn't watch her keynote speech after all, which was what I'd assured her I *would* do. I hated not keeping my word, but I hated even more not knowing whether she'd end it with her love sign. I went to bed sad, but also angry that Char withheld it earlier. Even if I deserved it for being such a wussy.

Weeks later, after news of what happened emerged, people gossiped about Char not making the sign when she finished her talk in the memorial garden. They wondered if it meant she somehow knew what was to come.

I was the only one who knew the truth.

I bore the blame for the pain each of her fans felt at what they'd lost.

Chapter 13

Char's refusal to signal her love was wrong, but my infraction was a doozy, so I tried to mitigate her pain through action. I cleaned the house, bought a package of Char's favorite dark chocolate, and set up towels and lotion near her spot on the couch for a foot massage. Fresh flowers went on the table, and a pot roast bubbled in the crock pot. I would have taken her out to dinner, but she'd want something homecooked and comfortable after traveling.

Everything was set and ready by the time I left for the airport. We'd taken the train when we went down together, but this time, I drove. I parked and wove through the labyrinth that is Boston Logan airport to get to Char's arrival area. The glittering mosaic sea creatures on the floor were a temporary distraction from my nervousness. I wondered about the artist who'd designed them, and the crafts people who installed them. Did their knees hurt at the end of the day? Were they local, so they could come visit their work? I'd gotten there early and had time and nervous jitters to kill. The art gave me something to think about other than Char's anger.

Shimmy had never been so mad at me before, and I wasn't sure how to process it. She was a wonderful communicator, always cutting to the key issue in any disagreement, seeking resolution, and wanting a return to unity. The fact that she'd been silent for three days was ominous and surprising. Char always tried to put herself in the other person's reality so she could understand their position. But over the past few days she hadn't tried to communicate at all. Char was acting like a child, but I couldn't stay mad. The house without her had lost its heartbeat. The colors and fabrics she'd chosen were there, but their vibrancy dimmed without her, as if she was the light that shined life into them.

I grabbed a cup of coffee from a kiosk on my way to baggage claim, then headed down the escalator to wait. The flight was on time, and when a flood of people appeared at the end of the hallway, my heart pounded from adrenaline. I stood and moved toward them, searching. The arriving passengers flowed around me like a human river, eager to greet the ones who waited for them, eager to get their bags and be done with this stage of their travels.

I searched for her when the crowd was thick. I watched for her as the stragglers came through. I waited for her when there was no one left to come out.

The carousel of bags spun endlessly. Her purple suitcase wasn't on it.

Char loved her life. She loved me. No matter how mad she might have gotten, she wouldn't abandon us. Would she?

I drove home, furious that she still wasn't answering her phone. When I got inside, I decided to call her hotel.

"Thank you for calling the Downtown Sojourner, how can I help you?" Bland music played behind the man's voice.

"Can you connect me with Charlotte Mitchell's room, please?"

"Certainly. One moment."

The background music was replaced by ringing. After the sixth ring, I heard "The guest you are trying to reach is not available. Please leave a message in their confidential mailbox."

I clicked off the call and slammed the phone down on the table in front of me. It was 8:00 PM, her time. Was she somewhere having supper? Who was she eating with?

I realized I should have left a message, and called back. The same guy answered, and we had the same conversation as the first time. When the voicemail message beeped, I began to talk. "Char. I'm so sorry about the whole plane thing. Is something wrong with your phone? I'm sorry I wasn't there, but I did catch part of your talk, and you were great! Really great." I paused, considering whether to do any complaining. "Listen. I don't understand why you didn't come home. Or why you didn't at least tell me you were staying longer. You knew I'd be at the airport to pick you up. I'm sorry I made you so mad, but this is kind of freaking me out. I miss you. Please forgive me?" I paused again, thinking of what else to say. "Please call me," was all I came up with.

I hung up, then paced between the kitchen and dining room. I kept my phone close so I could get it quickly, torn between the need to yell at her for treating me like this, and the need to hear her voice and get her to say she forgave me.

I turned off the pot roast and considered eating a chunk, but my stomach was sore and tight from the hours of tension. I tried Char's cell, but it went straight into voicemail, as it had for days. I thought about calling the hotel again but forced myself to wait until morning.

Eventually I went to bed, pulling Char's satin robe from its hook on the back of the bathroom door so I could breathe the scent of lotion, perfume, and her. I rubbed the silky fabric between my fingers, like a toddler with their blankie, until sleep eventually came. By some magic I slept all night, finally startling awake when I thought I heard Char calling me. "What's the matter?" I sat up, looking for her, but her special pillow was missing and her robe was lying next to me, so everything rushed back.

The phone showed she still hadn't called. I tried her cell again, with the same result as last time. After brushing my teeth so hard the gums bled, I dialed the hotel.

"Thank you for calling the Downtown Sojourner, how can I help you?"

"Could you connect me to Charlotte Mitchell's room, please?"

Maybe my panic attack was the final straw for Char. She'd put up with all my weirdness and occasional clinginess, and it seemed like she really loved me, despite all that. But maybe she'd just been really good at faking it all these years. Maybe I'd been driving her bonkers the whole time and was just too stupid to see it.

"Certainly. One moment."

The line went silent, the call tone rang, and the voicemail message recited. I hung up.

The coffee grounds smelled good, but making just two cups was lonely. The caffeine did its job but didn't inspire any brilliant solutions, so I went to work, figuring the distraction would be useful. I managed to last until lunchtime before calling the hotel again.

"Thank you for calling the Downtown Sojourner. How can I help you?" I was so sick of hearing that greeting that I wanted to tell her to shut up. But I didn't.

"I'm trying to find out if a guest has checked out yet. It's my wife." There was a good chance they'd think I was a stalker, so I qualified my explanation. "I'm not some sort of creep or anything." I shook my head, realizing that wasn't going to be helpful.

"What's the guest's name?"

"Charlotte Mitchell."

"Let me see… No, she hasn't checked out."

"Oh. Okay. That's good, I guess. Well, thank you."

"Actually, there's a note in the system. Let me get my manager."

"A note? What kind of note?"

"Can you hold for a moment? The hotel manager will be happy to explain."

"Sure." I had no idea what a note might mean. If it was a message for me, why didn't she just say so? Maybe it said to fuck off, and employees weren't allowed to say that to people on the phone. Maybe Char said they should tell me to stop calling.

"This is the Day Manager," a very professional female voice came on the line. "With whom do I have the pleasure of speaking?"

"I'm Maddie Wells. Charlotte Mitchell's wife."

"Thank you, Ms. Wells. Can you tell me what Ms. Mitchell's plans are for checking out? She was booked through Sunday night, and obviously today is Tuesday. She didn't let us know she'd planned to extend her stay. Housekeeping reports that her belongings are still in the room, but the system says she hasn't used her key to enter it since Saturday, late afternoon."

My brain processed what she was saying, and doing the math. Char hadn't been back to the hotel since the day of her talk.

Three days ago.

"What… what do you mean? Where could she be?"

"I'm sure I don't know, Ms. Wells. That's why I'm consulting with you."

"But I don't know either! I've been trying to reach her. We had a fight, but…" I stopped, because it hadn't really been a fight, and this woman didn't give a damn or have any right to hear the details of what had happened. "It doesn't matter," I finally concluded. I didn't know what else I could say.

"Could she be… staying with someone?"

My heart started to pound. Was it a stunt or had something happened? "Char doesn't know anybody down there." She told me she used to have anger issues, but I'd never seen them in play. Maybe my panic attack had kicked her old self back in gear?

"I'm sure everything is fine, Ms. Wells." I could hear condescension in her voice, and the sound of impatience. "Perhaps we'll just pack up her things and consider her checked out. Shall we do that? Or would you prefer to put additional days on a new card and keep the room open?"

I didn't know how to answer. I couldn't imagine what might have happened, or what she might be up to.

"Let me call you back, okay?"

"Certainly, Ms. Wells. I'll be here until 6:30 and you can let me know your preference any time before then."

"Thank you," I said, even though I felt like long-distance throat punching the bitch.

"Of course, if we don't hear back from you, we'll need to involve the police."

"No!" Char would be furious if a police report was issued. People would love to implicate her in a scandal to tarnish her reputation and pull her down. "I'll call you back shortly."

"That will be fine, Ms. Wells." If she said my name one more time, I knew I'd start screaming. A wave of anxiety threatened to overtake me, and I wanted to make it stop. "As I said, I'll be here…"

"Never mind," I interrupted. "Just pack up her things." It would serve Char right to get back and discover some stranger had been messing around with her makeup and bras.

"All right then. Thank you for your assistance."

"You're quite welcome." I swallowed down my panic, and forced my voice and language to sound like hers. "Miss…?"

"Mrs. Rodriguez. I'm the hotel manager."

"You're welcome, Mrs. Rodriguez. I trust this entire affair will be handled with discretion?" My forced formality sounded ridiculous.

"Of course, Ms. Wells."

"Good."

"Good day then?" she said.

"Good day." I hung up, embarrassed and vaguely ashamed, though I didn't know of what.

I was also confused. A frizzle of fear shivered up my spine and another wave of anxiety threatened to pull me under. My brain scrambled for explanations that weren't completely terrifying, and settled on this:

She must have hooked up with someone.

I allowed outrage to flare up, hot and fast, the fear acting as kindling. I let the idea settle in to my spirit and embraced it, the pain sharp and biting, an antidote to the fear niggling beneath it. People were always hitting on her. She was beautiful, charming, and famous; a natural target for attention. She must have met someone who was drawn to her flame, and this time, allowed them to be consumed.

She wouldn't do that, my heart insisted and my brain agreed. But I stomped the thought out because what lay beneath it was so much worse.

Chapter 14

I forced myself to get back to work but functioned like a robot while I was there. My phone rang an hour after I got home. It was Char's producer, a gorgeous Japanese guy named Yori.

"Have you heard from her yet?" he asked. His voice sounded both scared and eager.

Yori and Char were close. Sometimes I thought they might be too close. "No. Not a word. I assume you haven't either?" I'd even wondered if he might be involved in her silence.

"No. I can't believe this is happening." I examined the notes of his voice, trying to figure out if he knew more than he was letting on.

"You're sure she didn't tell you about someone she was meeting there?"

"She just talked about people in the Transgender Advocacy Network. People she's known a long time." Yori paused. "I should have gone with her."

I didn't want to be on team Yori, but there we were, rowing the same boat.

"She must have met someone," I said. The idea was ludicrous and we both knew it, but it was all I had, and I desperately needed to stick with it. "Maybe it was someone in the media down there. Maybe they offered her a job in between bouts of hot sex." I hadn't meant to say that last part out loud, but I kept going down the thought train, this time with my mouth closed. Maybe she'd be on the news soon in St. Louis, closing out each nightly broadcast with some new love-signal for her paramour. At least I *hoped* she'd come up with a new signal. Using mine would be truly heartless. Shimmy was a lot of things, but she wasn't that.

Yori sighed, loud and hard. I wondered if the idea made him jealous too. "You're being ridiculous," he said.

"This isn't exactly a moment for normalcy," I replied.

"Don't you think we should do something?"

"What else can we do? I filed the missing person report. She's obviously gone underground and doesn't want to be found."

"You aren't worried that something... happened to her?" Yori asked.

My mind began wandering down the dark alley which led to a cinema of possible horrors, but I stopped it in its tracks. There was nothing good to be found there. "She's too smart. She knows what happens to women like her, and how to protect herself. Obviously there's something else going on."

"That just doesn't ring true. She adores you."

The words may have been an attempt at reassurance, but there was an edge to his voice that told me what I already knew: Yori never thought I was good enough for Char. I agreed with him, but that didn't stop the flare of jealousy which rose from his statement. It was time to shut the conversation down. "We both know I kind of suck. And I didn't go with her. That must have been the last straw."

Yori sighed again, as if agreeing with my self-critique.

"I have to go," I said.

"I'll let you know if I hear anything," he said. "I sure hope I'll hear something."

I clicked off the call and looked around for a task that needed doing. The house had never been so clean. I did housework like it was my salvation. I turned on a podcast and mopped the kitchen floor, even though I'd mopped it that morning. Anything to stop the thoughts from over-taking me.

I slept badly despite the Ambien, just as I did every night during that time. And then I got the phone call.

Chapter 15

They wanted me to fly down to take a look at the poor woman who'd been murdered south of St. Louis. They thought it was Char, but obviously, it couldn't be. She had no reason to leave the city, and she was super smart, trained to be on the lookout in parking lots and dark streets. She carried her phone in one hand and a can of mace in the other. There was no way someone could catch her by surprise like that. So what if this particular victim was a trans woman of color? They were targets, and central Missouri was probably full of whackos bent on destroying things they didn't understand. Just because she was black and trans didn't mean it was Char. I sure as hell wasn't going to fly down there, rushing to see someone I didn't know. Flying for them when I couldn't fly for Shimmy.

Looking back, it's obvious I was delaying.

After checking out the options, I decided to take a train to St. Louis and then got a rental car to drive to a backwater called Byron's Mill, where the woman's body was being held. I felt sorry for the people who really *should* be going to view her, waiting and wondering where she might be. The thought of what it would be like to lose Char to murder made my brain spasm and my heart contract. The idea that she'd found a replacement lover was excruciating, but less painful. At least in that scenario she was in the world somewhere, shining her particular light.

I didn't tell Yori or anyone else about the call. He'd have gone into a frenzy and the last thing I needed was a bunch of cameras and reporters flocking down from Boston. All this was hard enough as it was. Once I'd done the viewing or whatever they called it, I'd head up to the hotel where the conference had been held to ask around and see if I could find clues about the charmer Char dumped me for.

A woman at the front desk of the tiny police station cum municipal center whispered my name nervously into a phone, and a few minutes later a gray-haired man with a beer belly and a uniform came out and shook my hand.

"Hello, Miss Wells. I'm so sorry to meet you under these circumstances. Hope you had a good trip down. I'm Chief Rogers."

"The trip was fine, thanks. Let's get this over with." I cut right to the chase. "I don't want to waste any more of your time because you'll need to find out who the woman is and reach her family."

"No worries about time wasting." His gray mustache was wiry and shot with black. His dark eyes were appraising. Cautious. "The deceased is over at the funeral home. We're too small a shop to have our own morgue." He gestured toward the door, putting one hand on my elbow as if to scoot me along. I stepped away from his touch but made for the door. The wind gusted hard as we exited. "We'll take Unit 1. Right here." Rogers started to open the passenger door of the patrol car.

"No thanks!" I said. "I'll follow you. That way I can drive straight back to the city when we're done."

"Are you sure? You might…" He paused and regrouped. "Sometimes people need to take a few minutes, afterward. To gather themselves."

"No, no. I'll be fine." He hesitated, assessing me again, and I could see he was about to continue his objections. "I'm sure it's not her. I'll be fine. Let's just go." I unlocked my rental to show him I wasn't changing my mind. Rogers shrugged his shoulders, went around to the other side of the cop car, and climbed in.

It was a short drive to the funeral home. The wind was still blowing furiously, and the funeral home door slammed backward against the front of the building as we entered. I shook the hair out of my face and looked around. Rogers exchanged hushed greetings with the receptionist, and we sat down to wait though I didn't know for what.

"You'll need to prepare yourself," Chief Rogers said once we'd settled into our seats. "The body has been mutilated."

Oh, God. I intentionally hadn't given much thought about what I might actually see, but I obviously couldn't put off thinking about it any longer. "What did they do?" I asked.

"They cut out his eyes."

Why? I thought. "Her," I said.

"What?" Rogers asked.

"*Her* eyes. They cut out *her* eyes."

"Okay," he responded, tipping his head to stretch his neck as if his collar was too tight.

"I wonder why they mutilate them?" I asked. Mutilation was one of the horrors trans women and their families often experienced. There were so many reasons Char did the work she did.

"I can't say." Rogers replied. "This is the first time we've dealt with someone like your… wife?"

"Yes. My wife. Her name is Charlotte." The guy was obviously confused by the whole thing. "But I'm sure this isn't her."

The muscles in his face moved, as if he was planning to say something else, but changed his mind. He watched me before continuing. "The eyes weren't the only thing," he said.

"What else did they do?"

"They cut off his penis."

"*Her.*"

"What?" he asked.

"*Her* penis."

He looked annoyed at being corrected again, and a bit like I was crazy. But the least I could do for the poor woman was to help educate this cop who clearly had no exposure to trans people. "Anything else I should know?"

"Those are the worst parts."

"Okay then. Where do we need to go? I have to wrap this up because my wife is still missing and I need to figure out what's going on." I was anxious to get it over with. I missed Charlotte and wanted to get back to her hotel to see what I could find out. Maybe once I found her, she'd listen to me. Forgive me. He nodded, stood, and waved toward a door a few feet away. Apparently we hadn't been waiting for anything other than his warnings. We passed through the door into a utilitarian corridor, clearly not a section of the building where paying customers generally traveled.

Rogers' shoes squeaked softly, the rubber or whatever it is cop soles are made of trying to grip the astringently clean surface of the floor and failing. I imagined the tiny suck of starfish feet gripping my finger and wished I was on the beach at Plum Island, or anywhere else really. My boots were quieter, the tread not bothering to cling, and I tried to see how quietly I could walk in comparison to the sticking, gripping mini squeak of his non-slip soles.

I thought again about how horrible it would be for the real family once they were found. How they'd walk down this hallway listening to the footsteps. For me it was some kind of sick sideshow. For them it would be tragedy. I rolled my shoulders from the tension of it, and turned my brain away from the idea of loss that huge.

Rogers led me to a room filled with stainless steel, then walked to a wall of drawers and pulled one out. I stepped closer, not looking forward to what I would see. But I stopped about three feet away from her.

I thought she'd be completely covered by a sheet, or be encased in a zippered bag, but she wasn't. She lay like she was tucked into the world's least comfortable bed.

Her eye sockets were red and raw, violated and torn, and I didn't know how I could keep looking. But the eyebrows were meticulous, those beautifully arched brows of which she was so vain. Perfectly smooth. Perfectly shaped. Perfectly filled in. Her makeup had always been flawless.

They were her eyebrows.

They couldn't be her eyebrows.

The lips were hers as well; full and curving, but one side was swollen and cut where she must have been punched.

They were her lips.

They couldn't be her lips.

My chest started to constrict, as if tentacles of stainless steel were snaking out from the tables and sinks and wrapping themselves around me to squeeze away my breath. I had to get out of there.

"Charlotte's missing. I need to go find her." I had to drive to the hotel right that minute. I turned to the door.

"Miss Wells…"

"This is a waste of time."

"Have you made a determination, Miss Wells?"

"This can't be her."

"Do you need to view more of… the deceased's body?"

"It can't be her."

"Does Charlotte have any distinguishing characteristics? Scars, or maybe a tattoo?"

"I have to go. Charlotte must have lost her phone."

"Perhaps if you check the torso?"

He pulled the white covering down and I couldn't help it; I glanced back. I saw her breasts with their tiny, dark, nipples. But they were deformed now. Sliced and cut. Deflated. Obscene.

They were her breasts.

They couldn't be her breasts.

"I have to go."

It was getting very hard to breathe. I looked lower and saw the mole beneath her right hip bone. The one I liked to kiss. Lower, to her groin, the dark triangle of hair now a frame for a grotesque, ragged stump.

My stomach churned. My face grew hot. My head began to swim.

Shimmy decided years ago that she didn't want bottom surgery. It was too harsh, too drastic, she said. She didn't hate her penis, and I loved it. She was so feminine except this one part of her. Her penis made her a chimera, magical in her half and halfness. Silken and honeyed while simultaneously rigid and pulsing. I called her Shimmy when I was happy with her, which was most of the time. Char when I was irritated or needed her to pay attention. Charlotte when I was pissed. But in my head, in my heart, she was always my miraculous chimera. My Shimmy.

I would have supported her if she'd wanted the surgery, even though I loved her dick. I loved every part of her, so much it scared me sometimes. I'd never told her, but I didn't want to lose any single bit of her. I saved her hair from the bathtub when she left any, which was rare. We used separate brushes, and I collected hair from hers every week. Not a full harvest because she'd notice. Before she went on trips, I'd strip it bare though, reasoning that she'd be too busy getting ready to pay attention, and if she did, she'd just think I was being helpful. I kept the hair in a mason jar in the basement. Our old house sat on a fieldstone-lined hole, and she hated spiders so she never went down there. I didn't want her to think I was creepy, or stranger than she already knew me to be, so it seemed safer to hide it.

I wished she'd cut her own finger and toenails, because if she did, I would collect those too. A jar would slowly fill up with them, tiny moon-shaped slivers lacquered in rainbow shades, nestling into each other the way lovers spooned. The way we spooned. Unfortunately, she considered manicures and pedicures a professional necessity. She didn't trim her nails at home.

I would have saved every scrap of hair, nails, and skin that I could. I envied the dust mites which consumed the particles of flesh which filtered into her pillow. I suddenly understood the Victorian mourning art made from hair which I'd seen at some of the historic properties I worked in, though I didn't know why that thought suddenly popped into my head, and I pushed it away as quickly as it had come.

Her body was sacred to me, a gift from heaven, my personal miracle.

And this poor woman in front of me, they'd taken her penis. They hadn't even cut it off flat against her mons pubis, the dumb fucks. They'd left half an inch like a ragged hose.

I wanted it back.

I wanted it back for her, for me. I wanted to save it in a jar, a relic to my beloved saint of a wife, to sit next to her hair and the empty jar which should have been filled with nail clippings.

"Where is it?" I finally said.

Rogers tried to look sympathetic. "We couldn't find it."

Thank God this wasn't Shimmy.

Couldn't be Shimmy.

"Are you all right?" Chief Rogers asked.

It was a stupid question. Who could ever be all right in a situation like this, looking over the dead body of someone's beloved? Wondering what sort of an animal would cut off a stranger's penis. The tentacles gripped tighter and my breathing came in abrupt gulps. "I'm fine."

"Almost done?"

"Almost."

I stroked the woman's torso, hoping her family wouldn't mind that I was touching her, testing for Shimmy's signature heat.

Char was like a furnace, a wonderful burning presence on cold New England winter nights. I burrowed up against her every time I woke, and she rolled us over, wrapping me in her arms and curling up against me, warm breasts pressed into my back, warm thighs pushing against my thighs. Sometimes it would excite her and we would make love just like that, falling asleep again, still connected. Her heat raged in the summer and I hated having to choose between torrential sweat or not feeling her skin. The compromise was running the air conditioning so high that the air made me shiver.

I realized I was shivering.

The dead woman's skin was cold. Really cold. And it didn't give like Shimmy's did. It was unyielding to my touch, where she was all giving, all rising to meet me. The hardness of her skin made my stomach heave and my head spin.

"Do you have confirmation?" Rogers asked. He was starting to sound impatient.

"One more thing to check."

One final proof that it wasn't her.

Couldn't be her.

I bent to look at the crook of her elbow, that intimate place where the skin was so thin, I could sometimes see the beat of her heart pumping blood though a blue vein on its way back to oxygenation. The veins on the woman's arm looked just like Shimmy's, which must mean that all our blood vessels are in the same positions and we are more like robots than we realize.

She was so classy, my Shimmy. She dabbed scent on just a few places of heat and pulse, not wanting to walk in a perfumed cloud but wearing just enough that when someone drew near, they caught a hint. I liked to think it was just for me, because of that. Kind of like her love signal when she ended her nightly broadcasts. A few people might whisper in her ear and catch a sniff, but I was the only one who laid my head on her shoulder and breathed deep. Only I could rest my head on her breast and smell the scent rising from her cleavage. I was the only one to kiss her wrists and trace the delicate cradle of her inner elbow with my tongue.

She was a furnace, my Shimmy, and the heat did something to the fragrance she applied, transforming it. I tried wearing it once, thinking I'd be able to smell her all day at work, but it didn't smell like it did on her. The exotic spiciness which mellowed and transformed from her heat smelled heavy and raw on me.

It wasn't just the alchemy of heat and perfume that made me want to sniff her all the time though. There was a scent beneath it, created by some sort of osmosis in which her skin absorbed oxygen and breathed out Char-ness. It smelled of citrus, honey, and musk, and was very much her. The scent was strongest in the morning, when we'd been covered up all night and her essence was still trapped beneath the linens rather than out and mixing with the air of the room. I breathed deep each morning. I missed it while she was traveling, every time and this time. I couldn't wait until she came back home and I could open the sheets to breathe her again.

I bent closer to the crook of the poor woman's elbow, lost in the thought of her scent in our bed. I bent to get one last reassurance, to give it one final test, and then I'd go back up to St. Louis and wait for Char to show up at her hotel.

I bent closer.

"Miss?"

So close I could feel the cold reach my nose as the air emptied of heat calories trying to warm her frigid presence.

So close I began to detect it, even though I wasn't sniffing.

And then I did sniff; an open-mouthed gulp of air.

It was her perfume.

It couldn't be her perfume.

It was cold and dulled but not gone, and not raw the way it smelled on me. It had been transformed by her alchemy, softened the way I could not soften it. I also smelled a faint hint of citrus, honey and musk, but it was so faint, barely there, not producing, not breathing out of her, just a fading ghost of former life and breath.

I smelled it all, and the tentacles cinched brutally around my chest like a torture device. I couldn't breathe, and as I tried to stand up, my vision went blank. I was as blind as the woman lying on the table in front of me, the woman whose eyes had been stolen. The woman who was Char.

In death her body spoke a language I did not want to understand.

I couldn't breathe, and I couldn't see, and after that, I couldn't think. The last thing I remembered was hitting the floor.

Chapter 16

I shook my head to break free from the hold of the memory. Horror and disbelief threatened to drown me. I had to shake it off and come back to where I sat in Maria's kitchen, or I'd be lost. "After that, all hell broke loose." I finally said. "Cameras and reporters arrived, and Yori came with them, thank God. I don't know how I would have gotten home without him." He'd been almost as heartbroken as I was, but he pulled himself together to take care of the details.

"I am glad he was there for you," Maria said. She stood and placed a warm hand on my shoulder. "I do not know how it is you survived this." The timer dinged, and she turned to the oven to remove the final tray of cookies. The lemon scent no longer smelled delicious. She transferred the cookies to a cooling rack.

I'd been right, of course. Telling Maria about the whole thing hadn't changed my mind. I wasn't emotionally cleansed and purified, simply through the telling. I still wanted vengeance. If anything, it fueled the fire.

"Then there was the funeral to organize and the press to fend off." I said. "It was busy for a few weeks, dealing with all the details. And then Christopher Jackson confessed."

"I saw much of this part, on the television, in the newspapers. And of course, around the town, where everyone was talking."

Clyde rubbed against my legs, and I bent to stroke the softness of his cheek. His purr was comfort, but not enough. The emptiness in my chest was a canyon of grief, impossible to fill.

"It all exploded again when he turned himself in. I hibernated in my house, with a lot of booze. Turned off all media so I wouldn't have to hear details about what happened. I didn't come back out until last spring. I don't think I would have survived otherwise."

"I am so glad you did survive, Madelaina," Maria said, sitting again now that the cookies were taken care of. She didn't offer me one, apparently sensing I couldn't possibly eat it now. She didn't eat either. "The world has work for you."

I didn't really give a fuck what the world needed from me. I had one goal.

"Do not discount this idea, Maddie. I see you poo pooping it, but it is hard to be happy and enjoy life without following the purpose Dio has for you."

She was a delusional optimist, duped by hope and the idea of God. But any God who permitted what happened to Char wasn't someone I wanted to know. Enjoying life obviously wasn't my fate. It would be hard to be happy in jail.

The thought made me sit up straight for a moment. Were women housed in the facility where Jackson was serving? If so, maybe I'd be sent there, and could find a way to get to the men's wing and kill him. I lifted my head to look at Maria. "Maybe you're right," I said. "Maybe I *do* have a purpose."

Her eyes narrowed and her lips tightened. "You are putting something up your sleeve, and it isn't a good something. You think I can't see this, but I can." I had to giggle then, and the giggle built into laughter. The laughing felt like relief and release. She watched me suspiciously for a minute, then joined in. "I wish I had known you then." Maria said, when our laughter subsided. "When all this was happening. I would have held your heart when you were not able to."

"I wish you did too, but nothing could have helped."

"Your heart, it still needs holding. Which is why you should stay here and not go on this fool's voyage you have planned."

I rolled my eyes and sighed, not wanting to go back down the same path again.

"It is obvious your head is like a boulder, and you are determined." Maria shook her head, still watching me. "So go. Hurry up, and get it over with, this thing you have planned." I nodded, grateful for her blessing. She'd become a center of warmth in the tundra of my life, and I didn't want to leave town carrying her anger. "As long as you come back, are we agreed?"

I'd have to get out of jail eventually, so it seemed safe to go along with it. "Agreed," I said.

"Bene!" she replied.

Two days later, I was driving to my new life.

Chapter 17

Deer carcasses deteriorated along the highways from Massachusetts to the Midwest. They came in all sizes, poses, and states of decomposition. The older corpses probably fled hunters in the woods only to die from motorists who had no desire to do them harm. More recent additions may have wandered into the road out of hunger, when winter snows made foraging for anything green and tender impossible to find.

In Illinois, I passed signs for the World's Largest Pitchfork. And rocking chair. And wind chime. And mailbox. It turned out that all these things were in the same place, a small town called Casey. I pulled over to check them out and grab lunch. The wind chimes hung, huge and silent. A sign described how to pull a long rope to make music. I took the handle, walked backward, and pulled the gigantic metal pipes into motion. They clanged with tones in several registers, their tolling low and dolorous, like church bells announcing the start of a funeral.

When I dipped south into Missouri, I drove past an oddly shaped patch of grass and early blooming flowers growing atop the pavement. Perhaps the garden had grown from one of the dead deer, transformed by time and weather into ashes and dust, eventually becoming breathing greenery which shifted and bent in the wind.

The whole trip was like that, funereal and full of dark discoveries, of oversized things and death and growth and decay. I didn't like thinking about decomposition. The dark mystery of a body filled with life suddenly having none, and then beginning its disintegration into eventual nothingness was too painful to contemplate. Luckily, I had a lot of other things to think about. Google reported that Jackson's wife still lived in Peytonsville, but that could have changed. I had to figure out how to find her, approach her, and eventually do what needed to be done.

Chapter 18

The place was smaller than it looked on TV; just a sharp triangle formed by the intersections of three scruffy streets, with a plastic recycling plant down the block, and graffiti rendering veiled wisdom on nearby brick walls. The young trees were planted close together. A wooden sign read "Transgender Memorial Garden."

I'd stopped on my way through St. Louis because it was the last place I'd seen Char alive. I should have been shivering because Char had been cold while she talked, but it was too warm. I walked to where the dais had been positioned so I could stand where she stood and try to feel her presence.

Char's memory was now stamped into the elemental fabric of the place. She'd changed the air that moved through it, and the ground on which she'd placed her feet. She died the same day she spoke there, talking about all the transgender people who had also died, known and unknown, murdered like her or felled by suicide when dysphoria or rejection by family, church, and society became too much to bear.

I wanted to feel her, but couldn't. I wanted to scream at her but didn't. I wanted to destroy the sign or gild it with something shining and indestructible. Instead, I kicked it.

Why, Shimmy? Why didn't you give me the love signal? Why wouldn't you forgive me?

I didn't understand how humans were supposed to survive this much guilt and grief. Why would Maria's God design us to love so much and then live on after losses this huge? Why didn't that God destroy me along with Char, or *instead* of her, if they required sacrifice? If it could change anything I would claw my own eyes out, slash my own breasts, and mutilate my own genitals. But the horror was that I could do all those things and it wouldn't make a bit of difference. Char wouldn't be restored. Time would not flow backward so I could take an extra Xanax and get on the damned plane. There was no treasure chest of a blue time-traveling mantel. The horror of it was that there are some things which can't be undone, no matter what you're willing to sacrifice at the altar of regret.

The only way to fight it was to succumb to the seductive power of revenge. When there's nothing left to do and there's no way to survive the grief without action, revenge is there. It wafts and whispers, pulling your mind away from mourning and into something different. Still dark, but actionable. And the wounded heart grabs hold and embraces it, breathing deep the intoxicating relief of distraction.

Jesse James had a lot to teach me. He'd made a name for himself by accepting the anesthetic revenge offered, and I was about to do the same thing. I got back in my car.

Chapter 19

I checked in to a cheap motel off the highway outside of St. Louis, and called the museum to let the Harrises know I'd be there mid-morning the next day. Staying at the Downtown Sojourner had been my initial plan, but after the depth of emotion experienced at the garden, I figured I'd be better off somewhere with no connection to Char.

She hated cheap hotels. Not because she was snooty, but she claimed a strange spiritual sensitivity, and said the human darkness played out in those places saturated the walls and made her skin crawl. I'd always been slightly empathic but didn't pick up shadow vibes from previous tenants. A cheap room with my car parked in front of the door was fine with me. The biggest problem with the place was the fabric of the bed covering. Ick.

It was my final day as a good person, or as good as I could, be, given what I'd let happen to Shimmy. The next day would set everything in play. I'd take over the museum, fertilize my tiny seed of a plan, and wait to trample the resulting vintage. It was my final night of freedom from what was to come.

To celebrate, I ordered a small pizza and filled a plastic cup from the box of red wine I'd brought with me on the drive. The TV delivered a deluge of porn channels. I flicked past those fast, worried the images would ignite the fire I struggled to keep banked. Making love with Shimmy had changed sex forever, and succumbing to the slapping flesh of pornography would only make me lonelier and more disgusted with myself than I already was. I went to bed early.

Breakfast was a donut and coffee from the lobby. St. Louis traffic was calm compared to Boston and the drive went by quickly. I found the museum with no trouble, and was surprised that it was so small. The sign was large and dated, but in remarkably good shape.

"Good morning!" A voice called out when I came through the door. "You must be Maddie?"

"Doris?" I replied, watching the woman pop up from her seat behind the checkout counter at the back of the gift shop. She was small but not as small as me, and spry, nearly bouncing as she came out to greet me.

"Yes, yes! I'm glad to meet you! So happy you're here to set us free for our next grand adventure." She extended her arms in what could only be an invitation to hug. Her perfume smelled powdery. The hug was nice. She let go, then looked me up and down. "Well," she said. "I guess we have a lot of territory to cover. Let's start with a tour. Unless you'd like to bring your things in first?"

"A tour sounds great. I can get my stuff later."

"All right then. Gerry ran to the bank to explain that you're taking over so they won't be surprised when you go in. He'll be back shortly."

I nodded.

"Obviously this is the gift shop. A lot of our revenue comes from the sale of these items, so if you can encourage patrons to look around, it's helpful."

"I can do that."

"This is the children's section, as you can tell." Doris led me into one of the front corners, gesturing toward a display of undersized cowboy hats, toy guns, and plastic horses. "We've been meaning to add some candy, because kids always want to buy *something*, and parents like cheap options. Gerry's worried about the potential mess though. So you'll have to decide about that later on."

"Got it."

"Over here we have the hot sellers. Coffee mugs, shot glasses, and spoons. Classic souvenirs never go out of style. You'll have to keep your eye on this stock, because it will move fast. We've got plenty out back so you shouldn't have to place an order for some time."

"Check." I figured my job for the moment was simply to watch and listen.

"This corner is for apparel. We sell lots of T-shirts and hats." There were several racks of hanging clothes, and a shelf displaying miniature flags, both American and rebel. "You should go through them once a week to make sure a variety of sizes are always available."

Doris continued walking me around the store, pointing out the challenges of particular items and offering notes about Gerry's preferences. Once my tour of the shop was complete, we went behind the counter and she walked me through the books. I asked enough questions to reassure her that I wasn't clueless about what she was describing, but not enough to slow down the process. I could figure out all the details once I was on my own. Doris showed me how to use the antique cash register, and I imagined Jesse James breaking into it to fund his gang's next escapade.

The whole thing took about an hour. No patrons came in during that time, but Gerry finally appeared, greeting me as warmly as Doris had, minus the hug. Instead, he gave me a long, firm handshake.

"You can tell a lot about a person by the way they shake your hand," he said. "That mostly applies to men, but you've got a good shake on you. You're not afraid of it. That's a good thing." He smiled at me, then gave me the once over just like Doris had. "You weren't kidding, were you? Just a little mite of a thing." He shook his head. "But smart. I can tell. We're glad to have you."

"I'm really glad to be here."

"Doris been filling you in on how things work?"

"Yes, she's been a great help. We covered a lot of ground already."

"Good, good. Has she shown you the museum yet?"

"Nope! We just went through the front of the house," I said.

"Thought you'd want to take her through your sanctum," Doris said.

"I surely do. Let's go." He waved me toward two doors at the back of the room. "This one's the storeroom. It's got your cleaning products, inventory, stuff like that." He closed the first door. The second was open and led past a poorly realized wax figure of a card-playing cowboy, which didn't seem to bode well for what was to come. I followed Gerry into the dimness, and he described the visitor experience, which started with a short film. He showed me how to access the equipment in case of problems. After patrons watched the flick, they walked through three rooms of displays. Wax figures in a variety of settings explained how Jesse James went rogue as an action of revenge, and then moved on to tell the tale of the man who claimed to have lived on even after Jesse was murdered. Similar scenes showed Billy the Kid and Wild Bill Longley, complete with a scaffold. These wax figures were a lot better than the one out front. They reminded me of Disney World's Hall of Presidents: just as creepy but without the motion. Gerry offered expansive stories about each display, and his passion for the tale the museum set out to tell was evident.

"Do any of the guns still work?" I asked as we walked past a glass cabinet full of firearms. I hadn't fully formulated my plan for Jackson's wife, and all the guns were giving me an itchy trigger finger.

"I've never tried them, and I wouldn't if I were you. Might blow your hand right off, or worse."

"Oh, I won't," I said. *At least not until I clean them.* "Hands are too useful to risk."

"A man's got to know his sidearm before he fires it," Gerry said, as if not listening. "Becomes an extension of him, that way." He reached around his back and pulled a pistol from the waistband of his polyester pants. The gun had been hidden by a navy blazer which probably fit well 15 years ago, before he started shrinking. "This fella's been my constant companion for a long time. Wouldn't leave home without it. You carry?"

"Nope." I bagged my fair share of game growing up, and was a decent shot. But I hadn't hunted as an adult, or felt the need to own a pistol.

"That's too bad." He tipped his head back to look down at me along the slope of his nose. "Little slip of a thing like you could probably use one."

"I rely on my wits and martial arts training." I'd never taken a martial arts class in my life, but now wasn't the time to quibble over particulars.

Gerry nodded, as if assessing how much damage my frame could inflict. "Glad you got that going for you."

I pushed back my shoulders, trying to look taller and street smart.

We stopped in front of a display of dolls wearing wedding dresses from the past two centuries. There were a wide mix of textiles, some of which were disintegrating. The few grooms were female dolls clad in the masculine garb of the era; their long hair cut short, feminine faces thinly disguised with faux mustachios.

I thought back to our wedding, when Char was clad in a gorgeous white sheath dress. I wore a suit tailored to emphasize my minimal curves. We'd talked about wearing matching dresses, but I would have looked ridiculous in that sheath. I'd tried on other gowns, but what I wore was really irrelevant. Shimmy was the star. She deserved to shine and I was happy just to be in her orbit. The suit was a good solution. It was practical and comfortable, and allowed me to focus on making her feel special.

I turned away from the weird collection of couples in their marital finery, and away from the thoughts of the wedding. I didn't want to cry on my first day at work.

We finished the tour and headed back out to the shop. "Is it going to be hard for you to leave all this?" I asked.

"It won't be easy," he replied. "Been at it a long time. But there's life yet to be lived, and we've lived this one pretty darn fully. Isn't that right, dear?"

"We sure have," Doris said from her spot behind the counter.

"Time waits for no one, and we want to see a little bit of the country before the man with the sickle comes after us."

"That makes a lot of sense," I said. I wondered why it took us humans so long to figure this reality out. The Harrises were elderly and just got it. I'd learned younger, but still too late. "I hope you enjoy yourselves."

"Oh, we will." Gerry opened a side door and pointed out back. "You said you're handy, so that's where you'll find tools and stuff." I looked out and saw a ramshackle shed. "Key's here on this hook." He pointed to a hook on the interior trim of the door.

"Did Doris explain that we don't take credit cards?" Gerry asked.

"Would you like to? I could get a system set up."

"No, no. We don't want to pay a bunch of fees and deal with that nonsense. We like to keep things simple."

"Okay."

"If they come in and only have plastic, send them over to the Quickie Mart. They've got an ATM."

"Sounds like a plan."

"And if you have questions about our history or the building, just talk to Chip over there. He's one of those oddball genius types, and he knows pretty much everything there is to know about the place. Works a lot of hours, so it's easy to catch him."

"Great." It would be good to have a knowledgeable codger nearby, given that this one was heading south soon.

"Ready to see where you'll be living?"

"Sure!" I said, wondering if either of them noticed how much I was speaking in one-word sentences.

I followed Gerry up a narrow staircase into a living space which was almost as much of a museum as downstairs. It had been cleaned recently though. We were met with the scent of bleach and pine.

"Here you go! Doris has been up here getting it ready for you," Gerry said.

The room was dark paneled and dim, which didn't thrill me, but I hoped in the height of summer the dimness would translate to cool. Missouri summers were supposed to be scorchers. "You guys don't live on site?" I asked.

"Oh, no. Much too small for a family. We had kids, and then grandkids. They wouldn't have fit." Gerry looked around. "Think it will do?"

I didn't much care where I'd be staying. I was in Missouri for one reason only. As crash pad and planning headquarters, the place was adequate. "It's perfect," I said. "Big enough to spread out a bit, small enough to clean in an hour."

"Well, that's just fine, then." Gerry turned to go back down the stairs. "Any last questions?" he asked. "If not, Doris and I will be getting on the road. Can't drive too long at our age. The bones start to ache."

We rejoined Doris in the gift shop. "You're leaving right away?"

"No time like the present!" he said.

"When Gerry had a date for your arrival, he got so excited he started lining everything up so we could head right out! He's so organized," Doris said.

"If we leave now, we can get some hours in and find a place to stop for the night before it gets dark." Gerry said.

"We don't like driving at night," Doris said.

The news was kind of a shock. I'd figured they'd have me shadow them on the job for a few days and get the routines down before they left. Given how much Gerry loved the museum it seemed odd how trusting he was. They didn't know me at all but were ready to hand over what had been his kingdom for decades. I felt a little guilty that I'd come for nefarious reasons, and that my interest in the museum was feigned. But obviously he'd moved on from this phase of his life, or he wouldn't be so eager to give me the keys to it all. It was strange, but I was perfectly happy to get started on my plans without observation.

"Well, by all means, get going!" I said. "I'm sure I'll have a million questions, but I can call with them, or go bug the gas station guy."

"Chip."

"Right. Chip."

"All rightee then, that's what we'll do. You'll want to stay downstairs until closing time. Museum's still open, after all!"

"I'll man the desk and go through the books again to make sure I've got it all straight."

"Now, remember what I told you about the lock-up procedures. We've got the place insured pretty good, but that doesn't mean you should be careless."

"Of course. I remember."

"One last thing," Gerry said. "Some know-it-alls will come in and try to get evidence that the outlaw survivors aren't who they said they were. You need to kick those bums to the curb."

"Okay," I assembled my features in what I hoped resembled sincerity.

"We've lived our lives here, protecting these stories, because you won't hear about them many other places. And people need to know. We're counting on you to get rid of the naysayers as soon as you spot them."

"I'll be on the lookout, and when I see them, their butts will bounce." Gerry squinted one eye at me as if trying to make sense of the phrase. "Out they'll go," I said.

"Good. Good." He seemed appeased, and I was relieved I hadn't had to agree to a blood oath.

The Harrises offered a few more parting pieces of wisdom, we said our goodbyes, and they disappeared down the highway. It was one of the oddest experiences of my life. I'd just taken custody of a tiny oddball museum after only a three-hour introduction.

Thinking about it all made me consider that maybe the universe was lining things up for me. Maybe the arc of justice was shorter for some things than others, and this arc might be shorter than I expected.

I spent the rest of the day as I said I would, greeting the two sets of visitors who came, and looking over the books. At closing time, I hauled my bags up the stairs and unpacked what was in them. Tiredness hit early and the bed was surprisingly comfortable. The sheets were white and clean, and the building was quiet. Traffic on the nearby highway was just frequent and loud enough to be soothing. I fell asleep thinking about how eerie it was, knowing that wax bodies were beneath me, telling their tall tales and hoping to be believed.

Chapter 20

A battered kettle was perched on the stove, and though I'd never been a tea drinker, it was the only caffeine option in the cupboard. I blinked the sleepiness out of my eyes and turned on the burner. The coil glowed orange beneath the pot, the smell of burning dust proclaiming it hadn't been used in a while. Morning light sifted through the net curtains above the sink, and the space was pleasant as I waited for the water to rumble and the tea to steep. Time must have leached the flavor out of the leaves, because the brew was nearly tasteless. Clearly it was time to introduce myself to Chip or whoever else was working at the Quickie Mart. The store's employees were likely to be my initial source of intel about Christopher Jackson and his family, so I planned to become a regular. And I needed coffee.

"Is Chip in?" I asked the young guy behind the counter. His face was down, tuned in to the thick textbook he was reading.

"I am he," the guy said. He glanced up and tossed his head to shake the hair away from his glasses. He was tall, cute, and built.

"*You're* Chip?" I said.

"I am indeed."

"I expected someone older. Crustier."

He tipped his head questioningly at that. "My crust level is probably below average." He lifted a hand and pushed his glasses up, putting a finger right on the lens, which explained why they looked so dirty. "Hygiene is generally understood to be quite important, socially."

"That's true, but it's not what I meant."

"Well, I assumed you weren't referring to pastry, or pizza, or other types of edible crusts, which is what led me to conclude you meant some sort of bodily accretions. I take it there's another meaning?"

"There is, sort of. I guess it's a colloquialism," I said. "I just didn't expect you to be a young guy. Gerry told me you'd fill me in on anything I had questions about, so I thought you'd be someone like him, only covered in engine grease or something. And maybe kind of sardonic."

"So to describe this older character you used the term 'crusty.'" Chip said, as if adding the new meaning to his neural dictionary.

"Yes."

"I am incapable of being intentionally sardonic. Sometimes things I say may inadvertently result in irony, but it's not one of my skills. But you are quite right; I'm not the crusty character you envisioned. I'm sorry if that disappoints you."

"Trust me, I'm not disappointed," I said, thrusting my hand toward him. "I'm Maddie. Nice to meet you, Chip."

He took my hand and shook it properly. "The pleasure is mine. Mr. Harris told me to expect you." He peered at me more closely. "You look vaguely familiar."

"Do I?" I hadn't thought much about whether local news coverage would include pictures of the grieving widow. "I hear that all the time," I said, trying to deflect his thought process. "Must have one of those faces." Hopefully that would be enough to send him off the track.

"Your face is quite unique, actually."

Unfortunately, I was all too aware of that reality. I decided changing the subject was the best move. "So, have you worked here long?" I asked.

"Since high school. Initially part time. Then when I graduated it was just logical to continue."

"How'd you get to be an expert on the museum?"

"I'm hardly an expert. Everyone who comes from here knows about it. Most people take the museum for granted. It's been here for decades and has become an institution. Mr. Harris came in every day to talk with the owner of this establishment, and we became friends. I'd go over there fairly often, help him with physical tasks, and he'd tell me things about the place and its artifacts."

"So you aren't a big fan of outlaws? Jesse James isn't your hero?" I asked.

"I am not. His life story seems quite futile, so much death and villainy driven by a desire for revenge. It all appears rather improvident. Of course, human passions are not my forte."

I wondered if they were mine. "I think the desire for revenge might feel like an addiction," I offered. "So maybe it was hard to resist." This was an understatement. The desire to inflict pain was consuming.

"You may be right. However, addictions must be combatted."

I realized this was another dangerous line of conversation. "Has the museum changed much over the years?" I asked, in an attempt to bring things back around to safer topics.

"Not really. The inventory in the gift shop shifted a bit, though not much. The displays have essentially been the same."

"As far as I can tell, the myths about Jesse James, Buffalo Bill Cody, and Bill Langley's survival were all met with disbelief by most historians," I said.

"Not just historians. The people around town have mixed feelings about it too. Everybody likes Mr. and Mrs. Harris, but I think that's why they had trouble finding someone to run the place. The only people who wanted the job were kids or meth addicts."

"That must have upset them."

Chip nodded. His handsome face was consistently devoid of expression. "It did indeed. They take the business quite seriously."

"Why'd they decide to leave in such a hurry? I figured they'd want to test me out, but they took off immediately."

"Six months ago, Gerry had a mild cerebrovascular accident."

I processed the phrase. "Do you mean a stroke?"

Chip nodded. "Yes. There don't seem to be lingering effects, but it appears to have frightened them. Apparently they've had a lifelong desire to reside in Florida, and their great grandchildren are there, so they decided it was now or potentially never."

The reality that death comes when it chooses was all too familiar. "There's certainly wisdom in not wasting time."

"Is there anything I can help you with today?" Chip asked, apparently ready to get back to reading.

"Not really. I just wanted to introduce myself. And get some coffee."

"The machines are right over there," he said pointing to the middle of the shop, before sitting back down and opening his textbook. "Instant and ground options are in the second aisle."

I grabbed my coffee and paid for it with cash. "I'm sure I'll see you again soon. Maybe you can help me understand the outlaw lore," I said.

"I'm reasonably familiar with the pertinent details."

I headed toward the door. "See you later."

"Keep your eyes open for wax worms. Mr. Harris never seemed concerned about them, which I consider lunacy."

"Wax worms?"

"It's unlikely that you'll experience an infestation. But it's best to be vigilant."

"I guess I'd better study up on them. Didn't realize they were a thing." Preventing insect damage was critical in textile preservation, but I'd never heard of wax worms.

"They are indeed a thing. Species: mellonella: genus: Galleria. I'm glad you'll be taking the issue seriously."

I left the store, shaking my head at the interaction and considering the possibility that worms were at that very minute chewing away at the wax bodies of the figures in the museum. I didn't like thinking of worms and bodies and the things they implied, so I shifted my thought to Chip. Gerry called him an oddball genius, and it was easy to see why. It seemed like he'd be a good source of information about Jackson. His practicality and lack of emotion hopefully meant he wouldn't tune in to my motives. And he was easy on the eyes, if you were into that sort of thing.

I decided I'd call him Chip Boulderpecks. At least in my own mind.

Chapter 21

"Why did you not tell me you have a black Madonna so close to where you are living out this plea of insanity?" Maria rarely bothered with conventional greetings when she called, and she didn't this time either.

"Hi Maria! How are you?"

"I am as fine as a woman my age can be. But that is not important. She is near you, and you did not tell me!"

"I don't actually know what you're talking about."

"You remember the card I gave you. Of Mamma Schiavona."

"Of course! I still carry it in my pocket."

"Well, a little bit lower than St. Louis is one of her homes. A shrine. It is near you! You must go visit her."

I appreciated Maria's heart, but religious places weren't exactly my thing. "It's hard to get time away from the museum. It's just me running it."

"Didn't you say you made a friend? Chips Rockysnack or something like that?"

"Boulderpecks. But that's not his real name. Plus, he works too."

"He can't all the time be working. Does he live in that inconvenient store like you do in that wax house?"

"No. But I still wouldn't want to bother him."

"Is it hard, this job of yours? Will he have problems doing what you do for two hours?"

She obviously didn't want to give up. "I'm sure he could handle it."

"Then either close up for the time you are gone, or get Mr. Boulders to help you. You don't have to be so 'I'll do it myself' all the time. Like a toddler."

"All right, I'll ask! Geez, you are pesky."

"Pesky in a good way. Pesky in a way that says I love you, Madelaina."

"I love you too."

"Dio knew you needed a bossy old Italian nonna in your life, and here I am."

My concept of God leaned toward the idea of a force which launched the universe into being and then sat back to let us do what we wanted within it. Given the evils which ran amuck, it didn't seem like God controlled much. Loved ones were murdered, fires and storms ravaged cities and countryside, and children died of starvation. A supreme being who thought about my needs was pretty unlikely, but it didn't seem wise to mention it. And I couldn't argue with the fact that I really *did* need an Italian grandmother. "I'm grateful he gave me you, even if you *are* bossy."

"God is so good, and he wants you to go to this shrine. You must visit her, this Mama Schiavona of Missouri."

I sighed recognizing defeat. "Okay, you win. I'll go."

"Grazie!"

"You are welcome. Give Clyde a cuddle for me."

"He is in a mood today, but I will try."

We ended the call, and I took out the holy card to read the inscription again. Maybe a trip to see a Madonna like that would turn out to be interesting.

Chapter 22

A grizzled old man in a sweatshirt and plaid pajama pants limped over to where I'd parked. "We close at 6:00," he said, thrusting a brochure at me. "Sun will be behind the hill by then anyway, and it'll be getting dark."

"Thanks," I replied, glancing at my watch. "An hour should be plenty."

He nodded, turned, and stumped away, disappearing into a long, low building. It looked like the tour would be self-guided, which was fine with me. I walked the grounds, visiting crystal-encrusted grottos and reading about a monk who died in the 1960s doing what he loved; building niches and setting up statues of saints. He'd done much of the construction during the "Jesse James survived!" frenzy. Cement held together stones and found objects, and the whole thing was gently crumbling. It was hard not to compare the wax figures at the museum and the shining white faces of the Mary and Jesus statues. Both places were fueled by passion and built over decades.

I settled for a few minutes in an open-air chapel, breathing the serenity which pooled there, and looking at the mosaic Madonna icon behind the altar. Her jeweled crown was held up by a pair of angels; apparently it was no easy thing to be the queen of heaven. Two gashes were prominent on one cheek. The brochure explained that there were efforts to steal the original icon throughout the centuries. During one attempt her face was slashed with a saber, and as the soldier pulled back his arm to strike again, he fell down dead. Caretakers tried to repair the image, but each time the marks would reappear, and something which looked like blood seeped from the wounds. Legend said Mary wanted her image to remain scarred as a reminder to anyone who tried to desecrate her shrine.

Char would have loved the place.

I wished there was a way for *my* scars to become permanent beacons of warning, though I wasn't sure against what. Maybe just coming too close. But my wounds were invisible, and anyone coming near was definitely at risk.

A fish on the mosaic wall behind the Madonna reminded me of the floors in Boston Logan airport, though it was just one symbol of many in the stone tapestry including a dove, lamb, and chalice.

Peace, innocence, and blood.

The sinking sun shone in toward the altar, settling gently on the Madonna's face. For a moment I thought I saw a tear on her cheek, sparkling like one of the jewels adorning her crown. But that was ridiculous. It must have been a shard of crystal from the crumbling grottos, broken down into dust and blown in by the wind. She was safe here, snuggled into her little chapel in the rural landscape, surrounded by trees, statues of saints, and peace. She had nothing to cry about.

Chapter 23

Later that week I put the "Back in 30 Minutes" sign on the door at noon and headed over to the gas station for my daily check-in. Chip was behind the counter, tapping two pens like drumsticks along with the piped-in music. The beat didn't match, but he was having a good time.

"Hey, Chip."

"Maddie." He looked up briefly, then went back to his percussion. I walked around the store, not really interested in buying anything but figuring I should get something to help justify his salary. He was the only companion I had who could make conversation, after all. I settled on a bag of sunflower seeds.

By the time I got back to the counter, the music had shifted to something softer and slower. He put down the pens. I set down my packet of seeds.

"Anything else? Cigarettes? Vaping devices? Condoms?" He pushed up his glasses the way he always did, flinging a hand toward his face and planting his index finger wherever it landed.

"Nope. Just these." I pushed the seeds toward him. "Why do you push your glasses up like that?" I asked.

"Efficiency."

I looked at the right lens, fogged with smudges. "But how can that be efficient? The lens gets covered in fingerprints."

"I did the math. It's more efficient." The glasses slid down his handsome nose again, and he used the same technique. "$1.07."

"What math?" I asked, pulling cash out of my pocket.

"I estimated how many times I push them up every day, and calculated how much time it would add to aim for the bridge. It would slow me down by at least 2 seconds each time. That adds up."

"But don't you have to clean them more this way?" I tossed two singles on the counter.

"I clean them once a day. When I brush my teeth before bed. No additional time needed. Would you like a bag?"

"Don't bother." I paused. "Why don't you get your glasses adjusted so they don't slip down so much?"

"I dislike optician offices. They smell peculiar."

I tried to think about what an optician's shop smelled like but couldn't come up with anything. Maybe the spray they used to clean the glasses? But Chip was still speaking. "Also, they'd make them too tight. I can't stand the sensation of pressure against my temples." His big green eyes glanced up at me briefly before flitting away again. The music shifted to a new song, and he picked up the pens. The drumming resumed.

I nodded. "It always takes a while to get them just right."

"I can't be bothered. It's not worth it. I did the math."

"I'm sure you did," I said.

"What's new at the waxworks?" Chip asked.

"Absolutely nothing."

"No worm infestations?"

"Not yet. But I'm keeping my eyes open."

"Vigilance pays. Not that it's likely. But it's possible. A female could travel in on some farmer's pants, and the next thing you know you're overrun."

"Maybe you could come check for me, when you get off work?" It would be nice to have company other than museum guests.

"Can't," he replied. The drumming continued. "They're not really interested in the wax itself, of course. Normally they just chew through honeycomb in order to eat the bee larvae and dead skin and whatnot. Protein. That's what they're after."

"So, it's unlikely."

"Yes. But you never know. If a pregnant one got stuck in there, she might think it's her only option. And before you know it, all their faces would be pockmarked." He looked up again, his normally expressionless face looking vaguely earnest.

"I'll check again when I get back."

"Good." Chip nodded and stood up. "I've got to restock that sunflower seed display, now that you've taken a pack."

"I'll be leaving then. Have a great day!"

"I will." He set the pens down parallel to each other, and walked toward the back of the store. His shoulders were wide and stretched the fabric of his tee shirt. If I were straight, I'd consider taking him to bed. I wondered if he was a virgin. His oddness made it a definite possibility.

"Hey Chip?" I called.

"What?"

"Are you a virgin?"

"My father taught me that it's impolite to talk about sex."

"Your father is a wise man."

"That's what he says."

"See you tomorrow." I left the store, ripped the top corner of the sunflower seed bag, and walked slowly back to the museum, sucking the salt off the seeds and spitting the husks out as I went.

Chapter 24

Working in the museum was like stepping into the 1960s. The place made me feel dislocated in time, just as being away from New England made me feel dislocated in space. Nothing felt normal, which was just what I needed.

The museum had the kind of over-the-top cheesiness that Char would have adored, but I tried not to think about her. For the first few weeks, I immersed myself in this new life, a life which had never included my wife. My persona as wax museum manager was more than just an act, it was a tool for survival and forward motion. The new me set out to learn everything I could about the outlaws, starting with Jesse James. There was a lot to learn.

His story started young. At 15, Jesse was whipped by Northern militiamen after they tried to hang his stepfather. His mother lost an arm when their family farm was bombed. I thought about the experience of losing a hand; the digits gone but not the muscle memory of things touched by it. The idea of body parts no longer connected to someone you loved was dangerous emotional territory, but excellent fuel for my fire.

The trauma kicked off Jesse's penchant for vindication, and he set about robbing banks and post offices, holding up trains, and generally not giving a fuck. I connected with the hunger for retribution. I was totally down with burning cities and shooting up trains full of Missourians. I didn't care about cash the way Jesse seemed to, though if I hadn't had all that insurance money, perhaps I'd have wanted to steal as well.

Historical record states that a man named Bob Ford shot Jesse in the back on April 3, 1882. Many of his contemporaries called Ford a coward for killing him that way, but wasn't he also a hero for stopping such an outrageous outlaw? Might history someday judge *me* as heroic?

The wax museum had another explanation for the Bob Ford story, and if you squinted sideways, you could almost believe it. Lots of people testified that Dalton was really Jesse. Affidavits were taken from surviving members of the James Gang, law enforcement officers, and a judge who said Missouri's governor helped Jesse fake his death so he wouldn't have to live like a fugitive.

J. Frank Dalton—old, frail, and potentially delusional—rekindled America's worship of Jesse James. Dalton's appearance and eventual death re-immortalized Jesse and reinforced his image as dark hero.

The museum was a shrine to revenge and violence. Through it outlaws were transformed into misunderstood saints, cloaked in gun smoke rather than incense.

It was twisted and farcical, but I understood the desperate cling to nostalgia. The Harris' predecessors came from the John Wayne era, and the museum connected them to all that, and made *them* feel heroic by connection. There was no heroism in any of it, but the call to nostalgia was similar to my love of cookbooks. The past always *seems* simpler, even though it wasn't.

Jesse's story resonated with me, deeply. He had a craving for justice, vigilante style. Sometimes having your enemy locked up just wasn't punishment enough. Jesse's loved ones were hurt, and he never stopped trying to get them back for it.

I could understand that.

Chapter 25

The museum closed early enough that I had plenty of free time in the evenings. More than enough really, in a place where I had no interest in taking adult ed classes, joining a church, or establishing friendships. I was here for one reason only, and trying to figure out how to accomplish my goal was driving me crazy.

I thought about the challenge while soaking in the turquoise tub of my time-capsule bathroom, considering Jesse's revenge-fueled violence. Did he feel better each time he watched a man jolt from the force of a bullet entering their body? Did the depth of his pain lessen when he spent money acquired through the fear and death of others?

When you struck back at a person who did profound evil, did it make you a hero? Would I feel like a hero when Jackson's wife suffered? Or would I feel just as flat and empty as I did then, rattling around in life, alone and irritated?

I couldn't answer the questions, but it didn't matter. I was going to do it. Jackson's wife was going to pay the price, and he would suffer just as I was suffering, only more so. He'd know that it was his actions that brought it about. He'd know she died because of what he'd done to Char. We'd both face the consequences in prison. I'd turn myself in, as he had. As Jesse hadn't done.

And who knew? Maybe one of his relatives would find a way to kill me while I was locked away, Hatfield and McCoy style. There'd be no one left after that to continue the battle. But I didn't care if it ended there, didn't care if I died as long as Jackson suffered.

The water trickled out the overflow drain while I soaked and thought, and I refilled it several times to keep the water super-hot, the way I liked it. So hot Char told me she was surprised my skin didn't peel off. I wished she was there to climb in with me, her long legs wrapping around mine as I leaned back into her, water sloshing on the floor from the additional mass. I felt her absence as an ache at the bottom of my ribs, a fist of ice which no antacid could melt. The pain was always there, though it receded from my awareness when I was distracted, and pulsed back into prominence at night or times like this when I was alone, and thinking.

There was too much free time on my hands. I had to get things moving. I'd had enough of waiting. It was time to get some information out of Chip.

The store was empty when I got there the next morning, which was handy though not unusual. I bought a soda but stayed at the counter to shoot the breeze like I usually did. My heart started to thrum and I could feel blood blooming its way toward the skin of my throat, but it was no time for a panic attack. I was grateful for Chip's lack of eye contact and hoped he didn't notice my attempt to self-soothe by deep breathing. We made small talk and when I had myself together, I shifted conversation to the news channel's stream of outrage, which worked well as segue. "I heard there was quite a controversy here a couple years ago," I said. "That newscaster's murder?"

Chip nodded and pushed up his glasses. "I was once surprised by the depths to which humanity plunges when facing discomfort of the unknown" he said. "But with stories like that becoming commonplace, surprise has transformed into something else. I don't quite have a word for it, though there's probably one in German."

My heart rate slowed slightly when I realized he didn't find the question odd. "What did you think about the victim being transgender?" I asked. Knowing his view would allow me to frame my questions in a way that wouldn't shut him down. He could be rabidly anti-LGBTQ, though he hadn't shown it yet.

"Can you clarify your question?"

"The woman who was murdered was trans."

"I'm aware of that."

Chip parsed sentences literally, and I regularly had to elaborate on what I was trying to say. "What do you think about transgender people?" I said.

"I began studying the issue a year or so before the murder, because it had become such a socially divisive topic. I don't generally converse about those sorts of things because people inevitably get emotional and it's impossible to engage in intelligent discourse with someone who is emotional. But I do like to 'have a take,' as they say, and that requires evaluating the validity of various arguments."

"What did you conclude?"

"The science suggests it's a biological phenomenon on a number of fronts. White matter differences in the brain, for one. Hormonal variance during and after gestation for another. The investigations of cause are ongoing, but it seems clear that there are physical issues which contribute to dysphoria related to one's sex assigned at birth."

I nodded as he spoke, and sipped my soda.

"Of course, not very many people object to transgender people based on science. Most objections come out of religion and obviously that's illogical," he continued.

"Do you believe in God?" I asked.

"I base my decisions and beliefs on evidence. With something like the idea of God, I haven't found enough proof."

"So, you're an atheist."

"I would consider whatever evidence became available, so I suppose you could call me an open-minded skeptic. But we've wandered off point. We were talking about religious objections to transgender people, and around here that means Christian objections."

"Glad you brought us back."

"The idea of God in the Christian context is that a being designed and created everything. In which case, that being would be responsible for variants and permutations, because evolution is demonstrable and measurable and therefore part of the design they demand exists." Chip stretched a rubber band between his thumb and index finger, and began strumming it like harp strings as he spoke. "The idea of a god who creates a system which is permitted to mutate being simultaneously angry at the variants it produces seems like either a significant logic problem or a description of a pathological mind."

I thought about what he was saying, and it was as good an apologetic as I'd heard in all the years Char and I had discussed the issue, despite having been summarized by an atheist. "That's a really good point."

"So objections to the idea of people being transgender aren't backed up by science, and the Christian understanding of God also doesn't support it. But of course, humans are intensely irrational, and so we have things like the brutal murder of a visiting transgender newscaster."

Thinking about Char's murder right then wasn't going to help achieve my goal, so I forced my brain to remain in the present. I'd gotten used to doing that. It was like not looking at the floaters which are always moving across your field of vision. "The guy who did it was local, right?"

"Christopher Jackson. Yes. He was from Peytonsville."

"Did you know him?"

"We were not acquainted."

"Does he still have family here?"

"Yes. His parents, assorted cousins, aunts, and uncles. They all live in Peytonsville. And his wife, of course."

"So, he's married." I knew the answer, obviously.

"He was at the time of the crime. I heard Sarah was divorcing him, but I'm not sure if it's been finalized."

"You know her name?"

"I know her person. We perform our physical fitness regimens at the same facility."

I tried to control my reaction. This was too good to be true. My heart started racing again, but this time with excitement. I had to think fast.

"Where do you work out?" I finally asked. "I've been thinking of joining a gym."

TRANSCRIPT

Davis: Tell us how you approached Charlotte Mitchell.

Jackson: The banquet was pretty much over when she gave her talk. I was still finishing my cheesecake. Wasn't bad either. Had kind of a skin on it, probably from sitting in a fridge, but once you busted through that it was good.

Davis: Did you stay in the ballroom the whole time?

Jackson: Yeah. Didn't have to take a whiz until later.

Davis: Tell us about her speech.

Jackson: I don't remember much. Seemed a lot like what she'd said at the garden, about needing to raise awareness that trannies are people too, yada yada. I didn't pay that much attention.

Young: What happened when she finished?

Jackson: A big crowd of people went up to meet her on the stage. She talked to them all, so it took a while, but eventually everyone left.

Young: How did you end up meeting her?

Jackson: I went up close when all the people were waiting to talk to her. Just smiled a lot and tried to look harmless.

Davis: Why were you worried about that?

Jackson: I don't know. Maybe I knew by then I was going to do something. I don't remember thinking about it. It sort of evolved. The whole thing did.

Davis: So, you figured smiling would make you seem less threatening?

Jackson: Yeah.

Young: You smiled a lot, and waited, and then what happened?

Jackson: When they'd all gone, I went up to say hello. I thought of a story while I was waiting. Figured I had to have something to say that would make her want to keep talking to me. So, I told her I had a nephew who's afraid to come out of the closet. Said she was the kid's idol, and that he'd wanted to come to her talk but couldn't because he had a football game.

Davis: Did she seem to believe you?

Jackson: Yep. She bought it. I could tell I had her when I mentioned he'd been talking about committing suicide. That was one of the topics in her speech. Trans people suicide rates. Kind of sad, actually. So yeah. She believed it. While I had her on the hook, I asked if I could buy her a drink to see if she had any suggestions.

Young: She said yes?

Jackson: I'm sure you know that already. Bartender undoubtedly filled you in that she'd been chatting with a guy who looked just like me.

Young: How many drinks did you have?

Jackson: Just one. I palmed the roofie powder and dumped it in her glass while the bartender was making my change. Place was crowded, so it was easy.

Davis: Are you pretty familiar with Rohypnol?

Jackson: It was my first time using it.

Young: Where'd you get it?

Jackson: A buddy gave me some a year or so ago. Said it loosens girls up when he's out clubbing. He's younger than me, so he goes out a lot. Told me it works like a charm, and he was right. At least about it making them loopy.

Davis: How long did you stay at the bar?

Jackson: Maybe 45 minutes? Not too long. It was getting late and I wanted to get going.

Young: What happened next?

Jackson: I could tell she was getting pretty buzzed, so I talked her into going out my truck to see a picture of my fictional nephew. Didn't want her passing out right there. We got to the parking garage, and I helped her get in. Told her she might as well sit while I looked for the picture.

Young: The drug was obviously working?

Jackson: Yeah. She kept blinking and sort of slipping sideways but she'd catch herself and straighten back up. I fumbled around for a few minutes, and when it looked like she'd fallen asleep I drove out of there.

Davis: Where'd you go after that?

Jackson: I drove straight to that witch shrine.

Davis: The black Madonna shrine in Knowltonsville?

Jackson: That's the place. Black magic's more like it though. Run by those Catholics. Christians don't believe in that kind of shit.

Young: Why'd you take Ms. Mitchell there?

Jackson: I had to think of somewhere to go, and I don't really know the city at all. Didn't know where might be safe. I knew the shrine would be deserted. The caretaker is my wife's uncle. Crazy old fuck. He kicks everyone off the property at 6:00 and then drinks himself into a stupor. I knew it would be deserted.

Davis: So, you drove to the shrine, and then what?

Jackson: I woke her up, or sort of did. It was like she was drunk. She kind of came awake, so I helped her out of the truck and into this outside chapel thing they have. It was cold out, but we were protected from the wind and I figured we could use one of the benches in case we wanted to lie down.

<Pause>

It got kind of weird in there. I sat her down, and she woke up a little more. Maybe from the cold? She was looking around, and it kind of jerked her alert. She looked at the statues and the paintings, and she smiled like she was happy to be there. It was like I wasn't even there.

Davis: Did she say anything?

Jackson: Maybe. I don't really remember. I was kind of focused. She got up and then dropped to her knees in front of the altar, which seemed like a sign, if you know what I mean. I walked around in front of her and it looked like she was praying. Not exactly the kind of thing to put you in the mood, but with her down there, I was still pretty excited. She looked beautiful.

Young: What did you do next?

Jackson: I started touching her because I wanted to find out how much of it was real. Like her tits. I wanted to find out if they were hers, or falsies, or what. So, I tried to pull up her dress.

<Pause>

Jackson: She jumped when I touched her. Like I said, I don't think she realized I was there until then. She saw me and started swinging.

Davis: So, she fought back?

Jackson: Sure as hell did. Punched me right in the gut while she was still down on her knees. I doubled over for a minute, and she came after me.

<Pause>

Jackson: I still don't understand. The drug worked enough to make her act drunk, but not enough to want to get fucked. Wasn't that supposed to be the point?

Young: False advertising, you think?

Jackson: Seriously. The whole thing might not have happened if I'd known she'd object.

Young: Were you planning to rape her from the beginning?

Jackson: I wanted to have sex with her, but I wanted her to want it. I thought that's what the drug did. Loosened them up. Made them more receptive.

Davis: It doesn't sound like she was receptive. Is that why you killed her?

Jackson: Things just got away from me. She kept punching me, and she was strong. Like, really strong. Thank God she was buzzed from the drug, or I would have been in big trouble. Her aim was a little off, so I grabbed one her of arms, and twisted it behind her back. Learned that move from a cop show. You know the one I mean, right?

Davis: I can imagine it.

Jackson: I wrestled her to the ground which took some work. She got her arm loose and tried to choke me then. Almost succeeded. See these marks? Her talons punctured my skin. Found two broken nails in there when I got home. Disgusting. They're still infected. Hurts like a bitch.

Davis: Those cuts do look pretty bad. Looks like your collar rubs them.

Jackson: It does. Drives me crazy, but at least it covers them up. I don't need the questions.

Davis: Have you sought medical treatment?

Jackson: Hell no, how would I explain it? My doctor knows Sarah. He would think she'd done it to me. Or some whore. Either way, I didn't want him knowing. Small towns can be tough.

Young: We can have someone take a look once we're done.

Davis: So how did you respond when Ms. Mitchell tried to choke you?

Jackson: I punched her. Right in the temple. Almost knocked her out.

Young: Almost?

Jackson: It should have knocked her out. Whoever made those drugs needs to be fired. She was still awake, but it was weird. She kept looking at that Madonna picture, and then at me. And her eyes, it was like they knew what was coming. She tried to push me off, but her arms were kind of floppy by then. Her eyes, though. They looked like they could see everything I'd ever done. Everywhere I'd ever been. All the good things and the bad stuff, all the things I couldn't control. She was buzzed as fuck, and punch drunk. But her eyes… They freaked me out. They made me want to cry. I never cry.

Davis: Did you do something about her eyes, Christopher?

Jackson: Jesus, why do you keep asking me things you know the answer to? You know I did. You have her body. So yeah, I did something about her eyes.

<Pause>

Jackson: I needed them to stop accusing me.

Davis: And then you kept on going? With the knife?

Jackson: She was a freak, all right? You know she was a freak. She was beautiful and it was all wrong, all of it, and I just kind of lost it.

\<Pause\>

Jackson: What? Why are you guys so quiet.

Young: Just taking it all in.

Jackson: There's a doll in a glass box there, too, did I tell you that? Place was fucking weird. Paintings and dolls, and statues of baby Jesus. Felt like there were eyes all over the place, watching me. Watching the whole thing. All those eyes. I couldn't take it. Had to make it stop.

Davis: I suppose that must have been disturbing.

Jackson: That's an understatement. Turns out taking her to the shrine was a bad decision. The whole thing was a bad decision, but there's nothing I can do about that now.

Chapter 26

I'd had the transcripts from Jackson's confession for a while, but the idea of reading them made me feel sick. I got access right after they became public, and saved the file, just in case. Until then, I'd had no interest in hearing what the scum bag had to say about what he'd done. I'd avoided all the news coverage about the trial while it was happening because I hadn't been able to face any details. Seeing Char so brutalized had been more than enough. The transcripts were like a dirty secret lurking in my tablet, a dark corner in a bad neighborhood. I liked to pretend the file wasn't there, but knowledge of its presence gnawed at me. It was almost like it was sending out radioactive waves, pulsing with hate and destruction.

I'd gotten the file, saved it, and tried to forget it. But roaming around the museum studying Jesse-James-style revenge and playing with scenarios wasn't getting me where I needed to be fast enough. I was tired of stasis. Tired of lingering in sorrow and churning around with no plan for how to move forward. Reading the transcript might offer insight to propel my plan forward. Maybe Jackson would say something about his life, or his wife, or something else he cared for that I could destroy. Maybe I'd get some pointers into what would cause him maximum pain.

It didn't seem smart to dive in while the museum was open. There was no telling what reading it would do to me, and the patrons who strolled in looking for cheesy side show distractions didn't need to be greeted by a sobbing lunatic. Once I'd closed up shop, I went upstairs, filled a tumbler with wine, and curled up in the corner of the copper-colored couch. I stared at the black screen of my tablet for a moment, working up my courage, and then clicked it on. The file was still there, pulsing with ugliness in its little corner of the file structure. I hadn't known where to put it when I initially saved it. I nearly made a folder named "Char" but didn't want him to have anything further to do with her, so I scratched that idea. Instead, I just titled the folder with his name. "Jackson." It sounded so innocuous, which just goes to show how blind we are to the reality of what hides beneath the surface of things. I opened the folder, and hovered over the document, considering, knowing there was no going back.

This whole adventure felt like a series of moments of not turning back. In this case, I feared the change would be internal. It wasn't that I'd be starting to put a plan into action, it was that my whole self could potentially be shattered, or at the very least, poisoned. But there was no turning back, only an inevitable grinding of gears toward doom.

The document opened like any other, as if oblivious to its nature. I read the description of Char's murder, and when I discovered where it took place, I had to stop reading.

I'd been in that shrine. I'd walked the grounds, and gone to each of the prayer stations. I'd read of the monk who died on a hot day. I'd sat before the black Madonna, communing with her and with a God I wasn't sure existed. That was the spot where Char died.

How had I not sensed it?

For the first time, I regretted not having followed the case. Did Maria know, when she sent me there? Was she that cruel?

She couldn't have known. She was good to the core.

Finding out renewed my intention. Someone had to pay. For all of it.

Chapter 27

To set things in motion, I needed more information, so I decided to invite Chip to dinner.

A skinny dude with empty eyes and a sore on his cheek brushed by me on his way out of the Quickie Mart door. Meth addiction was apparently as rampant in Missouri as it had been on the North Shore. The closest I'd come to addiction was the alcohol I'd relied on in the months following Shimmy's death. I was lucky it hadn't turned darker and longer lasting.

Chip was filling a rack with snack-sized bags of chips. "Hey!" I said.

"Afternoon," he replied.

"I was thinking. You're the closest thing I have to a friend around here, so you should come over for dinner some night."

"I would be honored to join you for a meal."

"Fantastic. Tuesday good?"

"Tuesday evening is currently unscheduled, as are most of my nights." He kept working as he spoke, slotting shiny bags behind the ones already on display.

"What kind of food do you like?" I asked. "Are you allergic to anything?"

"Unlike most neural-atypicals, I eat pretty much everything. Except bologna and hot dogs. Disgusting amalgamations of entrails and hooves."

"I knew they were kind of gross, but I didn't know about the hooves."

"It was an exaggeration, but barely."

"So no bologna or hot dogs. Anything else?"

"That's it. I wouldn't waste your money on shellfish, however. I'll eat it, but it's not in my top 30 favorite foods. Unless you enjoy it, of course."

My mind drifted to lobster rolls and steamed clams eaten with sea gulls swooping overhead. Grocery store seafood in the middle of the country didn't hold the same appeal. "I was thinking chicken."

"Perfectly acceptable."

"Do you drink?"

"I assume you mean alcohol, and yes, I do. Moderately."

"Then I'll get some wine."

"Allow me. While I've trained my palate to find a wide range of foods acceptable, wine is another matter."

"Sounds fantastic. See you Tuesday at 7:00?"

"Agreed."

I spent the next several days pouring over old cookbooks to select recipes, and thinking about how to drill Chip for information. Entertaining would be a challenge in my micro-kitchen, but I figured I could be creative even on two electric burners and a miniature oven.

The lemon meatball cookies took a while because there was only one cookie sheet. I made them Monday night and drizzled them with icing the next afternoon.

Chip showed up right on time, and thrust two bottles toward me when I greeted him at the door. "I foolishly didn't ask how you would prepare the chicken, so I selected a dry Riesling and a Cabernet Franc. Neither are terribly aggressive, and both pair well with a wide range of foods."

"It sounds like you've got us covered. Come on in." I led him up the narrow staircase and into my living room. "Welcome to my humble abode. Have a seat."

Chip sat on the couch. Its position ten feet from the kitchen made conversation easy while I finished up and set the table. "I see you haven't made many changes," he said, looking around at the room.

"You've been up here before?" I wondered if he thought it was odd that I didn't personalize the space. Chip nodded. "Hope you like chicken pot pie," I said to change the subject. "I went old school."

"I do enjoy it. And the Riesling is a match." He pulled a corkscrew out of his pocket and walked to the table to open the bottle.

"My, you *are* prepared."

"I wasn't sure the Harrises would have provided one."

"You were right. They didn't."

I pulled the layered salad out of the fridge and brought it to the table. We both sat. "The wine will be best if it's given a moment to breathe," Chip said as he poured an inch into our glasses.

I was eager to start grilling him, but figured drinking some wine would make it easier for us both. I should have had a glass before he came. "How long do you recommend?"

"Optimally we'd leave the bottle open for 30 minutes. In the glass, it needs less."

"Do you mind if I drink mine sub-optimally?"

"Not at all." He set a timer on his watch. "I choose to wait for 20 minutes, but be my guest."

I took a sip of water. "I'll give it five minutes of deep breathing, so as not to reveal myself as a complete Neanderthal."

"You lack the chin, forehead, and physique characterizing the Neanderthal. Clearly Homo sapien. Drink the wine when you choose." His manner of speaking frequently made me want to giggle, but I tried not to. I served the salad and chattered for a minute about how I'd found the recipes, wondering if flirting with him would help get the information I needed. But I quickly realized that would be stupid. He wouldn't recognize it, and I couldn't pull it off. I gulped some wine, hoping it had been five minutes.

"So, you were telling me about the gym you go to."

"Yes," he said.

"Where is it?"

"On Main St. in Peytonsville. It's adjacent to the Pizza Hub, which seems a bit cruel for those who have difficulty abstaining."

"That borders on sadistic," I replied, forking salad into my mouth and chewing madly to try to seem normal. It took me a minute to realize that it was actually pretty delicious. "Mmm. This is good."

"It is. Though hardly diet food. With all the cheese and dressing, it's possibly more highly caloric than a slice of pepperoni pizza."

"Did you see that woman much when you went to work out? The wife of the murderer?" I figured I might as well jump in and get it over with.

"Sarah Jackson. Yes. Last year I would see her every Monday, Wednesday and Friday."

"Your workout days, I take it."

"Yes."

"She was there at the same time?"

Chip nodded, swallowed, and patted his mouth with his napkin. He had very nice table manners. "We exercised at the same time, and crossed paths doing weight strengthening."

"Sounds like you don't see her any more. Did she stop coming?"

"My work schedule changed, which meant that my exercise schedule also needed to be adjusted. I have no way of knowing whether she stopped going, but I also have no reason to think she would have. Sarah is one of those people who dedicate a great deal of time to physical fitness. She went daily."

I tried to think of a way to ask a question without sounding like my focus was on Sarah. "Did it throw you to change your workout time?"

"Schedule changes are challenging, but I acclimated. The biggest problem is that there is increased competition for the machines earlier in the morning. People go there before work."

So, she went in the morning. "That makes sense," I said. I could work with that. Chip finished his salad, and I carried the plates to the sink. "Did you ever talk to her about the murder?"

"No, but you've undoubtedly ascertained that I'm not a typical conversationalist. She disappeared for a while when the news broke, and when she came back, we resumed our previous level of pleasantries common to acquaintances in that setting. I never questioned her about the event. I could only assume she was traumatized. My mother counseled a sympathetic expression which I attempted to employ upon her return."

The pot pie had been resting on the stove, and I carried it to the table and set it on a trivet. "I'm sure you did great," I said. "Shall I serve you?" Chip passed me his plate. The crust broke with a satisfying burst of golden flakes, and I spooned out a steaming scoop of chicken, gravy, and vegetables. I thought about whether or not to continue asking Sarah-related questions, but decided I'd gotten enough information to make a start. "Tell me more about those wax worms," I said. "Unless it's not appropriate dinner conversation."

"If discussing moth larvae doesn't bother you, I'm happy to comply."

"Fire away," I said.

"As I told you before, it's unlikely that there would be an infestation, for a number of reasons." Chip went on to explain those reasons, and a whole lot more. I allowed my thoughts to drift, making appropriate noises to show I was still with him, but mostly I planned my visit to the fitness center.

Chapter 28

Working with the wax figures became therapy as I thought through the things Chip told me. I did some gender-bending by swapping the positions of the characters in one diorama, so that the husband sat in front of the sewing machine wearing his wife's apron while she relaxed in a chair across the room, the sleeve of her missing arm pinned up to her elbow. I also feminized the face of several other figures, and stuffed the front of their shirts to hint at breasts.

But I didn't just mess with them. I also cared for them.

Dust accumulates quickly in a place filled with old things, with forced heat pushing molecules of ancient detritus around in the cool weather, and air conditioning doing the same when it was hot. The figures hadn't been dusted in a while. I discovered there was an optimal time between dustings. Too soon and the work wasn't satisfying. Too long and the skin lost luster. It made me think about lovemaking. If you do it too frequently, the sense of satisfaction was lessened. Not often enough and you had to trudge through all the accumulated baggage that got in the way of intimacy.

But thinking about sex was dangerous. Bodies speak in the language of hunger, and mine didn't seem to care that the love of my life was gone. It wanted what it wanted. Thinking about sex only made it cry out more insistently.

Wax bodies weren't so complicated.

When dusting, I gave the eyes the most attention. After all, the eyes are the windows of the soul. Or in this case, the soulless. I stared into them as if looking for answers, for guidance, for mentoring on vengeance. But they were empty, devoid of emotion or assistance. I wondered what they would look like, dug from the sockets of their plaster skulls.

Those glass orbs showed how hard it is to recreate the beautiful complexity of a human eye, with its flexing pupil and color-flecked iris. You could paint the tiniest network of capillaries with the utmost care and still never capture the life and love carried by them. Eyes were priceless, delicate, individual, powerful, intimate. I cleaned the glass eyes and tried not to be offended by the fact that they were located right there where they should be, nestled in the concavities designed for them.

Dust accumulated on the eyebrows and eyelashes of the still characters, and on the shoulders of their garments. I employed the proper cleaning techniques, vacuuming with a fine screen over the nozzle to capture any minute bits which might detach and otherwise disappear into a bag full of dirt.

Sometimes I relied on a childhood old trick of feigned blindness, feeling for the texture of dust with my fingertips, instead of with my eyes. Touching them that way made me hate them less, as if blocking the fakeness of what they represented allowed me to connect with their essence. With my eyes closed it was almost pleasurable; the sensation of smooth wax; dust pushing away like a film of talcum powder on the curve of a beloved buttock.

I was rougher with my eyes open. I buffed their skin with damp paper towels, and brazenly used a craft knife to pick at the dirt gathered in facial wrinkles Gerry obviously hadn't attended to, not giving a fuck if a curled shaving of wax came away with the knife. It was as if I was rebelling against all my curatorial training, actively damaging objects rather than doing everything in my power to protect them.

The characters generated an anger that I didn't want to think about, though different from the thoughts about sex. The waxen skin of the man who'd been Jesse's cook for years and who testified to Dalton's authenticity was an affront of falseness. It was the wrong shade, a color that never appeared on a human. The color was an insult to every African

American, blackface in wax form, completely missing the life glow that lit real people from the inside. The glow that burned so brightly from within Char's amazing skin. He looked shiny and fake and I was insulted on behalf of the man who wasn't able to object to his effigy.

The figure of the museum's creator pissed me off more than any of the others. His suit was the nicest, and his skin looked the most realistic. He stood by the bed of a fake Billy the Kid, slick and handsome, as if *he* was the star of the show, which in reality, he must have been. The museum seemed to be a monument to him in a way. *His* discoveries, *his* research. Meanwhile all those who mourned the loss of limbs or lives were transformed into props.

Early on I undid their pants, to see if any of them had penises, but there was nothing there. They had bodies like Ken dolls. Missouri seemed to cultivate the loss of penises. Their lack of genitalia irritated me and made me want to hurt them. I took the craft knife and carved the texture of pubic hair into the plastic mounds above where their dicks should be, wondering if the next museum manager would look down their pants and see my work. Of course, they wouldn't know *I'd* done it, and even if they did, I'd be in jail by then.

I looked closely at fingernails which never needed cutting, and hair which didn't need to be brushed, imagining locking up and walking off without telling anyone, leaving the whole thing to rot. Those cold bodies didn't need me and were probably better off drifting into entropy.

I'd do it, eventually. But I had things to accomplish before that day came.

Chapter 29

Fit This In smelled like testosterone and the disinfectant. The gym's light was an assault of fluorescent flickers, and if there was any latent epilepsy in my genes, I'm pretty sure it would have triggered a seizure.

What *was* triggered was my anxiety. Not so much because I'd soon be meeting Sarah Jackson, but because I could feel expectation pressing in on me from every gaze. Muscled dudes lifting complicated weights, women in expensive-looking spandex, the smiling girl behind the check-in desk. A sea of white faces, all of them watching with questions. They'd want to hear my story, offer advice on toning up, and tell me about their kids. Gyms were a foreign land to me. All those people knew how to act. To them it was no big deal. But to someone who's goal in being there was slightly more nefarious than taking off a few pounds or trying to extend a lifespan, knowing how to act was slightly more complicated. I recited a few lines of Poe's poem "The Raven" in my head to calm down.

As I looked around the room, I saw just one person of color, a black woman. Tall and athletic. Not tall enough though. Not dark enough. And her shoulders weren't broad enough.

Char didn't like her shoulders. They were too much of a reminder of life before. I wished I'd known her back then. Char had been married at the time, and her wife couldn't handle the transition, so Charlotte had shed Charles on her own, and come out the other side well into the path of wholeness by the time we met. I'd given up on ever finding the perfect someone by then. We met at a work function, and became first friends, then lovers, then finally, were married.

The wedding was a study in contrasts. Charlotte glowing, tall, calm, and grace-filled. Me, a nervous, fluttering little mouse, pale and transparent in comparison, but so happy! I was so buoyant I'm surprised I didn't lift right up off the ground and float above her, Char's hand the only thing keeping me from sailing away to burn up in the sun. She was my tether to the world. To life and light and sanity.

This woman's skin didn't glow, and her shoulders were too narrow. *Nevermore.*

A voice interrupted my thoughts. "Good morning!" The girl behind the reception desk beamed at me aggressively. "Come on over and say hello!" I took a deep breath and obeyed.

"Hi," I said.

"I'm Jeannie. Don't think I've seen you here before. What's your name? Would you like a tour?"

"Maddie. And yes, I would."

"Great!" She pushed through a little gate to escape from her pen and joined me. "Nice to meet you, Maddie. As you can see, most of our equipment is used in this open space." She gestured around the wide-open room, and I could feel the gaze of the sweating throng watching us. "Are you thinking of joining? I'm not supposed to ask that until the end of the tour, but I figure, why waste your time if you're not?"

"Yes. I think so. I need to…" I scrambled to come up with an explanation for my presence, realizing I should have thought of that beforehand, then noticed a large woman with a protruding rear end shaking a set of long ropes nearby. "…build up my butt," I continued. It sounded pretty lame, but didn't seem to faze Jeannie. She leaned to look at my back side.

"It *is* kinda flat. Lunges and squats should help with that. We'll hook you up with the trainer. He'll work out a routine for you." We kept walking while she spoke. "Otherwise you look like you're in pretty good shape." Obviously, Jeannie's assessment skills didn't run deep. The last thing I was was in good shape. Thin didn't mean healthy, especially when it came to emotional stability, and I was pretty close to certifiable. I offered a noncommittal grunt in response. She ignored it and kept talking. "Here's the cardio room. We've got all the standards. Bikes. Treadmills. Elliptical." A few people looked up, but most were focused on breathing and whatever noise was coming in their ear buds. "We have classes, of course. Schedule's online."

I was paying partial attention, but mostly scanning the space, looking for my target. We continued to a counter against a side wall, where a selection of protein bars and energy drink bottles were displayed. "Someone's usually here if you want a smoothie or whatever, but if they aren't, just ask whoever's manning the front desk." I nodded, and we kept walking. Jeannie led me through a door. "Here's where you'll find the restrooms, showers, and lockers." The place smelled good, like if a hundred women had exchanged their sweat for shampoo and body lotion. "Bring your own padlock."

Then *BAM*, there she was, sitting on a wooden bench in one of the rows of lockers. I recognized her right away. She hadn't really changed since the case had been in the news, except in the pictures I'd googled she'd worn more clothes. In the locker room she was wrapped in a towel. Her hair looked darker brown when wet, the curls pulled long from the weight of water. But it was definitely her. She had the same elven quality, the tipped-up nose and pointed chin. She glanced toward us.

"Hey, Sarah," Jeannie said.

"Hey," the woman replied with a brief smile.

How odd and wrong it was, that she could sit there, drying off and preparing to return to the tasks of the day, her flesh feeling satisfied at the work it had done and the sensation of blood pumping through her veins. How wrong that her life got to continue, that she could just keep on coming to the gym, getting her workouts in, tending to a body which still had the capacity to dance, laugh, make dinner, make love. I wondered what was on her agenda for the day, and if it included calling her nightmare of a husband. Bubbles of rage roiled within me as I stood there, too long, staring at Sarah's living, breathing flesh.

She glanced up at us again, and I forced muscles to turn away, reassuring myself that I would be back, that we would meet again, and that she would pay for what she'd allowed to happen. "Getting the lay of the land?" she asked.

Clearly she didn't recognize me. Apparently I hadn't deserved the kind of intense scrutiny I'd given her after it happened. I was simultaneously insulted and relieved. I nodded back, and mustered a smile which felt like a grimace. "I sure am."

Jeannie wrapped up the tour, and I paid the membership fee. I left before Sarah did, and hurried to get in my car where I could watch the door. She came out a few minutes later and climbed into a red pickup truck. It was at least a decade old, with rust spots on a few corners, and the sheen worn down so the paint looked soft and a little dusty. She drove away. Her driving was unremarkable.

I sat there in the parking lot for a few minutes, shocked that I'd found her the very first time I'd come. It seemed the gods were with me.

Or the demons.

Chapter 30

After waking up in the middle of the night sweaty, panting, and fighting off the vestiges of the recurring dream about making love to Char, I picked up the Mamma Schiavona prayer card. Her face was somber, her mouth small. The child Jesus clutched a handful of robe at her breast. I looked at the angels hovering near her crown, and the haloed heads of the saints at her feet. The image was comforting in a way I couldn't explain because it made no sense. It made me feel less alone to look at it. *She* made me feel less alone.

Nights were consistently hard. I'd lie in bed, thinking about meeting Sarah, simultaneously looking forward to and dreading it. Unlike me, Char loved meeting people. She couldn't avoid it of course, her flame burned bright and people couldn't help but be drawn. She told me about them at our 10:00 PM check-in every night. We'd head to bed and catch up on the small things of the day, like who she'd met and oddities I encountered at work. Even when she traveled, 10:00 was our time to trade stories from our separate beds, clicking off the phone after a final "I love you," and rolling into sleep. But there were no more soft cuddles, no more phone calls, no more stories of people she'd encountered. 10:00 PM had become an hour of sorrow for me. It took a while to escape its hold and enter into sleep.

Debating whether or not to commit murder is a strange experience. The anger pulses and you're convinced it's entirely warranted, but the part of you raised to be a decent human tries to talk you back from the precipice. I wanted to kill Sarah. I really did, so I had to push down the voices preaching decency.

Because of those voices, it wasn't clear I really *could* kill her. But I could damn sure take her eyes as punishment for being blind about the kind of monster she married. She might even be a monster herself, given her choice of mate. So, I'd kill her if I could, and if not, I'd take her eyes, and mail them to Jackson in prison, as payback for stealing Char's. I liked imagining him opening the box, recoiling, not understanding at first what he was seeing. I liked the horror on his face when he realized they were hers, and the breakdown he'd have when he made the connection about why.

The hunger for vengeance is powerful. I'd stumbled near to alcoholism in the months after Char was killed, and the ache of wanting to hurt Sarah echoed that need to drink. My mourning for Char was disabling. The only thing that made it survivable was thinking about payback.

During the day, I peered into the faces of outlaws in old photos, trying to read the language of murder, hoping their eyes would transmit wisdom about how to overcome basic decency. They weren't helpful. I wished there was a woman I could consult, because I felt no connection to any of the men in the pictures. But all I had was Jesse's one-armed wax mama, and she offered me nothing.

There were so many details to work out. If I just took Sarah's eyes, timing would be critical or she'd die. An ambulance would have to get there quickly. You couldn't very well tourniquet someone's head, but maybe there was a way to stem the bleeding. The whole line of thought reminded me of a biology class in high school where we'd dissected cow eyes and I'd almost thrown up. It would be a lot easier to just kill her. Either way it went, I'd call 911 afterward. When the police came, I'd turn myself in.

These rambling thoughts filled my head when 10:00 struck each night, instead of the drifting trail of Char's voice, and the scent of her neck as I burrowed into her safety and warmth. It was a horrible substitute, but it was all I had.

Chapter 31

The family was one of the annoying ones. "What's this?" the little girl shrieked as she picked up a glass vase containing red, white, and blue LED flowers. "I want it!" She gave it a shake which launched the electric blooms into the air, then dropped the vase on the floor, where it bounced on the grubby carpet. She rushed to the toy section, and pushed her brother away from the display of hobby horses. He was small and skinny, maybe four years old. No match for her adolescent girth and big-sister energy. He screwed up his little face and punched her in the stomach, and she screeched loud enough to make my eardrums rattle. "Maaaaaah!" she yelled. "Leroy hit me, for no reason!"

"Keep it up," the woman who'd entered with them replied mildly. She didn't bother looking to see what was going on. "Daddy will take you outside and burn both your asses." She kept sliding T-shirts along the circular rack, the noise a scratching glide as each one was rejected.

Daddy wasn't paying attention to any of it. Instead, he stood evaluating me where I sat behind the counter, wearing my dark glasses.

When I was a kid, most people thought I was deaf. My language skills were so hampered that when it came to communication, I might as well have been. My world had been rich with sound from the beginning, but the sounds were largely of nature. Mom and Dad were profoundly deaf, and didn't try to vocalize. Human sounds to me were more subtle; sighs and coughs, laughter, the passing of gas, or the scratching of a scalp. When they finally sent me to school, a world filled with human voices was overwhelming, and the first week of bus rides was pure torture.

I didn't understand the language, and with so many people trying to communicate at once, it was a deluge of competing noise, like Babel after the tower fell.

Learning speech came surprisingly easily. The more I did it, the more I wanted to learn.

The stillness of the museum when no one was there was a return to that early age when humans were quiet, though humans breathed and bumbled through the world unlike the depth of silence offered by the wax figures. I had too much time on my hands, time spent thinking about revenge and what it would be like to have no eyeballs. The idea of blindness became a kind of fascination. It was aggravated by the people who came to the museum and didn't seem to realize the place was a joke. The sight of them brought about what I now recognize was unreasonable anger. That's why I started shutting my eyes, and just listening. Some of the visitors got it, of course. They came in giggling and ready to be entertained. Others treated the place as if it was real history and Jesse and the other outlaws were heroes to be worshipped, and it was those who made me crazy. I closed my eyes and listened, and they didn't realize how much I could pick up. I'd had years of practice understanding people's inner world by watching their faces and body language. Watching my parents as they grew tense about each other's irritating habits. Watching their faces when they were upset with me. Watching the beautiful flow of language poured out through movements of hands, arms, and expression. I could tell a lot from the people who visited. The ones who were angry at each other when they walked in. The ones who were worried about life. The ones who didn't give a damn what anyone thought.

Closing my eyes turned a lot of it off. In simulated blindness, I was left to contemplate the world with merely sound to guide me. I thought it would be less complex, that it would pare down the irritants. I thought I might be scared by it, the loss of vision predicting a coming, complete darkness. But it wasn't that frightening. The world was saturated with sound. And it turned out to be fun to just pretend to be blind, some of the time. To watch when they didn't think I was watching.

The girl yanked the yo-yo Leroy attempted to use out of his hands, and this time it was him who wailed. Their mother threw her head back in the extremity of her martyrdom, then stomped toward them. "That's *it*, Olivia," she said, and walloped her across the face. "I told you to leave him alone. One more time and you can kiss your phone goodbye." She flounced back to the T-shirt rack.

As the drama unfolded, Daddy just stayed where he was, looking at me. I had my head tilted so it looked like I was focusing on the kids, but my eyes were on him the whole time. Guys like him were a reminder of Jackson. I fumbled my fingers around on the countertop as if feeling for my stapler, to reinforce the idea of unawareness. His hands were stuffed in his back pockets so his hips pushed forward beneath the bulge of his beer belly. It was hot and the air conditioning was acting up, so I was wearing a tank top. He finally pulled his gaze away from my boobs to check out the junk on the shelf beside him. He picked up a paperweight, looked back at me, then stuck the ugly thing in his pocket. "How you doin' today?" he called to me over the dwindling snuffle of his kids' tears.

"I'm great," I replied. "How are you fine folks?" He walked closer to the counter. "Come to see the exhibits?"

"We sure did," he said. "Heard about this place from my cousin Bobby. Big Wild West fans he and I. Throwbacks, I guess you could say."

"Not from around here, then?" I asked.

"We came up for some camping. Live on the Lake of the Ozarks," he said. "Been there?"

"Not yet, but I've heard it's very pretty."

"Nothing prettier." He glanced toward his wife. "'Cept maybe you." He tipped closer as he said it, and adjusted his crotch.

"It's going to be $8.00 each for you and the lady, and $5.00 for the kids," I said.

"Come see this one, Andrew." She held out a shirt for him to inspect, eyes like daggers. She must have gotten a whiff of his hormones. A burst of anger flared in my gut at her willingness to put up with his bullshit. Just like Sarah must have tolerated Jackson's.

"I'm getting our tickets," he called back. "Fucking bitch," he muttered.

"What was that?" I said.

"Nothing. Here you go." He pulled some bills out of his wallet, looking between the money and me as if evaluating which denominations to give me. After shuffling them a bit, he set some cash on the counter.

Pretending to be blind had a body language all its own. You had to consider how someone who is sightless would move when trying to extract clues about what's happening around them. Should you sniff the air when someone approaches? Should you comment on their cologne, or notice the lack of it? Should you tilt your head toward small sounds and shifts in the atmosphere? Should you avoid sitting close to fans or air conditioners because you can't hear what might be coming?

"Would you mind separating the denominations for me?" I asked, feeling for the cash. "We work on the honor system here, so if you could do that, I'd appreciate it."

"Sure." He placed the two bills side by side. Two singles. "There you go," he said. "A twenty and a ten. I just need four bucks back."

I took the singles, opened the cash register, and tucked them into the slots he'd listed, then pulled out four dollars to make his change. I fumbled four tickets from the pile next to the register and held them toward him with the money, at an angle slightly off from where he stood. "Thank you very much," I said. His face bore a satisfied grin. Wifey apparently didn't like what she saw, because she came strolling up carrying another shirt.

"Look at this one. Your daddy would love it," she said, cracking her gum and looking me up and down like I was the one trying to get away with something.

I'd practiced being blind with my eyes open, trying to not see even as my ocular organs processed data. I didn't enjoy what I was seeing in this couple, and tried to tune out their faces.

"Come on kids!" Andrew yelled. The pair had settled into quiet bickering near the puzzles. "We'll buy some shit after we come out," he said. The woman sighed, sneered at me, then returned the shirt to the rack.

"It's right through this door," I said, making a show of feeling my way around from behind the counter and over to the museum entrance. "Are you all set?" The clan had gathered, and the kids were complaining about wanting toys and being hungry. I walked them to the darkened theater, explained what they were about to experience, then left them to the show.

When they made their way toward the wax figures after the film, I hurried out the front door. They'd left their minivan unlocked. The back hatch rose, releasing a cloud of cigarette smoke. I rifled around to see what I could find. There was a cooler with sandwiches in it. The first one was ham and mustard. I took a few bites and it wasn't bad. The next was bologna and ketchup. It tasted even better, though the ketchup had soaked into one side of the spongy white bread like blood. I tossed the rest of the sandwiches in an empty shopping bag they'd stuffed in a side pocket, and rummaged to see what else I could take to annoy them. A bag of potato chips and a box of cookies joined the sandwiches, and I suddenly understood Yogi Bear on a deeper level. Several air mattresses were rolled up with an air pump on top, so I grabbed the pump too. I shut the hatch, walked to the rear of the building, and threw the goodies in the trashcan.

It wasn't my first time. No one suspects me, even when they go straight out to the car, planning to tailgate their lunches right then and there. They march back in with their confusion transforming to anger because most of these assholes dwell perpetually on the edge of fury. But they never suspect me, even though I'm the only person they see at the museum. I look too childlike, too angelic. My baby-fine curls glow like a halo from the can light above the counter. My skin is waxen and my lips and cheeks are a soft, rosy pink. My pale eyes look naked and slightly dazed in their faux blankness. They didn't have a clue how much I observed.

By the time I returned through the side door, the family had emerged from the museum. I slowed down my pace, and remembered to act my part. "Sorry about that," I said, feeling my way to the stool. "Had to take out some garbage."

The kids ran to the toy section to make their selections, and wifey brought a T-shirt back to the counter. "Do you want to get this or not?" she said to Andrew, who'd returned to his post nearby.

"Sure," he said. "And price is no object." He jerked his head toward me with a snigger, and her eyes grew wide as she realized what he meant. The kids brought up armloads of junk, and she argued with them until they settled for two items each. Andrew went through the money charade with me again, and they were finally ready to go. "You guys go use the bathrooms first. I know how you are. Have to pee all the fricking time."

"It's right over there," I said, turning to point vaguely in the direction of the restrooms.

"I *saw* them," the woman said, all snark and phony fingernails. She thrust their bag of loot at Andrew, and grabbed the kids by the hands. They all tromped off.

"So," Andrew said, sidling closer. "You ever get out at night? I was thinking of stopping by that bar we passed down the road later on." He suddenly seemed to realize I might have trouble getting there. "I could pick you up."

For a minute, I considered telling him yes and spending the rest of the day plotting what damage I could do to him once he was drunk. But I'd had enough fun for one day. "Wish I could," I replied. "But I've got to give Jesse a bath." His expression went from horny to confused and it was hard not to laugh. Thankfully, the kids exploded back into the gift shop.

"I want McDonald's," Olivia yelled.

"I want Taco Bell!" Leroy replied.

"Shut up!" the woman said. "I made sandwiches, remember?"

"I hate bologna!" Olivia whined as they went out the door. Little did she know she'd be thanking me a few miles down the road when they discovered their lunch was gone.

"Are you coming?" wifey said to Andrew, her arms crossed over her chest as she propped the door open with her hip. He gave me one last leer and headed for the door, pulling a pack of cigarettes out of his back pocket.

"Real nice to meet you," he said.

"Have a nice day," I replied.

Once they were finally gone, I transferred cash from my wallet to the cash register to make up the shortage, smiling as I imagined Andrew's anger when they stopped to camp for the night and he couldn't find the air pump.

While practicing the language of being blind I learned the patterns of the cicada as the buzzing started low and slow and shifted toward electric frenzy. I noticed the long—long—short—long bellows of train whistles, and marveled at the variation different engineers bring to that proscribed blaring. I focused my listening on the rattle of train cars once the engine passed by, making a game of identifying whether the cars were empty or full. I practiced for moments like that day, when horrible people came in, so I could outsmart them.

Or maybe I was practicing for something else. Maybe I'd pluck my own eyes out, once all this was over.

Chapter 32

The tip of the shovel sunk into the ground without much effort, which was a relief. Planting at home was an exercise in frustration because the ground was so stony. The June sun scalded my scalp. Getting a hat might be necessary if I was determined to be a gardener. The holes I made along the side of the shed were about a foot apart, enough space for the trumpet vines to spread out. Hopefully they'd take off quickly. I liked the smell of dirt and the scent of my sweat before it turned sour. The odors made me feel useful and connected to something, and the manual labor helped me think through options.

One option was to become friendly enough with Sarah Jackson to invite her to dinner. Executing my plan would be a whole lot easier at the museum than it would somewhere public. I could give her a tour, knock her out, and take care of everything downstairs where the blood on the floor could just be used as part of a new display. But building that kind of relationship would take time. You don't just meet someone and immediately invite them back to your place, but I didn't want to wait for a faux friendship to develop. I wanted to get the whole thing over with before the trumpet vines flowered next year.

Not that everything was terrible in Missouri. I didn't have to deal with traffic jams, or any traffic for that matter. I just jumped in the shower every morning, grabbed my coffee cup, and headed downstairs. The apartment had become my nest and I feathered it with a few things which made me happy: some old cookbooks, a sunny yellow blanket for the couch, and a hand-crafted card from my parents which had been forwarded from home. It made me miss my folks; being away from the bustle of Boston reminded me of growing up. The isolation was similar, though not as extreme.

Once all the holes were dug, I dragged a bag of topsoil to the first one and spread a few handfuls in the bottom. I placed a trumpet vine seedling in the hole, and topped it off with more dirt. The vine grew wild in those parts. When I had to leave the museum to make a bank deposit or buy groceries, I drove by the wood skeleton of an outbuilding being subsumed by the orange-blossomed vines. Hopefully the ones I was setting would attract hummingbirds, though it seemed a little crazy to plant something which grew so aggressively that other people tried to get rid of it. It was kind of like choosing to sew dandelions. Creating a garden of any kind was stupid, because I wouldn't be there to watch it come into its own, but I did it anyway. While driving, I scanned the sides of roads for blossoms, then dug them up and brought them back to place in the soil behind the museum, figuring anything that could survive exhaust fumes and asphalt runoff could survive in my new back yard. I stowed a trowel in the trunk for the purpose, along with a few old metal coffee cans which Gerry had stacked in the shed. Equipment was important.

I thought about the equipment I'd need to do the job with Sarah, but that was rushing things. The first goal was to get to know her. At least a little. Until that happened, the rest of my plans were useless.

I moved to the next hole and repeated the process: scattering dark soil, positioning the vulnerable green shoot, tucking it in with more dirt, and patting it down. The loam smelled like it looked; rich and old, ancient rot promising verdancy.

Mom never understood why people planted flowers, when so much energy had to be exerted for producing food. I'd already planted vegetables in honor of her; tomatoes, zucchini, and cucumbers. Quick producers. But Pops was a sucker for beauty, so I planted the flowers for him, including a bunch in big terra cotta pots near the museum's front entrance.

Some nights I sat out there smelling the spicy scent of marigolds, looking at the stars and watching as armadillos crept toward the highway. I wanted to warn them, but they were like armored lemmings, irresistibly called to their destruction.

I understood the feeling.

TRANSCRIPT

Young: So it felt like the eyes of the paintings and statues were watching you?

Jackson: I know it sounds crazy, but yes. It was like they'd all come alive. And that Jezebel's picture, I swear her face shifted.

Davis: What Jezebel?

Jackson: The black Madonna, or whatever they call her. The shrine demon.

Davis: Her face shifted?

Jackson: I swear to God. After she stopped breathing, the face in the painting looked like hers.

Young: You are referring to Charlotte Mitchell? After she stopped breathing?

Jackson: Yes. That's when the face changed.

Young: You're saying it looked like Charlotte Mitchell's face?

Jackson: Yes! Swear to God.

Davis: Did it stay that way?

Jackson: I don't know. I hoisted that bitch's body over my shoulder, and got out of there.

Davis: It sounds like you were scared.

Jackson: I almost shit myself. The place was obviously haunted. Or possessed. Something. Something really strange.

Chapter 33

At first I didn't know what the pupa was. My brain processed the thing hanging on the clematis vine I'd planted as an overgrown seedpod, or the leaf nest of an insect. But then it hit me.

I watched it every day after that. It started as a green so bright and electric it didn't look quite real. As time passed it took on golden spots, not the gold of goldenrod, but bright and shining, metallic. I wondered about the strange alchemy which could transform caterpillar fur into gold. Then the green became slightly translucent so I could see the outline of something within it. The shape also began to transform, pushing out in one place, curving in at another. Changing from a green tube to a thing of convexities and curves.

I didn't know how long it would take for the transformation to complete and didn't care, I just entered into the joy of watching.

Then one day, it was gone.

I went out as usual to deadhead and check on it, but there was nothing there. I searched the ground though it hadn't been windy, and looked for the stem which must have attached it, but couldn't find even that. I didn't think it was possible to feel more broken than I already did before discovering the missing pupa, but I was wrong.

The missing butterfly haunted me. It would have been a monarch, all showy tiger stripes slowly fluttering in summer heat. Chars eyelashes fluttering as she grew sleepy after making love, trying to stay awake because she knew I liked to talk afterward. The caterpillar, so masculine and awkward, naked and vulnerable, unhappy in its current state and longing for transformation. Each monarch making that shift, going internal, transforming before breaking free, finally, as their beautiful selves.

Monarch numbers were dwindling, and the gorgeous process of their becoming made them targets for death. I'd heard concerned people in the area grew milkweed around their yards in an attempt to help save them, but I realized growing it was a farce, or worse, a trap, saying "settle here for just a moment! Look what we have to offer. Share your beauty. Let us safeguard you."

Char had assured me that St. Louis was LGBTQ+ friendly, and that she'd be safe.

But the milkweed was a sham and no monarch was secure there, and I wanted to scream into the sky for all the butterflies to keep flying north, to all the caterpillars to crawl back south, to hide under brown leaves, to attach themselves in hiding, or maybe, better yet, to never seek transformation at all. To simply stay in that awkward, ill-fitting form. To be safe. To be alive. To be there, where I could visit and gaze at the spots of gold shining from the miracle of glowing skin, and see the life which moved and breathed within it.

With the pupa gone, some new thing broke inside me.

Chip told me later a bird must have eaten it, but that didn't help.

Chapter 34

Christopher and Sarah Jackson had something in common with Shimmy and me: we didn't have kids. Of course, it's silly to say there was just one parallel. We were all so interconnected. Sarah and I by the tumult and loss Jackson created in our lives. Char and Jackson were connected through her death. She'd become unable to love me and be loved by me just as he'd became unavailable to be loved by his wife. The guilt he bore would be echoed by the guilt I would bear once I did what I planned to do to Sarah. It was a web of ugly, intersecting connections.

Their childlessness made it easier to continue my plans, though. I didn't have to worry about what would happen to them if their mom didn't survive.

The parking lot was nearly full when I pulled in to *Fit This In*, and the air was refreshingly cool for summer. Ingratiating myself with Sarah was a slower process than I'd wanted, but patience was apparently a required virtue. I spotted Sarah's truck after a quick scan, and it wasn't until my car was parked that it hit me: the truck might be the one Jackson used to steal Char from the Downtown Sojourner. A wave of nausea welled up and nearly crested, but I hummed a few bars of "Let It Be" and it subsided again. The last thing I needed was a front seat full of vomit. I sat for a few minutes wondering how to find out if it was the same vehicle, but realized it wasn't necessary. I'd just add a can of gasoline to my supply list and set it on fire after taking care of Sarah. What would one more crime matter?

When I had my shit together, I grabbed my bag and went inside. Sarah wasn't in sight, so I headed to the locker room to stash my stuff. I found her in the cardio theater, walking on a treadmill. A few deep breaths prepared me to step up on the machine next to hers. She nodded, pulled an ear bud out, and said "Came back, I see." Her pixie face was pink and her breathing accelerated.

"Yep." The controls on the machine were perplexing, and I tried not to look like I'd never used one before. "Figured I'd start back here." I pressed a green button, assuming green meant go, and the conveyer started moving. But it was going fast, and I could only imagine what sort of hilarious footage would go viral if I tried to hop on like that. I pushed a down arrow a few times, and the angle of the thing changed, which wasn't the goal.

"Need any help? They're all a little different, aren't they?"

"Ha ha!" I replied, the noise popping out of my mouth like a laugh in a cartoon sound bubble. I jabbed another down arrow and the speed slowed. "I'm good! But thanks." I don't know why I didn't just ask her to explain it. People like to be useful, and it could have helped establish the bond needed to get where we were going. Sarah's eyes were still on me as I stood trying to remember videos of people getting on treadmills. My mind came up blank.

"Here," she said, dismounting from hers like a pro. "Let me show you. Turn that thing off." I followed her instructions. It looked like she was going to end up feeling helpful whether I asked her to or not. "Hop up and put your feet on those side rails." I did as she said. "Now push that down arrow on the left so you won't be walking up hill. Let's start you gently." The bed of the treadmill returned to level. "Are you ready?"

I wasn't sure how I felt about her taking charge like that. But I didn't have much choice. "Sure," I declared, feigning enthusiasm.

"Hold on to the handle there, and push the green button to turn it on. Once you're comfortable, just step on. It's going slow enough you should be okay." Now that she was up close, I could see wrinkles around her eyes and the corners of her mouth. I understood them. The weight of sadness pulls at your flesh like gravity. I gripped the handles, and stepped on to the machine, fumbling a little, which was embarrassing. "Next time, focus on placing one foot at a time," Sarah said. "You sort of jumped on," she said, looking like she wanted to laugh, which was irritating. I bit back a snippy response. It wasn't the time for that. I could store up all my angry lines and spew them at once, when the stage was set.

"Got it," I said. "Thanks for the help. It's been a while since I used one."

She tried to hide a smirk, and rolled her eyes as she turned away, which was helpful, because it pissed me off. *Roll them while you can, sweetheart,* I thought. The machine was going too slow, even for me, so I pumped up the pace while she remounted. We walked in tandem for a while, then she sped up to a jog. I didn't follow suit. It was, after all, my first day.

When Sarah was finished, she wiped her face with a towel, then glugged a bunch of water from a bright pink bottle. "Want to head over to strength with me? I could show you my favorite machines."

"Sure," I said. "Um… what's the best way to get off?"

"Two ways," Sarah said. "You can either reverse the way you got on, which can be tricky. Or you can just slowly reduce the speed. Whatever feels better." I ended up doing a combination of both. By the time the thing had slowed to a near crawl, it was relatively easy to step off. "Look at you!" She said. The vision reference hinted at surreal, but she didn't know that. I turned the machine off.

"Thanks for the help," I said. "I'm Maddie." I watched to see if her expression would change. Char and I had different last names, and the few reports which mentioned my existence referred to me as Madeline. It seemed unlikely that it would ding any dongs in her memory. I didn't get much coverage when everything went down because I'd refused to offer comments, and kept my doors shut and drapes drawn when reporters tried to find me.

"And I'm Sarah," she replied, not missing a beat.

"Glad to meet you. What sort of torture do you have for me next?"

Sarah laughed, and led me to the weight room, explaining which pieces of equipment she used to work on various body parts. I half listened, and followed her instructions for the half hour that followed. I watched her while she worked out, and saw the way her face fell into heaviness when she wasn't actively interacting with someone. I wondered if my face did the same thing, and worked on trying to maintain a cheerful expression. Or at least neutral.

When she thought I'd had enough for one day, we walked over to the snack bar, or whatever you called it in a fitness center. "Try the kiwi and greens smoothie," Sarah said. "It's my favorite. Doubles as breakfast." She pulled a credit card out of a nifty pocket in her leggings. I patted myself down as if looking for my own stash, even though I knew I didn't have anything on me. "My treat," she said.

"Thanks," I said. "I'll get yours next time." Sarah nodded and placed our order. The drink tasted sweet, tart, and like someone had made tea from the clippings in their lawn mower bag. "Mmmh," I hummed noncommittally, making a noise that was a cross between yummy and questioning.

"Good, right?" She said, obviously not recognizing my mixed critique.

We parted ways in the locker room, though I tuned in to the sounds of her opening her padlock, showering, and brushing her hair. I didn't want to come across as creepy, so I left before she was done dressing, tossing a "Bye, and thanks again," over my shoulder as I passed, noticing the freckled paleness of her skin, the thin angularity of her collarbones.

"See ya," she called back.

It took another twenty minutes for her to come out and climb into her truck.

That truck.

That maybe truck.

Watching it drive away restarted my anger. The encounter had gone exceptionally well for our first time. But how disgusting was it that she'd drive something which had been used as a vehicle of death?

She and her husband had to pay.

Chapter 35

Living in the museum was handy for my mission. While rummaging around in the storeroom, I found an old medical book buried in a stack of dusty tomes, titled *Modern Operative Surgery Practices*. It must have been beautiful in its day. The cover was tooled leather with gold accents, but it was well on its way to converting to dust. Gerry and Doris obviously hadn't been trained in proper methods of archival preservation. The interior pages were spotted, but the contents were a gold mine for someone like me.

There was a section on eye surgeries, but I had a hard time turning to it, remembering that old science class. I'd go back to that when it was closer to launch. The content that interested me was on anesthesia. I needed to find out how to knock Sarah out. The book offered a short description of how ether and chloroform had entered the surgical landscape, and instructions for their use. I'd read stories elsewhere about Jesse's gang using chloroform-soaked hankies to knock out their opponents, which made its use appealing. But diethyl ether was a pretty effective pain blocker. A bit of googling revealed that ether is still used as a solvent, which meant finding some would be pretty straightforward.

The book also described the uses of formaldehyde. Something would be needed to preserve Sarah's eyeballs. Worst case, I'd use a bottle of cheap vodka from the Quickie Mart.

This was all progress, but still left the question of how to get her somewhere private so I could ether hankie her.

It was a lot to process.

Chapter 36

"Madelaina!"

"Hi Maria, how are you?" It was a hot, quiet day mid-week in July. The A/C was acting up again, and it was a good thing there weren't many customers because the heat was making me crankier than usual. I was grateful for the distraction of Maria's call.

"My hip is acting like a wicked mostro, but this is not fascinating. I must tell you something."

"What is it?"

"I have found out for you something interesting, that I know you will want to know."

"Okay."

"It is about the prepuzio of Gesu. Jesus."

"What's a prepuzio?"

"The skin. Of the penis. The beforeskin?"

"The foreskin?"

"Yes! Of course! This is what I'm telling you."

"You found out something about the foreskin of Jesus?" I tried to modulate the incredulity from my voice.

"Si. It was stolen in 1983."

Maria had always been odd, but it seemed as if she'd completely lost her mind. I wasn't sure how to proceed with the conversation, and decided on humor. "Took them long enough."

"I suppose this is true. Il Vaticano should have made sure it was safe. But perhaps they were busy with other things."

"Can you rewind and give me a little more background?" I asked.

"Certainly! There was a foreskin. A relic. Of course, there were more of them at one point, but they disappeared and this was the last. It was in a church in Calcata, Italia since the 1500s. Many pilgrims would go and visit it. Many miracles took place. It is said that a cloud of perfume settled down around the city when it arrived there. Imagine!"

I pulled together a picture of an ancient city filled with aromatic vapor, and suddenly smelled patchouli, which didn't seem like a match. "But it was stolen?" I responded, trying to stick with her.

"Sì. Il Vaticano proclamated that discussion of Cristo's penis was not appropriate, and so the relic was put away. In a shoebox beneath the Padre's bed, or a closet, or somewhere. And then it was gone. Poof."

"Poof."

"Poof! And now no one knows where it is. The Holy Mother must be furioso."

I tried not to laugh at the idea of Mary's anger about the lost bit of flesh. "How did Jesus' foreskin get to Italy?" I asked.

"This is a five-dollar question you are asking. It was a long journey, I think. St. Caterina of Sienna had an experience once, of getting married to Cristo. On her finger he put a ring from his beforeskin. But that is another story. And perhaps it was simply a vision."

"Perhaps."

"But back to your question. Some soldier fled to Calcata and left it there when he died. Once it was found, it became the pilgrimage site."

The odds of someone at Jesus' bris tucking the bit of flesh away so it would survive centuries later seemed unlikely, to say the least. But Maria wanted to talk about it, so I tried to keep playing along. "And where was it all the years before then?"

"Who knows, Madelaina! Somehow it had been protected. Of *course* it would be protected! The tiny bambino's little privacy…"

"Of course," I said. "The fact that it made it safely through all those years is quite a miracle."

"Sì! Isn't that true? But I don't think you are paying attenzione."

151

"I'm sorry. What did I miss?"

Maria's sigh is loud and exasperated. "The *beforeskin* comes from the *penis*. And it's missing now."

I thought for a minute, trying to make sense of it. "I thought we already covered that?" I said.

"Sometimes I think you Americani are not so fast in the thinking department."

"You are undoubtedly right about that."

"Charlotte's pene. It is also missing. They have something in common, Charlotte and Gesu. And you have something in common with la Santa Madre."

"Mary?"

"Yes."

"Because Shimmy's penis was taken?"

"Sì. Someone took what was a sacred thing to our Madre. Someone took what was a sacred thing to you. The same sacred thing. The most personal thing. The most intimo thing."

The image of the torn place at Shimmy's groin took hold of my brain and grief and rage gripped my heart. I couldn't speak.

"Remember this, Madelaina. Remember that she knows how you are feeling. She will pray for you in this. She will pray for you to be able to manage this horrible grief. You can talk to her about it. She will listen. She will pray."

The idea of talking to the Mother of God about the penises of her son and Char was so bizarre that it disrupted the pain for a moment, and I wanted to laugh. But I didn't want to insult Maria, whose sincerity was so pure and intense. "All right," I said. "I will remember."

"It is nothing. It is only what we should do when we think of these things. Do you think the rememory of Jesus' prepuzio came from the middle of nowhere? Of course not. It was the Spirito Sancto whispering, so I would tell you. To bring you comfort. When the Spirit speaks, we must listen. And act."

"Thank you, Maria. You are a good friend."

"You are most welcome, Madelaina. You are always in my prayers."

"I'm grateful."

We ended the call, and I spent the rest of the afternoon thinking about the foreskin of Jesus and the heart of Mary as she contemplated its theft. My mind worked diligently to avoid thinking about the other thing.

Chapter 37

Sarah's truck was parked in front of *Fit This In* when I arrived. I pulled in a few cars away so I could walk past it and check out the truck bed. There was nothing there. The back was empty except for a spare tire, and the surface was ridged, with scraped areas where rust crept to fill the spaces paint once covered. No one else was outside, so I took a minute to peer more closely. There was no sign of blood.

Sarah was in the locker room, completely naked. She didn't see me at first, but it was obvious she didn't care. She rubbed lotion on her legs and upper arms, then took the towel off her head to rifle her hair dry. I couldn't believe the irony that the first person I saw nude after Char's death was someone I was planning to kill.

Or at least maim.

Her breasts were small but not like mine; they were big enough to sway with the motion. Her nipples were larger than Chars and the color of mocha. Mine were pink, of course, an absurd pastel which matched my lips, a color too tender and vulnerable for my comfort.

Char was never ashamed of her nakedness the way I was. She understood herself to be a creation, and rejected shame because she said God created us naked and rejoices in our bodies. In her view, feeling shame about ourselves was a rejection of the gift of existence. She wasn't proud of her body, though she could have been because it was gorgeous. She was simply grateful to have been given a suit of skin and sinew that functioned so well, grateful to have been able to transform it into something which made her feel more whole, grateful that the composition of her face facilitated getting a job doing what she loved. In contrast, I picked the details of life apart and resented being so slight and insignificant. Char's life was a song of gratitude. Mine was a saga of regret.

I'd never understood why she loved me.

Sarah's comfortable nakedness felt pragmatic from where I stood in the functional environment of the locker room. If I'd been the one drying off it would be fast and flustered. I'd listen for footfalls and hurry into my bra and panties before someone walked by. She put the towel on the bench next to her electric-green smoothie. My eyes moved lower, to her pelvis. The hair was dark against her skin, a contrast whereas Shimmy's two darknesses merged. Sarah's looked soft and relaxed against her mons pubis. Shimmy's curled tightly into themselves and her, as if burrowing against her warmth. Sarah's came together in emptiness. There was no soft curving of want waiting to rise to meet my touch.

An ache swelled in my throat, and I looked up to see Sarah's expression morph as she watched my eyes travel from her pelvis up. Her features moved from alarm to confusion to a false understanding of my hunger. Her body language also shifted, nervous attention sliding silkily into something else. Her shoulders softened. Her neck elongated. Her lips curled slightly at the corners.

She thought I desired her.

A wave of rage threatened to send me screeching to tear out her throat or rip off her patch of brown hair. I pushed it down, blinking rapidly and racing through my go-to anger poem, thinking it was a particularly good fit for this situation.

> *Shall she receive a bellyful of weeds*
> *And bear those tendril hands I touch across*
> *The agonized, two seas.*

"Well, hi," she finally said, looking nervous, but flattered. The verses had calmed me slightly, and her nervousness settled me further.

"Hi," I replied, feigning casualness. "Got here early today?"

Sara nodded and stepped into a pair of practical cotton panties. I worked at not watching her breasts, which is remarkably difficult when a naked woman you don't know very well talks to you. "I have a dentist appointment at 9:00," she said.

By this time, I'd come unfrozen enough to move past her to a locker. The door opened too quickly, slamming against its neighbor so hard I jumped. Planning to kill someone is nerve-wracking. "Fun times," I said, sliding my bag into the open space, and then shutting the door again, carefully this time. "Are you getting your teeth cleaned, or is torture in store?"

"Torture. I have to have a root canal."

"Hopefully they'll offer the good drugs," I said, still enjoying the taste of the word "torture." "Do you like laughing gas?"

"I'll probably just stick to Novocain. I'm not very experimental about that stuff."

Let me expand your horizons, I thought, clicking the padlock on my locker closed. She was nearly dressed by then in dark pants and a sweater, so I figured I'd play it cool and go do my workout. "Well good luck, and don't drive doped." I sounded like an idiot. Retreat was my best option, so I headed toward the gym.

"Thanks," she said. I could feel her watching me walk away. Her gaze made me uncomfortably aware of my cadence, which made me walk weird. I held up a hand in a backward salute, and escaped through the door.

Since she wasn't there, I only stayed on the treadmill ten minutes. It probably didn't do much good physically, but it helped me think more clearly, because while processing the embarrassment of it all, it hit me that I could use the look I'd seen on her face. That self-satisfied, flattered interest. That misplaced idea that I wanted her, and more importantly, the fact that she liked it. I could use it to get her alone.

I walked on the rotating belt to nowhere and considered the logistics of breaking into a dentist office to steal a tank of laughing gas. Modern drugs were a lot more convenient than the ones used in the days of the outlaws.

The thought gave me an idea.

Chapter 38

Maria's call got me thinking about penises again, and seeing Sarah naked probably hadn't helped. I'd never understood the draw of mechanical gizmos, but I wondered if purchasing a prosthetic for medicinal use would help stave off the dreams. They were horrible and wonderful, and I wasn't sure whether I even *wanted* them to stop. I'd tried masturbating a few times, working feverishly to get it over with as quickly as I could, feeling guilty and miserable the whole time. I missed Char so hard it ached, but the thought of a silicone robo-phallus filling the role of her missing penis was grotesque on a million levels. There was no replacing her, and no replacing the beauty of our lovemaking. She was gone, and her penis was even more gone, and a disembodied mechanical dick would undoubtedly do nothing but reduce me to rage and tears.

I wandered outside one quiet afternoon, planning to sit in the shade jutting out from the side of the shed where I could still hear the ding of the bell signaling museum visitors. Tiny hopping green things bounced away with each step I took across the grass. I was a giant disrupting the serenity of their grazing, the foe in a fairy tale. The lawn was heading toward beige due to lack of rain, but weirdly, a clump of pale purple lilies stood on thick stalks in a place they hadn't been two days before. I bent to check them out, and they were leafless, just a set of jutting stems topped by light purple blooms. I sniffed the blooms, and found they had no scent, which was disappointing. I'd anticipated a mysterious aroma to match the strangeness of their appearance, but there was nothing. In life so far, I'd been the deaf girl who could hear, and the blind woman who could see. Had I become a person who could not smell? I sniffed more deeply, certain a scent must be hiding if I snuffled hard enough.

The flowers required expert input, so I positioned the "back in ten minutes" sign on the door, locked up, and went to ask Chip about them. He was stocking canned goods.

"Felicitations, Ms. Wells," he said as I approached.

"Mighty fancy greeting from a guy whose hands are full of pseudo meat," I replied.

"Language provides the ability to hone a message so that it offers nuance and particularity, though few choose to use it that way." That seemed true, but I couldn't come up with anything particularly nuanced, so I said nothing. Chip continued. "For example, instead of saying a cube of freshly de-canned SPAM is gross, as your tone implied, you could point out that it is gelatinous, or note that the juices are viscous, or state that the texture and overwhelming salinity nauseates you. Vocabulary allows for specificity."

"Well, all of that is certainly true. Toss me a can of chicken noodle soup please. Salinity will still be an issue, but there will be fewer signs of the gelatinous." He passed the soup as requested. "At least not once it's heated."

"May I offer a cooking tip?"

I looked at the can in my hand. "For this?"

"Indeed."

"Feel free."

"In my years of consuming prepared foods, I've developed a few techniques, one of which applies to condensed soups. Instead of adding just one can of water, add another quarter can, and then simmer it slowly to evaporate the excess. It improves the flavor considerably."

I didn't understand how that could possibly be the case, but I hadn't come over for canned-soup debate. "I'll give it a try," I said, wondering if I really would. "I have a question."

"Please proceed." I told him about the weird flowers which had appeared so suddenly.

"They're called resurrection lilies," he said. "Also known as surprise lilies or naked ladies, though all of those names are misnomers, because it's not actually a lily at all. They're in the amaryllis genus."

I listened as he spoke, enjoying the intensity of the air conditioning in comparison to the fitful tepid air the museum's system produced. "Why don't they have leaves?" I asked. "They're kind of bizarre."

"They do have leaves. Just not simultaneously with the corollas which garner all the attention."

"You're saying the leaves of the flowers exist at a different time?"

"Indeed." Chip pushed up his glasses, adding a new smear to the lens.

"When do they come out?"

"In spring. April, I believe."

I thought back to what the yard had looked like shortly after my arrival in Missouri. Now that he'd mentioned it, I recalled a clump of glossy, round-ended spears where the flowers currently bloomed. They'd died off after a while, and I'd mowed over their remnants.

"I'd better get back. Thanks for the information," I said, turning away from the counter. "I knew you'd have an answer for me."

"At your service," Chip said, dipping his head chivalrously.

I walked back thinking about the wonder of a flower which existed in two different times and shapes. A plant of rising and falling. Of promise and death and then sudden, jutting resurrection. A phallic plant called the naked lady.

TRANSCRIPT

Davis: What happened next?

Jackson: I put her in the back of my pickup. Didn't want to her bleeding all over the seats.

Young: You weren't worried about blood in the back?

Jackson: It was hard to be worried about everything that needed worrying about. You ever killed somebody? You're a cop. You must have killed someone.

Young: No, I haven't.

Jackson: Then you don't understand all the stuff that goes through your mind. It's like a tornado of thoughts, and you can't keep up. The whole thing freaked me out. Still does.

Davis: So, you were concerned about blood, but just in the front.

Jackson: I guess so. It was deer hunting season. If Sarah saw blood, she'd assume it was from the doe I bagged the week before.

Young: And forensics? You weren't worried about evidence?

Jackson: Like I said, the thoughts, they were like a hurricane.

Young: Tornado.

Jackson: Exactly. I just knew I had to get her out of there, and the old haunted hotel seemed like a logical place to drop her. I figured once I'd gotten that far, I could worry about everything else.

Davis: Can you state the name of the place?

Jackson: There you go again. The Morris Mill Hotel. As if you don't know.

Young: Just doing our jobs.

Jackson: I'm sure.

Davis: Why did you call the hotel a logical place?

Jackson: Well for one, it's pretty deserted out there. They've been working on that building for seems like forever. Keep saying it's going to reopen for guests, but who knows when. I dropped her off late Saturday night, so I thought I'd have a few days before anyone found her. Figured the earliest would be Monday. Turned out it took longer than that. Not sure why. I'll have to ask Sammy if I ever get out of here.

Young: Who's Sammy?

Jackson: Sam Sanders. Another of my buddies. He's part of the crew working on the place off and on the last couple years.

Davis: Did you tell him you went there?

Jackson: Of course not! For Pete's sake. I didn't tell anybody jack shit. Think I'm stupid?

Davis: Where is Mr. Sanders from?

Jackson: Peytonsville. Same as me. We hang out at the same bar. Hung out, I guess.

Young: What's the name of the place?

Jackson: The Blue Angel.

Young: Got it.

Davis: So, you drove to the Morris Mill Hotel with Ms. Mitchell in the back. And then what?

Jackson: I looked around to make sure no one was there. No cars were around, not that I expected anyone. It was spooky as fuck there too. Even on the outside. I'd thought it was bad at the shrine, but that was nothing compared to what this place felt like.

Young: How'd you get inside?

Jackson: I tried the door next to the driveway, but it was locked, so I broke a window. One of the old ones they haven't replaced yet. Figured it was going to go anyway, so wouldn't be that big a deal. Took me a minute to find one. Had to smash the whole thing in, and break the little wood dividers so I could crawl in.

Davis: Didn't cut yourself?

Jackson: Nah. I used my elbow, and I was wearing a heavy jacket. Didn't bother me. Is it possible to get a cup of joe?

Young: What did you do once you got inside?

Jackson: I hurried up and went to open the door because that place sucked. Scarier than hell. It was empty, and you could smell the new wood and see where they'd been working, but still. Felt ominous. Like someone was watching but in a different way from the shrine. Made my skin crawl.

Davis: The place has a reputation, doesn't it?

Jackson: Sure does. They say Jesse James stayed there, back in the day. Plus some serial killer worked there. It was a long time ago, of course. Apparently she killed dozens of people with her cooking.

Davis: Bertha something, I think her name was. People say she haunts the place.

Jackson: I believe it. Place was filled with evil.

Young: So, you found the door.

Jackson: Finally. Felt like it took forever. I went out and hauled her out of the truck. She was gorgeous, but damn if she wasn't heavy. Dead weight, I guess. Now I know why they call it that.

Davis: How'd you get her in the house?

Jackson: I dragged her. It was gross, though. Dragging someone like that across the ground. Kind of bumpy. I didn't like it. Made me feel bad. It was easier inside. Floors are smooth. I pulled her through the kitchen into what I assume was the dining room. Had a fancy chandelier. There was a fireplace, and I dragged her next to it.

Young: There was a symbol next to her body.

Jackson: Yeah, that was part of my plan. There'd been news about whackos carrying out Satanic rituals in the area. Got worse at Halloween. They were sacrificing animals, rabbits, cats. Sick fucks. It gave me the idea that if I put one of those pentagons by it, they'd think it was the witches or whatever they are.

Young: Pentagrams?

Jackson: That's it. I took a chunk of charred wood from the fireplace and drew it as best I could remember. Then I sort of arranged her around it. I figured that was the best I could do without researching what the hell those nuts do, and I obviously didn't have time for that.

Davis: I think there'd been a rash of stories about vandalism in the graveyards around there.

Jackson: Killed cats and dogs. Can you believe that? Sick fucks. Hey, is it possible to get a cup of joe?

Chapter 39

I hadn't looked at the transcript again since I first opened it, but eventually couldn't resist its lure. Jackson was a rat bastard, and I was furious at the way he'd treated my beloved after leaving the shrine.

I'd never been superstitious, but the thought of visiting a haunted building wasn't high on my list of things to do. But Char was eternally connected to the place, so there was no choice but to push through all the different kinds of discomfort, and go. I considered asking Chip to come along, but that would lead to impossible conversations. A solo trip was my only option.

The drive took me down twisting, tree-encroached back roads. The leaves changed color later in Missouri than they did in New England, and less dramatically. Chip said the color varied around the state, but in the area near the museum and on the drive, it was drab in late October, as if Mother Nature didn't perform her wild harvest dance there. Maybe she knew the land didn't deserve her attention, after what its home-grown boy had done. I missed the blazing scarlets and electric yellows which exploded all over the Merrimack River valley. It hit like a dim echo of my soul's hunger for Char. I mourned the reality that I might not see it all again, because I'd either be dead or in jail for God knew how long.

The hotel's driveway was muddy from recent rain and the sky was a gray that matched my spirits. I parked and looked around, simultaneously eager and hesitant to circle around the back where Jackson had parked next to the kitchen door. Eager, but hesitant to charge inside and see if I could find her. If you haven't experienced the loss of someone close, you probably won't understand the irrational shit that goes through your head, like it did that day. Despite the intellectual knowledge that it wasn't true, I felt like being there gave me a chance to save her, to step in and stop everything from continuing. To stop time, I guess. Driving there, I'd felt a sense of urgency, like I should be hurrying, even though it had been nearly two years, and I'd been in Missouri for months, and Char was long buried. I still felt the urge to hurry, to do something, to stop it all.

The looming building was notorious. The town had been a tourist destination until a flood in the 1990s washed much of it away. In its heyday, celebrities like Charlie Chaplin and Al Capone stayed there, as had Jesse and Frank James. Plus, a charming old cook called Bertha Gifford, who'd murdered dozens of children and adults by feeding them arsenic-laced chocolates.

It looked more like a big house than a hotel. The building shed paint flakes and an air of ruin despite the bits of new wood shining bright against the place's infirmity, a wrinkled grande dame in blue eye shadow and red lipstick, run down from a century and a half of travail.

I scanned the blank eyes of the building's windows, then pulled around to where Jackson's truck must have stopped. It was a Saturday, so there was no work crew. The museum should have been open, but I said fuck it, because I wanted to be there when no one was around. The hotel was still under construction, just as Jackson had reported, but it had been for years, as if it were trapped in time, always being worked on; the lodging it was supposed to provide was an ever-present offering of jam yesterday and jam tomorrow. But the perpetual delay suited the place. Given its history of death and suffering, it was probably a good thing people couldn't stay there.

I got out and looked at the steps, forcing myself to not think about how he'd dragged Char up them, and praying that he'd pulled her by her arms rather than her feet, so that her head would have been lifted. Her sweet, beautiful head, so full of wisdom and compassion. So full of knowledge and humor. So violated.

The air outside smelled like mud, and something dirtier. Maybe it was the portable outhouse in the side yard.

I walked toward the house, and the building felt like it was hunkering over me. Not in the protective way a hen shelters a chick, but in an ominous way, as if it wanted to devour me. There were windows on both sides of the small porch, and I didn't want to turn my back on either one. I could feel pressure between my shoulder blades. Pressure built in my sinuses, and my stomach started to churn. The weathered wood of the porch floor was gray with ancient traces of white paint. Char would have hated being pulled across it, getting dirt all over her coat.

Was she wearing a coat? Did the bastard at least get her coat before they left the Downtown Sojourner?

When I'd last seen her, she was naked. It pained me to think of the forensics crew seeing her naked, but apparently Jackson hadn't. Not entirely. That was a blessing.

The door had a lock box, and while I was prepared to break a window like Jackson had, I figured it was worth trying a few combinations first. It opened on my third try, which was the house number. So much for security.

Inside smelled like dust and fresh cut wood, a scent I found intensely insulting. It was the smell Jackson had smelled, and was too fresh, too filled with promise of newness. He didn't deserve to smell it then, and the house didn't deserve it now. That outhouse stink should have filled the place, like a warning.

The kitchen seemed untouched by recent hands. Yellowed cupboards hung along one wall, and an old cook stove with multiple ovens and openings for pots and supplies of wood or coal to keep the beast going gathered dust. It looked old enough to have been the one Bertha used when making her chocolates. I imagined her cackling like a witch as she stirred, thinking about what her victims had done to earn her ire. The scent of chocolate drifted by briefly, but it must have been my imagination. Chocolate had no place in this experience.

My nausea increased. It felt like a weightlifter was stepping on my face, the pressure was so intense.

The room was too dark. A bit of dismal light came through the windows, but the porch roof blocked a lot of it. I headed for a door which I hoped led to the dining room, forcing myself not to turn around and look behind me. It didn't feel good to not check, but there couldn't be anything there.

Char may have still been alive by the time they got to Morris Mill. The timing of everything wasn't clear, so it was possible. I hoped she wasn't, because if she couldn't handle the spiritual darkness of cheap motels, this place would totally freak her out.

It was jarring to think a situation existed in which having Char dead was preferable.

I wondered what Char's death would add to the place, because it already felt like breathing cyanide. I wished I had one of Shimmy's sacramentals with me. A rosary would have felt really good in my hand. I reached for the Mamma Schiavona card in my pocket as a backup. It felt strangely warm. I resisted the urge to thrust it out in front of me like a crucifix held by a vampire hunter, because it just seemed ridiculous.

The hallway was darker than the kitchen, and the darkness deepened as I walked toward a set of swinging doors. I took a deep breath when I reached them, fearing what I'd find on the other side, maybe the ghost of the murderous cook, or maybe Jesse himself, pissed off at my lack of respect for his legacy. I wanted to turn around and run to my car. I pushed through the swinging doors with a creak, and the room was just as empty as the kitchen had been. No Jesse, no Bertha, no Shimmy.

The peachy yellow glow of fresh two-by-fours created stripes in the dimness at one end of the room. The old floorboards were wide, and the remnants of a deteriorated floral vinyl carpet adhered in several spots. The fireplace was huge, with a surround made of tile and a stone mantle. I smelled smoke, and saw a few chunks of charred wood in the opening. I knelt to look at it more closely, wondering if fires had burned since Jackson came to commit his outrage.

I scanned the floor near the fireplace, and there it was; part of a circle marked in black, next to a large, dark stain.

My forehead felt like it was going to explode, and I felt increasingly sick. I crawled closer and pressed my nose against the stain, but there was nothing. I lay down, pressing my cheek against what must have been, what surely was, her blood, seeped into floorboards which didn't deserve her, wanting to push my arms deep into the wood, between the surrounding boards and under them, to pull the wood slats close, to tear them out and take them home with me. Really home. Not to the museum, but to our house, in New England, the place we'd loved, where the floorboards were even older, centuries older, and where our fireplace was shorter and wider, where we'd sat and warming our toes and our souls, making plans and talking about nothing, and simply living. I wanted to take the boards and put them in our bed so that I could sleep with her again. I dug my fingernails into the wood, hoping my hands would slide through and I'd be given superhuman strength to rip them out.

But of course, that didn't happen.

I felt a nail pull free from the nail bed. The pain was searing but miniscule compared to what Char would have endured, her blood pooling on this undeserving floor.

I breathed the dust and couldn't smell her and my tears intensified the pounding behind my eyes. I passed out, from the thrum of my head or the nausea or the relentless breaking of my heart.

The room was growing dark when I woke. The walls felt like they were pressing in, and the open door to the adjacent room near the fresh wood was menacing. I kissed the stain and scrambled up, heading away from that menacing door and through the swinging panels which led to freedom from that awful place.

Chapter 40

My old car had never looked as safe and welcoming as it did when I ran down the steps of that haunted hotel. I climbed in and pulled out quickly, wanting to get back to the kitschy sanctuary of the museum and my nest above it all. The drive took less time than it should have given the twisting road and gathering darkness.

I breathed in the scents of coffee and the lemon air fresheners I'd placed around my living room, feeling the nausea recede and the pressure leach from behind my eyes. When I felt mostly back to normal, I called Maria.

"This is Good Goods, Buonasera!"

"I have so much to tell you." I jumped right in without any niceties, just like she often did.

"Madelaina! What is wrong? I hear it in your voice. Something is on your foot."

"On my foot?" I suddenly realized what she meant. "Oh. Afoot."

"That's what I said! What have you done? I can tell this has to do with a bad decisione."

"I went to the hotel. The place Jackson took Char, after he…"

"Madelaina. Why would you do such a thing to your heart? Do you think it deserves such torture?"

I wanted to say yes, but figured that would lead us down a rabbit hole. "Do you believe in ghosts, Maria?"

"Ghosts?"

"Yes."

"We are eternal creatures, bella. Made to last forever."

171

"That doesn't answer my question."

"There are many things beyond our understanding. The souls of the dead who waste their chance to dance with the stars and instead lurk around the places where they were hurt are just one of them."

"So you *do* believe in them?"

"Well that's a silly question. It is like you are asking do I believe in scorpions. Of course! Now tell me what happened."

I explained what I'd felt while I was there, and told her about seeing where Shimmy had lain. But I didn't tell her everything.

"It sounds like the house is some sort of magnet for darkness. All those things happening there, in that one place. No wonder it made you nauseante."

"It was horrible."

"There may have been ghosts as you called them. There may also have been demoni, lurking to try to create more tragedy. Those who are sensitive can feel them. You must be sensitive."

I thought about the way it felt on the porch, in the kitchen, and waking up on the dining room floor. She didn't need to know about all that. I was just glad to be out of there. "It was…," I trailed off, not sure what to say without saying too much. "…bad," I concluded.

"It was a rock-head thing to go there, and I do not want you to do it again. But, you can turn this bad thing you experienced into goodness."

I wasn't promising not to go back, but figured I'd play along. "How do I do that?"

"You should pray for the souls you felt in that place. Maybe they are stuck."

"Stuck?"

"Sì. Like glue they are holding to the building, trying to work out whatever it is they need to work out." I could understand the idea. If I died in Missouri, I'd probably join the souls trapped in that place, angry I hadn't fulfilled the vengeance I had in mind. But Maria was still talking. "Perhaps it is forgiveness. Pray that they could let go of the old pain. Unforgiveness is like poison, and like glue. What a horrible thing."

I considered her words, imagining the tacky nature of unforgiveness, with a force of adherence so strong it could tie things with no matter to a world of matter. Clyde suddenly meowed loud enough to travel across the states, which gave me an out from discussing it further.

"What's up with Clydesdale? That was a pretty noisy complaint."

"Oh, he is angry with me because I put him on a diet. His belly is so low it will soon be dragging across the floor, like a fur broom."

"Poor Clyde."

Maria snorted. "Poor is the last thing is this cat. He is rotting spoiled. No. He needs to trim down his stomach, so he can battle the tiny rodents which have decided to move in to my storeroom. So far he pretends they are cat television."

"You want him to eat them?"

"I do not like traps. There is no grandeur in them. It is not fair to outwit a simple creature with technology. Better to fight a grand battle with a predator. If it gets away, imagine the tales it will tell the bambini of their bambini!"

I laughed at the image, and we said our goodbyes.

After the horror of the day, it was hard to settle into the relaxation of an old cookbook. My wine glass emptied quickly as I relived the experience and thought about what Maria said. I decided to pray for the dark presences looming invisibly near the windows and around corners of that dank spot in the middle of nowhere. I prayed in part because if I *did* die while trying to strike back at Jackson, I hoped someone would pray for me and reduce the time I'd need to spend lurking there.

Chapter 41

Daylight finally broke after a night full of creaking bed springs from my fruitless search for sleep. I rose, started some coffee to take with me, and got dressed. If I didn't go right then I'd have to wait another week to return, and that just wasn't acceptable.

Mist had settled in the back yard of the museum, nestling into the base of the slight hill. The shed rose up from the fog like a ship in a sea of ghosts. Opening the door pushed the mist away for a moment, but it drifted in as I rooted around for tools. It didn't take long to find what I needed, and the coffee maker was still burbling its final burbles when I got back to the kitchen. I poured a cup and considered a few containers before grabbing a gallon-sized zip lock bag.

Driving through the fog added a level of surreal danger which fit my task. The hotel itself was perched on a rise with a moat of cloud flowing beneath it. I pulled in to the same place as the day before, gathered my supplies, and went in, hurrying across the porch to avoid the heaviness waiting to land on me. Nothing had changed in the kitchen, and the dining room was just as it had been the day before.

My head began to ache.

I moved to the stain by the fireplace, settling on my knees to run my hands over the surface, assessing the breadth of the loss as measured by the spill of her blood. My breath hitched in my chest.

I shook out the tote bag of supplies I'd brought, emptying the contents on the floor. A putty knife. A black square of course sandpaper. A paint scraper. I looked at them, realizing the only one which would be effective was the scraper. The putty knife was dull and would do nothing. The sandpaper would take the blood off but pulverize it too much. What I really needed was a plane, and I hadn't thought to bring one. I opened the zip lock bag, settling it so the mouth gaped, then picked up the scraper.

The coffee in my empty stomach felt aggressively acidic, and rising nausea didn't help. I had to hurry if I didn't want to pass out again.

My first scrape was too shallow. I'm sure the thing was never meant to be used as I was using it; scraping off curls from the top layer of wood, scraping in the cracks between the boards, gouging and scratching to get every dark particle.

As I worked, I thought about the truck Sarah drove, and how the bed of it might bear a stain like that one. But not exactly like it, because the bed was made of metal, so the blood would have pooled rather than seeping in. I needed to get a closer look at the back of her truck. Her blood could still be in those rusted spots, dried out and blowing away in the wind, or diluting as rain pooled over it.

My fury rose knowing that her blood on that wooden floor was mingling with the dirt of all the people who'd walked these planks, some just passing through on holiday, some laboring to restore the building, others working and murdering here. They had no right. The dirt from their unworthy shoes had no reasonable connection to Char, and no right to contact with her very essence. Fury fueled the work. The pounding in my head grew worse but I ignored it. When I was nearly done, the nausea had grown so strong that I moved to the corner of the room and retched, vomiting up a small brown pool of acid, and hoping it would leave a bitter stain to stand guard over the one I was removing.

The baggie settled as its base filled with a ballast of wood shavings. My hands grew sore. The sore spots turned into blisters. I hadn't thought to bring work gloves, though I wouldn't have worn them even if I'd thought of it.

I brushed as much as I could into the edge of the baggie, kicking myself for not thinking to bring a whisk broom to sweep up the smallest bits. A tiny pile remained, a ledge of brown dust and deeper, darker particles.

They couldn't stay here. If I'd been sweeping at home I would have just wooshed the small remaining line so that it dissipated around the room, permeating the space with even more of her. But the hotel floor already contained too much of Char. I knew I didn't get every bit of her from the cracks, and part of me still liked the idea of pulling up the floorboards. Even then, molecules of Shimmy would sift down to whatever lay below. She had become an irrevocable part of the building and there was nothing I could do about it. But I *could* control that little pile of dust.

I bent close to the floor. The dirt was gritty on my tongue, and small bits of wood were sharp in my throat when I worked up enough saliva to swallow. The taste of copper was faint.

Too faint.

I wanted there to be more of it.

I wanted her blood to fill my mouth, the taste of her entering me one final time in a dark, new way. The round splatters of my tears left spots of a different color in the wood. I licked the floor again until the small pile was gone.

I got up jerkily from the floor, feeling older than I'd ever felt, my body not used to that kind of labor, not used to being on my hands and knees for so long. My back ached, my eyes ached, and my heart ached. But the job was done. Where Shimmy's blood had been was a rough outline of raw wood, the edges jagged, a choppy yellow sea, clean and shining against all the darkness that surrounded it.

The baggie wasn't as full as I'd expected it to be. I tipped the sacred contents into an old, glass-topped mason jar where the chunks and particles sifted and settled, ready to wait out eternity with me. My hands smarted as they pushed supplies back in the tote bag. I'd done what I could.

I made it home safely, which was a surprise given how shaky I was from caffeine and exhaustion. My hands trembled as I placed the jar on the sill of the one window which got sun each morning, but I moved it later. Working in museums taught me you had to be careful with light. Light broke down fibers and leached objects of color. I didn't want Shimmy's blood to undergo any further metamorphosis.

While waiting for museum visitors that afternoon, I extracted slivers which had pushed into the soft skin of my palms when I tried to sweep up the loose particles. I stacked them on the counter, debating whether to add them to the jar, not wanting to contaminate the holiness of her blood with the defilement of mine. But I couldn't throw them away. I ended up eating them, my brain too tired to come up with a better option. One particularly long, dark dagger remained in the meat at the base of my thumb as a reminder, the skin around it irritated and complaining.

I returned to the hotel a few more times in the months which followed, walking around looking for uneven spots in the ground. Places where her eyes might be. Jackson's interrogators never asked where he'd put them, at least not in the sections of the transcript I'd read so far. I knew it didn't make sense to go looking. Every day that passed meant signs would grow fainter, and the flesh of her eyes would have... deteriorated after so much time. But I couldn't seem to help it.

Maybe I wasn't just there for the eyes. Maybe I went there to see if she'd joined forces with the ghosts who haunted the place. Maybe I hoped she had, because then I could at least visit her. But I couldn't imagine her keeping space with such darkness.

I never felt her there at all.

Chapter 42

A skinny meth addict went to the Quickie Mart all the time. The side window in the museum gift shop gave me a good view of the comings and goings over there. He arrived on foot every other day, and came back out tapping a pack of cigarettes on his wrist. He'd sit down on the curb and smoke one before walking off again. I didn't know where he came from or where he went. Our little spot was pretty deserted. He disappeared up the unpaved road that headed over the slope behind our buildings after his smoke. Once in a while a car would pull up while he was there, and he'd walk over to it, lean in, and exchange something for cash, which he counted after standing back up. He never bothered to hide it.

Obviously, this was the guy for me.

After he'd gone back over the hill one day, I wandered over to see what Chip could tell me about him. Chip was reading a paperback and tapping his pen. "Good afternoon, Maddie," he said, without looking up.

"How did you know it was me?"

"That's easy. Your shoes."

I looked down at my feet. The day was warm for fall, and I was wearing the one pair of sandals I'd brought with me when I moved.

"Plus, your colors. They're always the same," he said.

I realized he'd never seen me wear anything other than khaki pants or shorts and the navy polo which made up the museum's uniform. There wasn't much point in putting anything else on. The clothes were comfortable, and I was always ready for work. "But you didn't look up at me," I said.

"I have excellent peripheral vision." He kept tapping, and I could see the muscle flexing in his impressively shaped forearm and bicep.

"You couldn't have seen my shoes in your peripheral vision though." At least, I didn't *think* he could.

"That was auditory data."

"And here I thought I was a quiet walker," I said.

"It's not the volume. It's the slipping. When you walk, your shoes slide just a tiny bit."

He was right. Stepping off the welcome mat always felt like stepping on to the ice at a rink. I kind of liked it, and played to the sliding. It made me feel like a kid. But I didn't realize it had been that obvious.

"Might want to replace the pair you are wearing. Could be dangerous," Chip continued.

"You're probably right."

I could smell food cooking, so I figured Chip must be heating up his lunch. The gas station was big enough for fountain sodas, but not big enough for chrome hot dog spinners. A gadget like that would go to waste there, anyway. The dogs would turn into mummy penises before anyone showed up to buy one. "Smells good in here," I said. "What's for lunch?"

"Chili." Chip looked up for a minute. "Would you like to join me?"

"Nah." I was honored. Chip didn't generally demonstrate that kind of hospitality. "I already ate. Thanks though."

Chip shrugged "Very well then." A beeping sound began, and he set the book down and walked from the back of the counter to the microwave set up for customer use. "What can I get for you today?" he asked.

"I was just in the mood for some company."

"The museum is slow, I take it?"

"It's slow most days. But yes."

"The Route 66 tourist traffic always dies down in the fall. It will be quiet until summer break next year." Chip carried a napkin-wrapped container of chili back to his post.

"Great." The museum visitors were often irritating, but they gave me something to do while I carried out my plan for Sarah. "Hey." I cleared my throat. "Who's that guy who comes in all the time?"

"Description please. We have quite a few regular customers. I'll need more information in order to narrow it down."

"Tall, thin, army jacket. Mid-twenties. Looks like a druggie."

"You mean Allister." He opened a sleeve of saltines and crushed one on top of the steaming chili, then scooped up a spoonful, taking most of the cracker shards with it.

"Dude's name is Allister?"

"Yes. It's an unusual moniker in this region."

"Huh. Well, I wondered if it bothers you. That he sells here."

"Allister does not conduct business inside the store. If he did, I would be required to act. What he does outside is not my concern." Chip crumbled up another cracker and ate a second bite.

"Even though he's selling on Quickie Mart property?"

"I find that life is infinitely easier if I leave people to their own destinies, and they leave me to mine."

The philosophy was generally a good one, but I was surprised Chip hadn't gotten in trouble for letting it happen all this time.

"Last week I saw a cop car pull up while he was inside, and then he went flying out the back of the building. He shot off into the trees faster than I thought he could move."

"It appears that you spend a good deal of time observing the store."

"Some days," I said. "Slow days."

"Allister worked here a few years ago. He knows where the back door is. I don't object if he uses it occasionally. He's always been honest with me."

"You *do* know that could change at any time, right? Addicts often turn on their friends and families to pay for drugs." I realized I sounded like a mom.

Chip looked up at me for a moment, which was a rare thing. "I am quite familiar with the behavior of addicts, Maddie. Your lecture is unnecessary." He was about halfway done with the can by then, and had put a serious dent in the sleeve of crackers.

I realized I was making some significant tactical errors given that my goal was to get information. "Sorry. You're right, and it's cool that you're someone he can trust. Besides, I think the guy is interesting." I had to come up with some kind of cover given that I planned to talk to Allister very soon. "Maybe you can introduce me sometime. Bet he could use another friend."

"I hope I don't offend you with the observation that you could use more friends as well."

There were a lot of things I needed, but I wasn't sure friends at that time and place were some of them. "You have a point," I said, because there was no reason to disagree with him. Chip continued his methodical eating. "Aren't you worried about sodium?"

"When one of my meals contains this much salt, I adjust the remainder of my consumption for a day or two to accommodate it. Life is, after all, a series of accommodations."

Sometimes Chip was quite profound. "It is indeed," I said. "It is indeed."

Chapter 43

Every morning I put a big black X over the previous day on the paper calendar which hung on the wall behind my stool in the museum. Each month featured a stunning landscape photo coupled with an inspirational word in block letters, like DETERMINATION and PERSPECTIVE. When I flipped the page on November 1st, I expected it to read VENGEANCE, instead it shouted LEADERSHIP, which I found quite disappointing. The plan was to get Sarah alone on November 20; the day Jackson killed Char. Having the right drug in hand would make everything more real, and the days disappearing on the calendar were my fuel.

In the meantime, there were details to take care of. I set up automatic payments for the person who was acting as caretaker for our house in Merrivliet and transferred enough cash to cover it for 30 years, which sounds more dramatic than it was. I was only paying him $50 a month to keep an eye on the place and mow the grass often enough to keep the neighbors from complaining. I also set up payments for utilities, taxes, and homeowners' insurance. Once I was arrested, I wouldn't need car insurance, so I didn't bother arranging those. There was at least some chance that Sarah would rally and tote a gun. If there was one thing Jesse James' story taught me, it was that you never knew when a caper was going to go tits up. There was a good chance I wouldn't make it out of Missouri alive. Sarah might have a pistol miraculously hidden in another one of those ingenious pockets in her workout gear. She might be the type who could focus despite being drugged, and shoot me before I was done hurting her. I kind of hoped it would go that way. If the stars aligned and God was actually in his heaven, Sarah would be maimed or worse, Jackson would be suicidal with guilt, and I'd be dead.

It seemed best to be an optimist for once, so I wrote a new will. It took some back and forth because our attorney was in Massachusetts, but since Char was gone, I needed to change it anyway. There was a shit-ton of money which wasn't designated to anyone. It was time, particularly given the potential for my demise.

Maria would get $300K. Maybe she was all set for her future, but that shop couldn't be providing a ton of cash, and who knew how long she'd be able to keep going. I figured having a little bit of a backup might help. The rest would go to the Transgender Advocacy Network. I was still pissed at them for honoring Char and luring her to her death, but I knew they did good work, and she'd be happy with the decision.

As far as the museum went, I didn't much care what happened to it. Chip could fill in Gerry and Doris, and they'd just have to figure out a new plan for keeping the place open.

With all that settled, it was time to rock and roll.

Chapter 44

"Hey Allister," I called, slightly out of breath from my graceless jog across the road to the Quickie Mart. He glanced up from where he sat on the stoop, smoking his cigarette.

He looked me up and down, then squinted from beneath the worn bill of his hat. "Do I know you?" he said.

"I'm a friend of Chip's. I work at the museum."

"Oh. The new chick." He stopped scrutinizing me like I was a skunk who'd wandered into his backyard, and turned his face back to the concrete beneath his feet.

"That's me," I said, quelling the urge to toss back a verbal hand grenade at the label. I stood there for a moment, trying to figure out how to pose my question. My hesitation seemed to make him nervous.

"Can I help you?" His voice came out sarcastic and overly polite.

"Actually, I hope you can. I was wondering if you could maybe get me something."

"You said you're a friend of Chip's? He'll vouch for you?"

"I'd prefer you didn't tell him about what I'm looking for, but yes. I think so."

"You want something exotic?"

I wasn't sure how to answer that. I'd done some hurried research about date rape drugs, but people kept walking by which was awkward. "Not sure you'd call it exotic, exactly." There were several kinds, turned out. Some were fast acting. Some caused amnesia. Some caused temporary paralysis. "I need Rohypnol." His expression shifted, looking slightly incredulous. "Unless you suggest an alternate pharmaceutical," I said, sounding idiotic but figuring he knew more than me about that stuff.

"Roofies."

"Yes."

"Here I pegged you for a coke girl."

"Nope."

Allister's gaze was penetrating, examining me as it had when I first approached him. "Never had a chick ask me for roofies before."

"First time for everything," I said, reprising my role as village idiot. "So what do you think? Can you hook me up?" I hadn't used that phrase since shortly after college, when asking friends if they knew where to get some pot.

"How soon you want it?" he said, stubbing his cigarette out on the curb beside his hip.

"How soon can you get it?"

"Be back in here on Tuesday."

"Sounds good. How much?"

"How many do you want?"

That was a good question. I really only needed one dose because it was a one-time thing, after all. It wasn't like I was going to keep on drugging her. On the other hand, there was a chance something could go wrong, so I figured a few extra wouldn't hurt. "Three," I said. "No, four."

"Twenty bucks," Allister said. "Since you're a friend of Chip's."

I nodded. "You want the money now?"

His expression turned incredulous. "You don't do this much, do you?"

"I do not."

He stood and brushed off the back of his pants. "See you Tuesday. Pay me then." Allister walked off the way he always did, disappearing around the corner of the store, and presumably up over the hill. I wondered where he'd get the drugs. Maybe he had his own supplier. Maybe he ordered them from the dark web. Either way, I was one step closer to Sarah paying the price.

I considered going in to say hello to Chip, but my mind was in too dark a place. Dark and coiled. Waiting. Instead, I headed back to the museum, just as a car pulled into the parking lot, unloading an elderly couple who'd come to pay homage to a bunch of serial-killer heroes.

Chapter 45

Two days later I found Chip washing the glass on the soda cooler doors. "Hand me a ginger ale?" I asked. He complied, then returned to polishing. The section of paper towel he held was sodden, and a cloud of ammonia filled the air. I watched him for a moment, noticing how carefully he checked for smears. "Hey, why don't you ever come to the museum to say hello? I'm over *here* all the time."

"You come here because it is full of things you want or need. I don't need anything from the museum."

"There is always the pleasure of my company," I said, unscrewing the cap of the soda. My stomach had been bothering me for several days, and I hoped the ginger would help settle it. Nervousness did that to me.

"Company is not something I tend to search out. Though I hope that doesn't offend you."

"I'll choose to assume it's not an insult."

"I assure you it is not." Chip moved to the next cooler door and began cleaning it with a fresh paper towel. "So, I've learned that you are a recreational marijuana user," he said.

His statement jarred me, though I should have seen something like it coming. "I take it you've been chatting with Allister." Thankfully he'd changed my order from roofies to pot.

"He informed me that you requested his services. He wanted an assurance about your character."

"What did you tell him?"

"The truth. That I'd only known you for a few months, but that you seemed unlikely to be an undercover police officer."

The absurdity of the idea made me giggle. If I was, I'd surely have to put myself under arrest for conspiring to commit several crimes. "I'm about as far from a cop as you can get. Thanks for that."

"You're welcome."

"Have you tried it?" I asked.

"Marijuana? Of course."

"Did you like it?" I tried to imagine Chip high, wondering what a methodical case of the munchies would look like.

"No. I don't enjoy feeling out of control. It was not pleasurable."

"But you're okay with wine?"

"Intoxication is controllable. The body processes one drink per hour, so as long as I consume only slightly more than that amount, I can achieve a slight softening without moving into significant loss of cognition or physical capability."

"That makes sense."

"Of course it does. What use is there in having intelligence if it isn't applied?"

"Very little. But most of us don't think about things like the proper use of sentience."

"And the world is the worse for it." Chip pushed his glasses up. I wished he'd clean them as assiduously as he polished the glass.

"I'll leave money for the soda on my way out," I said, turning to leave.

"I'll come ring you up," he replied. "I need to throw these out anyway." He followed me toward the front of the store, his fists full of damp paper.

Chapter 46

Allister was at the Quickie Mart on Tuesday, just like he'd said. He pulled a miniature baggie from the front breast pocket of his army jacket. "Here you go," he said. I shoved it in my own pocket, looking around guiltily, and figuring I'd check out the pills once I had privacy. "Big plans this weekend?" His expression was a cross between an assessment and a smirk.

"Not this weekend, no." There were still ten days until the 20th, and while I was itching to get it over with, the date was important. It would bring things full circle. Allister lit a cigarette and blew out a dragon's lungful of smoke above my head, still assessing me. "I appreciate that you didn't mention what I was getting to Chip," I said, handing him a twenty.

"No problem. Let me know if you need anything else."

I thought about the variety of drugs which might make life easier in the days to come. "I'll do that. Thanks again." I walked back to the museum, rubbing my fingers against the pills in my pocket, a braille message of what was to come.

Chapter 47

Sarah and I fell into a routine at the gym. I'd arrive shortly after she did, and join her at the treadmills. For a few sessions she'd watched my mounting technique, but that stopped when she realized I wasn't going to break my neck. It was easier for her because her legs were longer. Short people had to spread farther to stand on the sides of the machine, getting ready to step on to the magic carpet to no place.

"Hey," she said in our normal greeting. I nodded in response.

Sarah wasn't as big a milquetoast as I'd expected. She had a good sense of humor. Kind of dark, which I liked. She was into sports, which I wasn't. She was polite and deferential, which might be a requirement when you marry a murderer. From reading the transcript, it sounded like he was quite a prince. So, I got that she wasn't a forceful personality. It made sense. But she wasn't as wimpy as I thought she'd be.

Sometimes we chatted, sometimes she listened to music. I never did though. My concentration was always on watching, thinking, paying attention. I didn't have the luxury of music.

The day after Allister handed over the roofies, Sarah was in the mood to natter. "Didja catch the Chiefs game last night?" she asked.

It was my own fault, having previously pretended an interest in football. "Nope, I missed it," I said. "How'd they do?"

She wiggled her upper body in happiness, like a wriggling puppy. "24 to 10! They killed them."

"Dang."

Sarah prattled on about field goals and holding. I made what I hoped were appropriate responses, but mostly just listened to the sound of her voice. It was soothing in its steady excitement. It was soothing to be in the presence of femininity.

I'd never been athletic, but my endurance was increasing after weeks of workouts. Walking became jogging, and while I didn't go fast or long, at least I went. She didn't sweat as much as I did, which was one more thing to resent. Her slightly round face with its pointy nose barely got pink. My face in contrast immediately beaded with sweat, and my upper lip generated a water mustache within the first 3 minutes.

I stopped when Sarah stopped, and we moved on to the weight room. She talked me through a circuit and we worked our way around the machines, my peripheral vision on her even if my gaze wasn't directly. She was watching me as well, because she saw me flinch during one of my reps. My hand pulsed with pain from the sliver that was beginning to fester in the base of my thumb.

"Wait," Sarah clunked down her own weights, and stepped over to me. She reached for my hand. "What's this?" she said, concern pouring from her eyes. She ran a finger gently over the reddened flesh. "It's hot! Could be infected."

"It's no big deal." I'd left the bit of wood from the haunted hotel floor in there, weirdly enjoying the pain, and wondering if a person could die from a sliver.

She looked at me like I was stupid. "It's on its way to being a pretty big deal. Come on," she said, pulling me toward the door. "They'll have a first aid kit up front." She marched me to the reception desk and got the kit. I stood there like an oversized child while she fussed, trying to figure out how to get her off track. The wood fragment could be saturated with Shimmy's blood. I wanted to leave it in me.

"How's my body going to know how to fight off serious diseases if I don't let it handle the small stuff?" I said, not expecting her to fall for it.

"That thing's going to turn super nasty if you don't get it out. See how angry it looks? You could be headed for blood poisoning." I doubted her prognosis, but the splinter did throb and she wasn't letting up. Sarah used an alcohol swab to clean the end of a pair of tweezers, then picked up my hand and scraped gently at both ends of the splinter. "Looks like neither end is sticking out."

"I could have told you that."

"And I could have guessed that you'd be a crabby patient. Hold still!" Sarah squeezed the flesh to see if an end would appear.

"Oww!" My bellow was loud, but not nearly as loud as the pain warranted. "Damn, that hurts."

"Shh…" she said, her voice soothing despite the recent irritation with me. She released my hand and pulled a safety pin from the kit, repeating the alcohol rub. "I'm sorry I'm hurting you. It wouldn't be so bad if you'd removed it right away. Now your poor hand is a mess."

It felt really good to have someone fussing over me. The last person to do it was Maria, months ago, but that had been a whole different experience. Maria was older. Maternal. Sarah was older than me, but only by a decade. Plus, she was pretty in a girl-next-door kind of way. And she was actually touching me. I could feel the warmth emanating from her hand as it held mine. I could smell her as she stood close. Her scent was a combination of fresh sweat and berry-perfumed body products. Like she'd been out in the brambles picking berries in August. I pictured a fresh-plucked raspberry landing on her tongue just as the sharp point of a thorn punctured my palm.

It wasn't a thorn, of course, it was the safety pin, but it was effective in chasing away that line of thought.

"Sorry," she said, her voice sincere and soft with concentration. She was trying to make me like her. Trying to soften me up, almost like she knew what was coming. But I couldn't fall for it. What I could do was *pretend* I liked it, because people love to feel needed. She dug around with the pin and I watched her face and felt the pain, trying not to jerk away, not so much because I didn't want the pin to tear my skin, but because I liked her breath on my wrist. "I think I got it," Sarah said. She used the tip of the pin to lift one end of the splinter. "Hand me the tweezers." I complied, and she used them to pull the wood out. "There we go!" she said with excitement at her victory. She set the tweezers back on the counter and I squinted to look for a little fragment of wood on it. I couldn't see anything, but still hoped. "Now we'll just get you bandaged up. Does it feel better yet?"

"Are you kidding?" I asked, forgetting for a moment that I was supposed to be grateful. "That kind of stirred it up," I said, backtracking from my anxiousness about the wood remnant. "It'll calm down in a minute."

Sarah smiled in response, then wiped my wound with alcohol, which felt like a second needle being inserted. "This will hurt too," she said, a moment late. I held in my yelp this time, and she patched my hand up with some ointment and an oversized adhesive bandage. It looked like the sliver probably wouldn't be the death of me, which was disappointing. "There you go!" she announced.

"Do you have kids? You'd be great with them." I knew the answer of course, but wanted to steer the scenario toward a compliment.

"No. Tried for a while when I was your age, but then gave up. And now…" Sadness washed over her face before she reined it back in. "Now I'm single so it's a done deal. I teach Sunday school though. Does that count?"

"Absolutely. The kids must love you. You're very nurturing." I thought of her face tilted toward my wrist again, and of the image of a raspberry on her lips. But the lips were Char's, her teeth brilliantly white behind them, and I remembered the sliver of wood, waiting for me to collect it. I turned toward the reception desk and began cleaning up. "Thank you. It feels a lot better. And you probably saved me." Yet one more thing to hate her for. I gathered up the empty foil pouches and curling bandage wrapper. My eyes were on the tweezers the whole time, considering what to do about the sliver. My bag was in the locker room, and it would get lost in the pockets of my shorts. But there was one safe place. "I'll get all this." I paused to look back up at Sarah and forced a smile, hoping to release her to finish her workout. I'd peel back the edge of the bandage and stick the sliver against the stickiness of the adhesive. It would stay there securely until I got home, where I could decide what to do with it.

"I'll help," Sarah said, scooping up the tweezers and swiping them yet again with an alcohol pad, which she tossed in a trash can offered by the kid who had desk duty. I wanted to scream then, for real. She watched me closely, as if seeing the emotions morphing behind my eyes.

"Can I have that?" I asked, extending my good hand to take the waste-basket from her before she answered. "You go do your reps. I'll be there shortly." I tossed the bits of trash into the can. "Go on," I said. "You've done more than enough."

She tipped her head to one side, seeing God knows what, then smiled back. "Okay," she said, and started walking off. "See you in a minute."

The kid was busy staring at a couple of girls who pretended they didn't see him, so he wasn't paying attention to me, which was a relief. I pawed through the wastebasket, collecting the gauze pads and looking for the sliver. It wasn't on either one.

I thought about stealing the can and burning it so Char's essence wouldn't remain in that room, under that desk, in the glaring lights and the smells of receptionist farts and household cleaner. But the basket was plastic so how would it burn, and taking it would be kind of obvious, so I stood there frozen trying to figure out what to do. The kid finally turned around to look at me again. "You done with this?" he asked, gesturing toward the first aid kit. I nodded robotically, still scrambling to come up with a solution. He tucked it back into its place below the ledge, then held out his hand for the trash bin. I just stared at him until he put his hand back down, then turned away from me like I was insane.

"I'll bring it right back," I blurted, then crab-shuffled away to the locker room, where I dumped the contents into my bag, and fruitlessly searched the empty can for the tiny, precious relic. I sat down on a bench, growling with grief and rage, glad the place was empty.

When I returned the empty bin to the front, my shoulders were back and my heart was resolved. Jackson was going to pay, and so was Sarah.

She was almost done with her routine by the time I arrived in the weight room, and she beamed a smile at me that was warmer and more intimate than previous smiles. "Took you long enough," she said. I smiled back, faking it again.

"Had to make a pit stop," I replied, glad I wouldn't have to fake it much longer.

Chapter 48

Chip wasn't behind the counter when I entered the Quickie Mart. "Hello?" I called. There wasn't an answer, so I walked to the soda machines and scanned the cup sizes which ranged from large to ridicu-gulp. The kind I needed was at the smaller end of the range.

Chip appeared around the end of the aisle and greeted me. "Maddie," he said with a nod. "Are you in need of assistance?"

"Not really. I was just going to say hello." I took a stack of five cups that looked to be the right size. "Mind if I take some of these?"

"Be my guest. However, the accumulation of discarded plastics is becoming significantly disruptive across the globe. Not to mention the petroleum dependence and pollution which results from plastic production."

"I'll be sure to recycle them."

Chip shrugged and turned to pull a rag from the cupboard beneath the coffee stand, along with a spray bottle. "That's better than throwing them in the trash, but it doesn't do much to alleviate the problem." He pumped a mist of something that smelled clean but greasy on the stainless-steel surface adjacent to the soda machines, and polished until the whole thing shined.

I considered my stack of cups, and added two more along with matching lids. Straws shouldn't be necessary. "I'll make a contribution to an environmental fund to offset this lapse in judgment," I said. Chip's lack of curiosity about what other people did had turned out to be a useful trait. Most people would ask what I needed all the cups for, if only to make conversation.

"Good," he said with a nod. "I've been reading about the effect of charitable actions, and how if we were logical rather than emotional with our decision-making, we could affect significant change in the world. Perhaps the same is true for a situation like this. Donating funds would essentially be a grassroots carbon credit transaction."

Talking with Chip was always fascinating, but I had things to do. "Just doing what I can, where I can," I said, resorting to cliché. "Take care!"

"I shall." He put the bottle and rag back in the cupboard, and used another cloth and product to clean the laminated surface of the coffee bar. I took my cups back to the museum, debating about where to conduct my tests. Outside would be the least messy, but would require trips back and forth to the kitchen. I'd made a bunch of ice ahead of time. The kitchen didn't include a blender, so the contents of the cup would have to be approximated, but I thought it should be okay. Chip would have had a theory for me of course. He'd tell me a slurry would exert more force than a thin liquid combined with ice cubes, or vice versa, because water weighed more than ice. But I obviously couldn't tell him what I was doing, and figured the approximation was good enough.

I decided to conduct the test in the bathroom, and prepped all of the cups, filling them with water and ice and lining them up on the kitchen counter like soldiers awaiting their call to duty. I carried the first one to the bathroom and put it down on the flat edge of the tub, then knocked it inside. The lid came flying off when it hit the worn ceramic in a satisfying sploosh. *That was easy!* I thought, but I couldn't assume it would always do what it was supposed to, so I brought in another cup and that time the top didn't come off. I repeated the test with the remaining soldiers, channeling Chip and figuring there might be variations in the manufacturing tolerance of cup and lid which would make some more prone to popping off than others. The results showed that six out of seven lids came off, which wasn't flattering to the packaging designers. Lids should stay on tighter.

I left the ice in the tub to melt, gathered up the plastic for recycling, and crossed the test off my pre-murder checklist.

Chapter 49

Things started to speed up after that. I'd crushed the pills into easily dissolvable dust, and it was time to assemble my weapons, or surgical gear, depending on how you looked at it. I'd found an industrial supplier that carried ether and placed an order, wondering if purchasing it kicked off some sort of federal investigation unit to track me. It didn't really matter if it did. The stuff came in four gallon-sized bottles, which was way more than needed, but I couldn't be bothered to find another source. When the shipment came, I poured some into a water bottle. I added a trash bag, some spray cleaner, rubber gloves, and a bunch of rags for cleaning up afterward. Fingerprints weren't a concern, but I didn't want to leave a big mess to traumatize whoever happened on the scene later. After thinking about it a little longer, I threw in one of those disposable rain ponchos they sold in the gift shop, thinking it could protect my clothes, because I had no interest in going to jail covered in Sarah's blood. The first aid kit stored under the cash register caught my eye, and my blood boiled again at the thought of the still-missing sliver. I tossed it in the big gym bag along with everything else.

On the day I'd arrived, Gerry showed me a locked box behind the storeroom door, where the keys to the artifact cases were hung. "Not that you'll need them," he said. "Everything is arranged perfectly the way it is. It's all just the way the founder wanted it. Brilliant mind, he had. And you never have to dust those objects. That's the beauty of being under glass."

"Not sure Snow White would agree," I quipped, thinking about the cartoon version of the princess in her glass coffin. I'd pictured Char lying in state on a bed of white satin, whole and suspended rather than dead, waiting for me to come and pull the bit of poison apple from between her beautiful lips. Gerry's wooly eyebrows pulled together like two caterpillars kissing. He didn't get the reference. "You'll have to tell me the secret for dusting barbed wire," I joked, trying to relieve his confusion. That display wasn't behind glass.

"Ha!" he chuffed. "Funny girl, are you?"

The keys were right where they'd been that day, though none of them were labeled. None of the cases were labeled either, which would make it harder. If this had been a real job, I would have created a chart and put signs on the cases to map each key to its lock, but this wasn't a real job. I grabbed both key rings and went to the exhibit room to check out the knives. I wasn't educated about blades and their uses, so I had to imagine the task and picture which size and shape seemed like it would work best. Limited collateral damage I suppose they'd call it if this were war. I wondered if there was anything to practice on, and considered various foods in the supermarket, but couldn't come up with anything. Some things in life could only be learned by doing.

After considering the knives on offer, three looked promising. Then came the task of testing keys to get the cases open.

One thing I hadn't counted on was the depressions the knives had created on the fabric which covered the bottoms of the displays. Each one left its imprint behind, like one of the ghosts at the haunted hotel, refusing to give up their connection to a specific place and time. I pushed and prodded to rearrange the material as best I could, but the color was even different. The red behind the knives was vibrant and shining, while the fabric around them had faded. There was no hiding the fact that some were missing.

But time was short, and I had to prepare, so when a patron asked me about the missing items the next day, I just said they were out for maintenance. The dude nodded before mansplaining to me about the gun adjacent to one blank space. I let him blather on, and then went back out to the gift shop to kill time until he left. In the scheme of visitors, he was pretty nice, so I hadn't tried to fuck with him by feigning blindness.

The last thing on my to-do list was to call Maria and say goodbye. I wasn't sure if I'd ever talk to her again, which was going to make the conversation hard. All the cop shows made it sound like you got to make one phone call, and I had my lawyer's number ready in the pocket of my murder pants for when the time came. I didn't want him to fight the charges, but criminals had to have lawyers. Besides, what could I say to Maria after everything went down? "I'm sorry" wouldn't exactly cut it.

She picked up on the third ring. "Buongiorno, this is Good Goods."

"Hi Maria." I cleared my throat.

"Madelaina? Is that you? You sound strange, like there is something wrong with your throat. Are you sick? I will send you some zuppa."

"I'm not sick. Just had a little tickle." I cleared my throat again, and took a deep breath, willing myself not to cry. The idea that I was losing Maria was even more painful than expected. Hearing the care in her voice undid me.

"A tickle is nothing to be discarding. It is often the sign that something worse is coming. Do you have honey?"

"All I have is sugar and stevia, I think."

"Stevia? What nonsense is a Stevia?"

"It's a sweetener. Low calorie. Supposed to be healthy."

"You are as small as a child already. You are trying to disappear into a poof of bones and dust? Mio Dio. You young people and your obsessions about size. Go to the store. Get some honey. Good honey, from the bees that are your neighbors."

"Local honey?"

"And limoni."

"Lemons?"

"Si. And whiskey. Do you have whiskey?"

"Nope. No whiskey either."

"What kind of life is it that you are living? Like a religiosa, a monk in the desert. Next you'll be telling me you eat locusts and are wearing a shirt made of the hair of a goat."

The idea of a hair shirt sounded appealing, and led to thoughts of self-flagellation. I pictured a whip covered with tiny metal points like the ones on the barbed wire display. I'd whip it down my back while saying "mea culpa, mea culpa, Jackson maxima culpa." I'd whip him too, if I could. Should I whip Sarah?

"Are your ears also sick? Can you not hear me?"

"My ears are fine, Maria. I'm just distracted. Life here is… odd." It was an understatement, but it was the best I could come up with. I figured I'd better just hop on the Maria train. "I'll get some honey. And the whiskey."

"Don't forget the limoni."

"Right."

"Fill a mug with hot water. And don't use one of those micro machines. Using radio waves to cook your food cannot be good for the body. All that sound getting stirred up and electric. It has to be bad. Please tell me you have a tea kettle."

"That I *do* have."

"Grazie Dio! Fill the cup with the boiling water, but leave room. Maybe one inch. Add a spoon of honey and squeeze in the limoni. Then top it with whiskey. Like magic, it will help your throat."

What might help was if I filled a mug with whiskey, and left room for a splash of water and lemon. But it wasn't time to argue. "All right, I'll do that." I didn't like lying to her, but couldn't see another way out.

"Also make some zuppa di pollo. Do you need me to tell you how to do this?"

"No, I'm actually pretty good with soup." I was, though I had no intention of making any. It would just sit in the refrigerator and transform into something more foul than fowl by the time anyone bothered to clean it out.

"All the time I must be worrying about you, down there where there is no one to take care of you." I thought of Sarah's ministrations, and her raspberry scent, and the missing sliver, which brought me around to rage again. But Maria was still speaking. "When are you coming home?"

The thought of New England made my throat close up again, the ache of missing it was so strong. I missed the smell of Boston harbor when I walked from the T to my office. I missed checking out the big boats that pulled up along the boardwalk in the town next to Merrivliet. I missed the joy and rage of Red Sox and Patriots fans. I missed our house. But I didn't deserve any of those comforts, and I had to do this thing I'd come to do.

"I miss you, too, Maria," I managed to mutter.

"So!" she said. "You want to come home!"

"Of course I do."

"Then why do you not do it? Why are you torturing me, and yourself? Come home." The worry in Maria's voice was evident. "Please." It was almost like she knew she needed to do more than just send soup to save me.

"Because there's still unfinished business here."

"Business. What business is it of yours to be messing around in some wild wax museum. What business is it that you spend all day talking to people made of candles. What sort of good is this thing you think will help you recover?"

"I…" It would be so much easier if I could just tell her what I was there to do, but she'd find a way to stop it. Even with her lack of technology and thin understanding of where I was, she'd figure out a way. And even if she couldn't, she'd fret her head off. I hadn't prepped anything ahead of time to tell her, which was stupid, so I was floundering. "I'm almost done here," I finally blurted. "It won't be long, okay?"

"What won't be long? This is what I am trying to ask you."

"I'm on the verge of a breakthrough. I can feel it." That much was certainly true. I could feel it throughout my body. My nerves were jangling with it, and my hands and feet were buzzing with the itch to take action.

Maria sighed, long and loud. "I am praying for you, Madelaina. May the angels in heaven fly with you and keep you from falling right on your head into your own stupidity."

A bell jangled in the background, and I realized it was my way out. "Sounds like you have a customer," I said.

"Si."

I didn't like that her response was so short. I didn't want us to part like that.

"Listen. I hear what you're telling me, and I respect what you're saying. I'll be back as soon as I possibly can, okay?" It might be decades, or it could be sooner, when my spirit soared to the places I loved in search of my beloved.

"Do you promise me this thing?"

"Yes. I promise."

"Then this is all I can do. I will continue praying, Madelaina."

"Thank you."

"Do not forget the soup. And the hot toady. They will make you feel better."

"Okay. Now go tend to your customer." I focused on the image of a toad in a cup of hot whiskey to try to stop my voice from quavering.

"Call me again soon. On Friday. To tell me how you are feeling."

"Friday it is. I love you, Maria." It was the first time I'd said it.

"I love you too, piccolo."

I hung up the phone, and wept. It wasn't quite noon. I didn't know how I was supposed to make it through to the morning without having a nervous breakdown.

Chapter 50

The kitchen was dark when I finally gave up on sleep and went out to make coffee on the second anniversary of Char's death. It was so early the birds hadn't started singing. The only sounds were the hiss of the coffee maker and the ticking of the red and black kitchen clock above the sink. So early the Quickie Mart wasn't open.

The tiles on the bathroom floor were cool beneath my bare feet. I sat on the edge of the tub to fill it. Baths weren't part of my normal routine, but today wasn't normal and I didn't know when I'd be able to soak again rather than stand on some alien tile with other naked women, all of us counting down time beneath the pounding of water. There weren't any fancy bath oils or salts, so I glugged in a bunch of the strawberry shampoo I'd purchased on a whim. The scent reminded me of products the girls in middle school had in their suburban bathrooms. Like strawberries, but not. It smelled like innocence.

The water was extremely hot. I sunk in until only my head rose above the sea of foam. The light was off so I could focus on my thoughts, and I imagined my skin turning as pink as the scent rising from the bubbles.

Vengeance takes a lot of planning. Studying the outlaws showed me how much work must have gone into their heists. Very little planning went in to killing Charlotte, and I wished, perversely, that it had taken a great deal of time. The idea of it being spontaneous was enraging. She deserved full attention.

The bubbles around my ears exploded in crackling pops, reminding me of the concert of tiny snaps when waves drew back from the wet sand back home. I missed walking on the beach and smelling the ocean mix of rotted things and fresh air. I missed scanning the ground for sea glass or old fishing lures, corners of buried lobster pots and dying sea creatures. The sound of waves pulled the fractiousness from my heart, and left me calm. In Missouri I felt untethered from reality. Everything I was doing felt like something watched rather than enacted. All of it was Jackson's fault, but this place had something to do with it. Location mattered.

I thought the tub would clarify my thoughts, but the warmth and scent lulled me toward stupor, and it was no time for relaxing. It was time to pick a location.

Coffee helped, the black bite an antidote to sleep, and after a few sips my brain was alert enough to return to the question. Bringing Sarah to the museum had a certain logic, since it was a monument to revenge, but museum visitors could be pesky. I considered Meramec Caverns, where Jesse James had hidden out and where Mr. Turilli first encountered the phony Jesse, but I was unfamiliar with the place and needed to have my plan nailed down. The haunted hotel was frequently vacant, but I didn't want Sarah's blood polluting whatever particles of Char remained.

The Mamma Schiavona shrine was the answer. No blood remained on the clean tile floor of the chapel. Jackson's transcript said the caretaker was a drunk, so if we went early, he'd still be sleeping off his evening bender. By killing Sarah there, the whole thing would be reversed. She'd experience the same kind of fear Char had, the same cloudiness, the same confusion.

And then, the same pain.

The rising of the sun was permission to get going. I dressed, grabbed my goody bag, and trotted down the stairs, feeling the strength in my legs from all the exercise I'd been getting.

While driving, I rehearsed my plan and thought through the timing. If things ran as normal, Sarah wouldn't rush after her workout. She usually sat in her car for a few minutes, finishing her smoothie and scrolling through her phone before heading to the accounting office where she was a partner. She'd told me her schedule was flexible, which made it nearly perfect. No one would panic if she didn't show up at her usual time. So many things lined up in favor of my plan that I sometimes wondered if the whole thing was ordained.

I was super nervous during our weight training. "Do you have some time before work today?" I asked when we moved to the final machine.

"A little," she replied. "What do you have in mind?"

"Just wanted to show you something." Sarah tipped her head, evaluating me. "It's a surprise," I said.

"A surprise? And it's not even my birthday." She looked pleased, as if anticipating a present.

"When *is* your birthday?" I asked, hoping to change the subject. It seemed as if she was saying yes, and I preferred to keep her mind right there in that happy place rather than risk her questioning my plan.

"Oh, not for months. July 14."

We continued to chatter as we completed our routines, then headed to the snack bar like normal. Once in the locker room, Sarah put her smoothie down on the bench in its usual place. When she turned to open her locker, I knocked it to the floor. By some quirk of fate, it happened to be a one-out-of-seven lid which didn't pop off. My heart stopped beating for a minute before my body took over. I stomped on the cup. "Oh my gosh!" I said, just as she was turning to look. "I'm so sorry!"

Sarah's eyes traveled from the floor to my feet. "Wow, that's quite a mess," she said. The green gloop had splattered from the zealousness of my stomp. "It's all over your shoes. I'll grab some paper towels." She hurried toward the sinks.

I bent to pick up the dented cup, trying to use the lid to scoop some of the mess back in while making apologetic noises. "I'll go get you another smoothie. I'm so sorry," I repeated.

"Don't worry about it," she said, handing me a wad of paper and bending to wipe up the mess. I stooped near her, and the smell of our sweat merged with the grassy, fruity smell of the spilled drink.

"No, I'm definitely getting you a replacement. You go hop in the shower. I'll clean this up." We were almost finished, so she complied.

"Okay. But it's not necessary. I don't absolutely need one. I can just drink some of yours." She took the sodden towels to a trashcan.

You absolutely do *need one*, I thought. "I guess I didn't tell you I'm a germaphobe," I quipped. "I'll get you your own. You keep your cooties to yourself." I followed the sentence with an awkward laugh, but she didn't seem to catch its falseness.

Sarah pulled her sports bra over her head, muffling her voice. "No, you never mentioned it." She kicked off her shoes and peeled down her leggings. "I'm hitting the shower." She grabbed her towel and left, and I nearly ran back to the snack bar. I didn't have much time. Luckily, the attendant was there to take my order immediately, and I hustled back to the locker room clutching the replacement drink. Sarah was humming in the shower, so I still had a few moments. I pulled the baggie of powdered Rohypnol out of my sports bra. It was slick with workout sweat and nervous perspiration. The sound of water spraying on tile stopped, and Sarah cleared her throat. My hand was shaking as I struggled with the tiny plastic zip top.

The door of the locker room banged open and a woman I'd seen but not met walked past, heading to another row. She nodded as she passed. My heart pounded. I palmed the baglet and smiled back like an automaton. When she was gone, I snapped off the lid of the new smoothie as the shower curtain rings rattled, signaling that Sarah would be back momentarily. I got the bag open, and the powder poured in like the sand of an evil hourglass, counting down Sarah's time. My hand was shaking so hard I dropped the baggie, and a small cloud of powder puffed out on the floor, sticking to the dampness remaining from the spilled smoothie. I heard Sarah sniff, and glanced behind me. She'd stopped to look at herself in the mirror above a sink, tipping her face to examine the skin near her nose. I grabbed the baggie and shoved it back in my bra, then stirred the drink with the straw, praying she didn't have a sensitive palate. She arrived at the bench beside me just as I snapped the lid closed. A drop of sweat dripped from my nose to the lid, and I wiped it off before turning toward Sarah. "Here you go!" I said, super chipper and jerky, happy I'd gotten that far but eager to keep the ball rolling. It was important that Sarah take a few sips now and begin to loosen up. If I started acting even more stupid, or if the drive to the shrine seemed to stretch, she might start getting nervous. She took the cup, and sucked a small mouthful up through the straw. She'd need a lot more, but it was a start.

I watched her face to see if she detected any bitterness.

"Thanks," she said. "But you really didn't have to." She put the cup on the bench, then took off her towel, draping it so she could sit down. She looked me full in the eye, confident in her nakedness and more than a little challenging. Anger rose from beneath my diaphragm, along with a desire to laugh out loud; an obnoxious laugh of superiority and a different kind of confidence. The kind that comes from knowing something important the other person doesn't know.

I turned away before she could see the derision in my face, and started gathering my stuff. "My turn in the shower. I'll only be a second though. Don't leave without me."

"I won't." She took another drink.

I rinsed off fast and got my hair wet, not particularly caring about cleanliness. I'd need a shower again once this was wrapped up. But the appearance of normalcy was important, so I let the water pound for a minute and did a quick rehearsal of the plan.

Sarah was dressed and brushing her hair by the time I returned. I dried off and put my murder clothes on, super conscious of her gaze on my skinny limbs. "Not sure those butt exercises are working," she said. "It's still pretty flat." She'd been sipping steadily, and about a quarter of the smoothie was gone.

"It's hard to fight genetics," I said. "Ready?"

"Let's go."

We walked to the parking lot and I led her toward my car. "I'll drive," I said. "It's part of the surprise." The beep of the car unlocking was a warning she couldn't hear. "How's your drink today? Delicious as usual?"

Sarah went obediently to the passenger side and got in. I'd cleaned out the front and hung a fancy air freshener, so the interior smelled like apples and cinnamon. "Very funny. I can tell you don't really like them."

"They taste exceedingly green."

"That's the flavor of nutrients," she said.

"More like the flavor of photosynthesis." I took a sip of my own smoothie before placing it in the holder, hoping to lead by example. The car started smoothly as usual, and we pulled out of the parking lot.

"So when are you going to tell me where we're going?"

"Maybe I won't tell you at all. Maybe we'll just arrive."

"This feels a little weird," Sarah said. "I don't know whether to be excited or nervous."

"I'm both right now." I was driving faster than I should, so I slowed down. The last thing I needed was to get pulled over. Sarah would probably slip into full-fledged loopiness while the cops called in my license, which would create a lot of questions. I glanced in the rearview mirror, glad for once to be living in the middle of nowhere. The road behind us was empty.

Sarah kept drinking, sticking with her typical routine of finishing the whole thing. "We should have stopped for coffee," she said, sucking up the last bit of the smoothie until the straw bubbled with emptiness. I couldn't be certain, but it sounded like her voice was mellowing. She leaned her head back against the headrest. "This is nice," she said. "I usually have to drive myself everywhere."

"I'll do the driving today," I replied, which sounded super creepy even in my own ears. "Radio okay?" I asked.

"Sure." Sarah closed her eyes, and I flicked on the radio. Conversation was increasingly challenging, and I didn't want to say something stupid when we were just a few miles away. She didn't open her eyes again until we bumped over the unpaved entrance to the shrine's empty parking area. She blinked a few times as if working to focus. "Wait. Why are we here?"

"Let's go for a walk." I unbuckled myself and walked to the back of the car to soak a washcloth with ether and seal it tight in a baggie, then hurried around to make sure she got out. The place was quiet except for the sounds of birds in the surrounding trees. There was no sign of the caretaker. The air smelled earthy from rain captured in the fallen leaves on their transformation into soil.

"Wait," Sarah said again. "I know where we are." Sarah said. Her feet didn't move with their usual grace, so I took her elbow.

"You do?"

"Yes. I'm not sure I want to be here." Sarah stumbled a little bit on the uneven stone path. She wore impractical suede boots with a high wedge. Walking alongside the path might be easier, but the ground was kind of muddy. It could ruin her boots.

"It's beautiful," I said. "Come look at the chapel." I guided her off the stone walkway, realizing that ruined boots wouldn't be terribly important in about twenty minutes.

"I know it's beautiful. Or used to be. My drunkle works here."

"Your 'drunkle'?"

"That's what my ex used to call him. Short for drunk uncle."

"That's kind of funny."

"He wasn't funny very often." Sarah looked around, her expression a mix of confusion and unhappiness. "I don't think I want to be here." She kept walking with me despite the objections, and I led her to the stone bench right in front of the altar. The mosaic glistened in the sunlight streaming in from behind us. The eyes of the black Madonna gazed at me, the scratches on her face prominent. Her expression was calm and a little sad, and the for the first time I noticed her hand, lifted and curved toward her, as if gesturing for me to approach.

"Let's sit," I said, pulling us down on the bench, and placing my bag on the ground.

"I don't like it here." The effects of the drug were increasingly pronounced. The time had come.

"I've been meaning to tell you something," I said.

"What," she said, turning her face too look at me, her tone flat and slightly drunken.

"I've been keeping a secret."

Sarah laughed. "Uh oh. What is it? You're a drug dealer. IRS agent?"

"Nope." I thought I'd enjoy this part more.

"Spy for my husband? Christopher. My ex." She saw I wasn't laughing. "I have some secrets too," she said. The humor left her face, whether from her own thought trails or because she picked up my somberness.

I huffed at the suggestion. "Your husband isn't much of a secret." The thought of him made my heart pound harder.

"I s'pose you're right. Everyone knows." Her face turned toward the ground again, but I couldn't tell if it was voluntary. I'd better hurry up if I wanted her to experience at least a little bit of terror about what was coming.

"I'm not who you think I am," I said.

"Who are you?"

"My name never rang a bell?"

She looked confused, and blinked at me. "Maddie Wells, right?" I nodded. "I got nothing," she said.

"Two years ago? Two years ago, *today*?" I asked. My heart was pounding harder and I couldn't tell if it was from anger, fear, or adrenalin. I wanted to recite a poem to try to calm down, but couldn't focus. Sarah just looked more confused, and vaguely irritated, like she wanted me to cut to the chase. The date didn't have the same significance for her that it had for me, and that was additionally enraging. "Two years ago. Right here."

I always thought the idea of someone's face blanching was figurative. It isn't. As I watched, her complexion did the opposite of blush. "Maddie," she said. "Means Madeline. Okay." Sarah nodded as if to confirm having figured that much out. "But her last name was Mitchell."

"We didn't change our names when we got married."

Sarah shook her head, like a dog trying to get a fly out of its ear. Her movements were increasingly slurry. "Oh my God...It's you..."

"Yes." I bent to take a few items from my bag and shifted them to my pockets.

She looked like she was about to cry. "Look. I don't know how to say this. I've really wanted to get in touch with you." She looked so earnest, I almost believed her.

"To get in touch with me?" I fingered the handle of the knife. The ether-soaked washcloth bag in my other pocket felt like a stress-relieving squish toy.

"Yes," she said.

"Why?" I pulled the knife out where she could see it. It didn't look as sharp as it had back at the museum.

"What are you doing?" she asked.

I didn't answer, just watched her face as the emotions traveled across it. Confusion. Concern. Fear. I saw the fear in Sarah's eyes and thought about the fear which must have been in Char's 730 days ago. Thinking about that made me want to make the fear go away. I didn't want to have to see it. I wanted to make those eyes stop looking at me.

Was that what Jackson felt?

It disgusted me to experience anything he'd experienced. I pulled the soaked rag from its baggie. The sweet, chemically fumes rose up immediately. The smell was nauseating

Sarah's expression settled into a sort of sad resignation. I wondered if she could read minds and knew what I planned. The flesh of her face drooped, a wax figure melting in a heatwave, the weight of emotion too much to hold up under the strain. She looked decades older than she had ten minutes ago. "Do it," she said.

"Do what?"

"Whatever it is you have planned for that knife." I couldn't believe she was still that lucid. Jackson must have given Char a whole lot more than the one pill I'd broken up for Sarah. She was confusing me. I didn't like it.

"Okay," I said, and pushed her down on the bench so she was lying on it. I crouched over her and took a few deep breaths, readying myself to follow through, to knock her out, to kill her and get it all over with. I needed to calm down. My hands were shaking. It was getting hard to breathe, and the stink of the either wasn't helping.

Mark but this flea, and mark in this,
How little that which thou deniest me is;
Me it sucked first, and now sucks thee,
And in this flea our two bloods mingled be;

Sarah laughed, the sound loose in her throat.

"Did I just say that out loud?"

"Yes, you did. Weirdest shit I ever heard."

"It's just something I do when I'm nervous," I said, not knowing why I was explaining myself. "Why don't you shut up?" If she stopped talking, I might be able to think straight.

I tried to tell myself I was doing this for Char, but I knew that was a lie. Shimmy would never approve. She'd be furious, was furious right that minute if her theology was true, stomping her beautiful foot somewhere in a state where she didn't really have a foot, where she was merged with the creator and the raindrops and the souls of others like her who'd been murdered. If that foot was still in the physical world my action would destroy our relationship. I wondered if she'd forgive me, and if she'd greet me when I eventually came, or if she'd hide between the particles of a sunflower somewhere in western Canada, knowing what a punishment it would be for me to spend all of eternity searching for her.

It was too late though. I'd come too far. It was time. I moved the stinking cloth up toward Sarah's face. I couldn't believe she wasn't fighting at all, even if she *was* drugged.

"Hey," a gruff voice interjected behind me. I stiffened, and kept my hands where they were, out of sight and blocked from view by my body. I looked over my shoulder at the old caretaker who stood just under the edge of the open chapel's roofline. "What are you doing in here?" His eyes were almost as red as his nose, and his gray hair stood up in hedgehog spikes. "What kind of perverts have sex in a sanctuary?" His voice was a mix of outrage and resignation. He shook his head, then crossed his arms over his chest. "Get out of here."

Sarah lurched up to rest on one elbow. "It's just me, Uncle Frank."

He narrowed his eyes and jutted his neck to peer toward her. "Sarah?"

"Yup." She slumped down again.

"Are you drunk? And what are you doing with a woman?"

"Leave us alone. Okay?"

Weirdly enough, he did. He shook his head then turned and plodded away, shoulders hunched as if trying to offer shelter for his beer belly.

"He got old," Sarah said. "And he thinks we're here to fuck."

"We're not."

"Hurry up. I'm tired. I want to go to sleep."

She was making it too easy. Was it murder if someone asked you to do it? I tried to recall the instructions in that fusty old surgical book, but the reality of her lying there, prone and willing, was messing with my head.

"Do it!" She was nearly screaming now, loud enough that it might draw her druncle's attention. "Kill me so I won't have to think about it anymore. Or see how people look at me. 'The murderer's wife.'"

It hit me then that if I killed Jackson's wife, it would do to him what Jesse's murderer had done. It would turn him into a legend. He didn't deserve to have any more fame than he'd already accrued. People needed to say Shimmy's name, not his.

Sarah broke into jagged crying. The sound of her sorrow echoed the cries I cried in the months following Char's murder. It was an exhausted sound which I recognized viscerally.

I tossed down the knife, and heard it clatter against the tile.

I couldn't do it.

Vengeance takes a lot of planning, and even so, things don't always go the way you think. Just ask Jesse James.

Chapter 51

"Hurry up!" Sarah's voice was half wail, half impatient complaint, the letters of the word 'up' stretched to take the space of five words. She sounded like an annoyed adolescent.

"I'm not doing it," I said. Sarah responded with that hiccupping gasp toddlers make when they've had a crying jag, which I ignored. "Get up," I said. But it wasn't clear if she *could* get up, so I heaved a theatrical sigh and started shoving murder tools back in my bag. When the stuff was stowed, I pulled at Sarah's arm. "Come on. Let's go."

"Too tired."

"Too bad. We're getting out of here. I can't just leave you lying there, though I'd like to. If Frank comes back, he'll think you're dead." The irony of the fact that this was the scenario I'd intended wasn't lost on me. "Come on!" Sarah flopped to one side and pushed herself up to a sitting position. "Good girl. Keep going." I scooped my arm under her armpit to try to give her a boost, but she was taller than me so I could only pull her so far. Luckily, she kept moving from the momentum.

"Where're we going?" she asked. "I need to get to work."

"You're going to call in sick. I'll help."

"Okay." By that time, we were headed toward the parking lot. The going was rougher that direction than it had been coming down. I poured her into the passenger seat and buckled her in. "I'm going to sleep now," she said when I got in my side.

"Sounds good," I said. It would be easier to think with her asleep. "Let's just call your office first, so no one freaks out." I started the car and pulled out of the parking lot. "Hand me your phone." Sarah fumbled around to find it, then gave it to me. "What's the number?"

"It's under 'work.'" Her head tipped sideways. "Tell Sam I'm going to puke."

"*Are* you going to puke? Should I pull over?"

"Maybe," she said. Her eyes were closing and she didn't show any external signs of nausea, but I decided not to risk it and pulled off the road. It would be safer for making the call anyway. I found the number, called the office, and wove an illness tale for the receptionist that answered.

"Wow, Sarah's sure lucky you were there at the gym with her!" the woman said. Lucky wasn't the word I would have chosen but whatever. "Tell her I hope she feels better."

"Will do. Thanks." I disconnected the call, slipped Sarah's phone in her purse, and got back on the road. I hadn't been able to follow through with murdering her, because I was a giant pussy. And I wasn't going to bother trying again, because deep down I knew killing Sarah didn't make any kind of sense. Maybe I should have just cut out her eyes, then taken her to the hospital. At least then I'd still get arrested. What would I do with the rest of my life if I wasn't going to be in jail?

It started to rain, and the drops hit the windows, dripping down as if the sky was crying as Sarah had. And crying with me. The rhythmic pattern of the wipers was soothing though, the steady back and forth, scrape and thump, like a heartbeat, the car like a womb, with Sarah my twin passed out beside me.

Should I take her to a police station and turn myself in? Confess that I'd drugged her and planned murder? It was an option, but it left me with a huge problem. All the sorrow and anger were still in play. I still wanted to hurt someone. Jackson still needed to pay. I'd be in jail, which would be a good thing because it was at least part of the plan. But if it happened without accomplishing some kind of revenge, what would have been the point of this whole disaster? I didn't know how to decide what to do.

"Sarah," I said, shaking her shoulder. She lifted her head and tried to open her eyes, but they were bleary and had trouble focusing on my face. "Sarah! I need you to wake up. Just for a minute."

"I'm awake. Geesh."

She didn't look very awake, but I didn't have much choice other than to keep going. "Do you want to go to the police?"

"Why?"

"Because I just tried to kill you."

"Fucking loser couldn't do it," she said.

Harsh, but true. "I'm sorry. It's not as easy as you think," I said. "Should I take you to talk to the cops?"

"No. I want to go to sleep."

I sighed again, because there wasn't much point in talking to her in this state. I had to figure this one out myself, at least for now. "Okay. Go back to sleep. I'm taking you to my place." I'd wait until she sobered up, and see what she wanted to do then.

"Whoopee."

The remainder of the drive was smooth. Sarah's breathing grew heavier, turning into a slight snore which mingled with the sounds of rain and wiper blades. When I helped her out at the museum, I noticed mud all over the passenger side floor. Her cute boots had taken a toll.

Getting her up the stairs to my apartment was rough, but we made it without breaking our necks, and I let her flop across the couch to sleep it off. I was tired too. Exhausted really, from lack of sleep, too much adrenalin, and the sense of failure. I threw an afghan over her and headed to bed, not looking forward to whatever stage of nightmare was coming next.

Sleep came fast and I submerged deep. It felt like a dream when I opened my eyes to Sarah tugging on my hair. "Get up," she said. "What am I doing here?"

"Oww! Is that how you usually wake people up?"

"I don't usually have to wake *anyone* up. And can you please keep your voice down? My head is killing me. What am I doing here? I assume it's your apartment?"

I pushed the bed coverings out of the way and climbed out. "I'll get you some aspirin."

"Can you close the blinds out there? It's so fucking bright."

I hadn't thought to research the effects of coming down from roofies, but figured I was observing them. Late afternoon light angled in through the living area windows, and I pulled the curtains closed. "There you go. Do you want some coffee?"

"What I *want* is to know what I'm doing here."

"How much do you remember?" I called from the bathroom. My face looked sad and tired in the medicine cabinet mirror. I yanked open the door and pulled out the aspirin bottle.

Sarah was back on the couch when I came out. I went to the kitchen for a glass of water, and handed it to her with the pills. She gulped them down, then drained the glass. "I don't know what's going on. You were going to take me somewhere." Her eyes focused on the middle distance, trying to recall what had transpired. I wondered if I was going to have to decide whether or not to tell her. "I dreamt about my uncle Frank, which was weird." She looked up at me. "Did we get in an accident or something?"

"You didn't dream about Frank. We saw him."

She looked incredulous, her expressions still overblown and cartoonish, so the drug was apparently still partially in play. "Not sure if you want coffee, but I need it, bad." Sarah handed me the glass and I went back to the kitchen alcove, keeping busy while she figured out what she remembered.

"We saw him," she said.

"Yes." I could almost feel the force of her thoughts, scrambling to assemble themselves into cohesion.

"So, we *were* at the shrine?"

"Yes."

"Why do I feel like shit?"

I dumped coffee grounds into the filter basket, and flipped the switch. "I hope you aren't used to fancy coffee, because I just buy whatever's on sale." I was stalling for time, trying to decide how much to say.

"I'll manage. Maddie, you have to tell me what's going on!"

The coffee machine gurgled and the scented steam puffing out smelled like false hope. I wondered what prison coffee would taste like. "Here's the deal." I turned to face Sarah. "I drugged you, then drove you to the shrine, where we saw your uncle. That's why you feel like shit. It's the drugs."

"What?" Her face screwed up in disbelief. "Why would you drug me? Why take me to the shrine?"

"God, I don't want to have to go through this all again." The coffee was done, so I filled two mugs. "How do you take your joe?"

"Fuck the coffee!" She was sitting rigidly upright, her body radiating outrage.

"I need some, and I'll bring it to you black unless you tell me otherwise." But I could see she wasn't in the mood for further delays. I carried the cups to the lounge area and placed hers on the coffee table, then sat down in an armchair across from the couch. "Okay." I took a burning gulp. "So first, I need to tell you that I'm Charlotte Mitchell's wife."

"Wait…" Sarah looked away from me to think about what I'd said. Her eyes scanned back and forth as she thought it through. She didn't display the same shock she had at the shrine. "You told me that, right? Earlier today?"

"Yes."

"I thought so." Her head swung back up to face me again, demanding. "What else?"

"I came down here from Massachusetts. To hurt you. As revenge for what your husband did."

Sarah picked up her mug and leaned back against the couch pillows. She could never be a poker player, because her thoughts were so clearly displayed across her features. She nodded as the story sank in, guilt transforming her confused anger to something softer. She took a few sips before looking at me again. "Why didn't you do it?" she asked. Her voice had also softened. Sorrow could be heard behind the words, in her timbre's tenuousness. "Was it Uncle Frank?"

"No. He left us alone. I could have done it after that." I couldn't explain something I hadn't had a chance to process yet, and I wasn't sure how to even say that much. "I might… I might need some time before I can answer you. I don't really know why. Everything was set. I was ready to do it."

"I wish you had."

"That's part of why I stopped. I didn't expect you to be so willing. You were begging me to hurry up."

Sarah was silent for a moment. "It's not easy, being a survivor," she finally said. The words made my rage flare again. How dare she try to glom on to what was clearly my territory? But she was still talking. "I feel so stupid. Like I should have known." She sat her mug on the table again. "I *should* have known!" She crossed her arms over her chest, as if clutching herself together. "All those stories of mass murderers, where the neighbors describe the guy as 'a quiet man?' That's how I feel. He was just a regular guy. Full of shit like most of the men I know. Thought he was always right. Thought he was funnier than he was." She paused. "Is. He's still alive, but it's hard to think of him that way."

"You don't talk?"

"No. I have no interest in communicating with him. I divorced him as soon as I could," she said.

I was glad. Not that there was any reason to be glad, but still.

"There were just no signs, you know? He didn't talk about being violent. Didn't talk about gay people."

"You do know that being trans isn't the same as being gay, right?"

"Yes. I guess. But you know what I mean. We don't have trans people around here. There are gays, but he didn't talk shit about them."

"There *are* trans people, you just don't realize it."

Sarah closed her eyes and shook her head slightly. "I'm not trying to pretend I know anything. I realize I'm ignorant about all this stuff. I'm just trying to tell you how it was."

"Okay."

"If he'd been openly discriminatory, maybe I would have seen it coming. Maybe I could have done something to stop it." I wanted to agree with her, but in reality, she probably couldn't have done much. But

I completely understood the terrible power of "if only." Tears were dripping down her face. "I don't even know how I feel about any of that stuff. I'm not religious. I wasn't raised in church like he was, so I've never had a strong opinion. I just like to leave people alone and let them live their lives. Since Chris didn't talk about it, I figured he felt the same way. Turns out I was very wrong."

I tipped my face toward my coffee, inhaling the warmth and letting her words settle into my brain. She was taking away my ability to blame her and I didn't like it. Sarah kept talking, acting like I was some sort of confessor. A murdering priestess, listening to the perceived sins of the penitent victim. "Did he tell you what he did?" I asked.

"No. Not until he'd confessed to the police. He called me and blurted out the story, real fast. I couldn't believe what I was hearing. They let me see him a while later, and I went down because I had to understand what the hell had happened. I assumed Charlotte had tried to hurt him or something, and he was just defending himself." I almost threw my coffee at her then, wishing it wasn't still scalding. She saw my face and realized her error. "I didn't mean it like that," she said. "I didn't know anything at the time. I didn't know who Charlotte was, or what he'd done to her. I didn't know *anything*. I just knew that he killed her and wasn't going to get out of jail. I had to go find out more."

I breathed deep, and told myself that what she said was all logical. "When did you find out the truth?" I asked.

"He told me when I got there. Spilled the whole thing." Tears continued to slide from her eyes, over the curve of her cheek, down to the jaw, finally sliding to drip from her chin. "I'm so sorry," she said. "No one deserves what he did."

My anger flared again. It was beginning to feel like flashes of heat lightning, striking suddenly in a summer sky to stun the cicadas and birds into silence. "You're fucking right she didn't deserve it. She was completely innocent. On every possible level." The image of Char's mutilated face formed, and I pushed it away, calling up Jackson's image instead. "I was going to cut *your* eyes out. Did you know that?" I stared at her, wishing menace would flow out to surround her like a poisonous miasma. Sarah shook her head. "Of course you didn't know," I continued. "I was going to cut them out, and put them in a jar, and send them to your husband. 'Chris,'" I drew his name out long and slow, derision dripping from every consonant. She blinked several times and leaned away from me, slowly. "That idea bothers you more than the thought of being killed?" I asked. Sarah nodded. "Gross, isn't it?"

She tipped her head into her hands, shoulders slumped, exhausted. "Yes," she finally said. "It's gross." Silence unwound between us for several minutes, a silence full of increased understanding, of shared disgust, anger, and remorse. A silence that was somehow binding. I wasn't sure what to do with any of it.

I put my cup down and stood up. "Come on. It doesn't look like you're going to die or pass out again. I'm taking you home." I grabbed my jacket and keys from their places near the door. "Unless you'd rather go to the police station. Because I'm fine with that."

Sarah stood too, and slipped on her own coat. "No," she said slowly, shaking her head. "Home is good. I have to think."

"That makes two of us."

TRANSCRIPT

Young: We didn't find Ms. Mitchell's phone or bag. Did you do something with those?

Jackson: I threw her purse in a dumpster out back of a Baptist church in Cedar Hill. Tossed my jacket away too, because it had a lot of blood on it. I liked that jacket.

Davis: Do you remember the name of the church?

Jackson: Nah. It was just on the drive. Saw the parking lot and decided it would be a good place to get rid of it. Who'd think to look in a church dumpster?

Young: Where'd you put the penis?

<Noise of crumbling plastic.>

Davis: Did you hear the question?

Jackson: Yes.

<Slurping noise.>

Davis: That coffee good?

Jackson: It's not bad, actually. Thanks.

Davis: No problem.

Young: Where'd you put the penis, Christopher?

Jackson: I wish you'd call me Chris. I only get called Christopher when I'm in trouble.

Young: Chris then. Where is it?

<Sound of sighing.>

Jackson: You guys are like mosquitos. All you do is buzz around, making the same sounds. It's irritating. Anyone ever tell you that?

Davis: I'm sure it is.

Jackson: How am I supposed to remember every little detail? And why does this part matter?

Davis: You're saying you don't remember?

<Grunting noise>

Young: Tell you what, let's back up a step. What did you use to cut it off?

Jackson: My jackknife. Used to be my granddad's. Blade's as thin as paper and sharp as a scalpel.

Young: You remember using it?

Jackson: Yes, I remember! I dropped it on the ground after.

Davis: The knife or the penis?

Jackson: The knife. Wish I hadn't left it. It's the only thing I have from him.

Young: Why did you cut off the penis?

Jackson: I was pissed.

Davis: You were mad?

Jackson: Very.

Young: What were you mad about?

Jackson: It should have been hard. He should have been turned on by me. I'm a good-looking guy, don't you think? Women are always hitting on me.

Davis: Sure, Christopher. You're a good-looking guy.

Jackson: Right? So why wasn't the bitch turned on by me? I still don't get it. He was supposed to be a woman now, and women always like me. But he had a dick, so he should have had an erection. But he didn't.

Young: And that made you mad?

Jackson: Wouldn't it have made you mad? She had to be a tramp. Living that kind of lifestyle. Famous. Rich, no doubt. Sleeping with anyone who came along, most likely. So what was wrong with me?

Davis: So you cut it off. Her penis.

Jackson: Yes! Jesus, haven't we been over this? Besides, you know damn well I did. Her body sure didn't have a dick on it when you found it.

Davis: And you remember cutting it off, with your grandfather's jackknife.

Jackson: Yes. Christ. The blood.

Davis: It bled a lot?

Jackson: I always thought head wounds were the ones that did all the bleeding. But this was crazy.

Young: What did you do with it?

Jackson: You know, you'd think people in my situation would deserve a little dignity. Not much, just a tiny shred. We're all human, right? We all do things we regret.

Davis: You're right. We do.

Jackson: So why do you have to grill me about every fucking detail? I confessed. I've told you my story. Why do you keep harping on about her dick? Jesus wept, your names should be Freud.

Young: Why is this part so difficult, Chris?

Jackson: Fuck! I'll tell you. I was hard as a rock, okay? Hard as fucking granite. I was so turned on I thought I wasn't going to make it inside her. I was so fucking excited I was shaking.

Young: And that made you mad?

Jackson: Of course it made me mad! What kind of guy do you think I am? A fag? I only went and got her to prove her kind wouldn't do it for me.

Davis: You wanted to find out if you found her sexually attractive?

Jackson: Yes. Christ.

<Pause>

Jackson: All those times, you know? In the locker room at the gym. Seeing the guys buck naked on their way to the shower. I'm straight. I told you that already. I love pussy. Can't get enough of it.

Young: But the guys at the gym?

Jackson: They do something to me. And I don't understand why, because I'm not a fag, and I know all the Bible verses about abomination, and I don't want to go to hell.

Davis: How did that bring Charlotte Mitchell into the picture?

Jackson: I figured she was the perfect test case. I could prove that when it came down to it, I wasn't into guys. Besides, she was sort of a woman, too.

Young: And the test…? How'd it go?

Jackson. Hard as a fucking rock. I told you that already.

Young: What did you do with her penis, Chris?

Jackson: Not even a shred of dignity.

Davis: Come on Chris.

<Sound of sighing.>

Jackson: I kept it, all right? I wrapped it in an empty potato chip bag I had left over from lunch and took it home with me.

Davis: Why'd you do that?

<Pause>

Davis: Chris?

Jackson: Because I wanted to taste it! I've always wanted to taste one. Are you happy now? Made me crawl like a worm? You guys are sick.

Young: Do you still have it?

Jackson: Obviously I got rid of it. What would Sarah have thought if she'd found it?

Young: I'm sure she would have been confused.

Davis: What did you do with it?

Jackson: I sent it out to sea! <Laughs.> Just like a dead goldfish. <Laughs.>

Young: You flushed it down the toilet?

Jackson: Sure did. Bye-bye.

Davis: When was this?

Jackson: The next day. I kept it in my car and it was cold out, so I figured it would keep. I tasted it and it tasted like soap and perfume. She must have been really clean. The texture was strange though. Now I know what Sarah goes through when she gives me a blow job. Sort of.

Davis: So, you got it out of your car, and flushed it down the toilet. Where was that?

Jackson: At work. Did it during lunch. It looked kind of weird by then.

Young: I think we can take a break now.

Jackson: Sounds good to me. What are you going to ask me about next? How often I pick my nose?

Chapter 52

In all my reading about Jesse James, I didn't come across anything that said he backed down. There were at least 19 robberies of banks, stage-coaches, and trains, with twenty or so people dying as a result. He certainly wouldn't have stopped out of empathy for those who hurt his family. By some weird coincidence, Jesse was 34 when he was killed, and I was also 34. He was shot a few other times throughout the years, but it took a lot to kill him. Unlike Jesse, I was ready to die. I wished Sarah had taken the knife out of my hand and thrust it into my heart instead of turning those big fawn eyes my way, acting all Christ-like and ready for martyrdom.

The place where my heart was supposed to be ached like it was full of something acidic and bubbling, something poisonous rather than blood, like ether, maybe. I considered tearing out my own eyes, but decided that would render me unable to take further acts of retribution against Jackson. I ached to take away the blindness Char experienced, and willed her to feel me standing beside her in that loss of sight. I would have lived the rest of my life happily standing next to her with elbow crooked, a place to rest her long-tapered fingers, a human guide dog who would die happy just to sit adoringly at her feet.

Some people believed Jesse's exposure to the violence of war inured him to evil so he was able to commit the crimes he did. Maybe that was my problem. Char's poor, mutilated body had shattered me, but perhaps not enough. I decided to read more of Jackson's confession and see if it would push me to finish what I came to do. And a few days after my failure, I pulled out my tablet and clicked open the file, scrolling down to where I'd stopped previously. I read for a few minutes, swallowing convulsively to avoid vomiting.

I set the tablet back down, gently, gently, as if it were an explosive. It was too much to take in. Too much horror. Too much loss. Too much nonchalance on Jackson's part when he talked about what he did to Shimmy's penis, as if it was a minor detail. His twisted view of sexuality reduced her to a fetish which somehow justified his actions.

It enraged and sickened me, but even then, I knew I wouldn't be able to mutilate Sarah the way Jackson mutilated Char. I liked her too much. I'd been seeking an eye for an eye, a response equivalent to the loss endured. The aptness of the phrase brought on a bout of hysterical laughter, and the laughter transformed to tears.

When I was cried out, a strange clarity settled. I wouldn't steal Sarah's genitalia the way Jackson had. But I could take her another way.

Chapter 53

"Welcome to *Fit This In*," the kid at the front desk parroted as I entered. "Haven't seen you in a while. You been sick?" he asked.

That was a good question, but I didn't think he'd want the real answer. "Nope. Just… busy." Sarah was nowhere to be seen, but I was early. "Have you seen Sarah Jackson around?"

"Not yet this morning, but she was here yesterday as usual." That was a relief. It would be a lot easier to try to restart some sort of relationship in a familiar setting. God knows what she would have thought if I'd shown up at her office, or worse, her house.

"Great, thanks," I said, already walking to the locker room to store my stuff.

An older man was using the treadmill I considered mine. We exchanged nods as I claimed one at the opposite end of the room, hoping Sarah would position herself beside me when she arrived. I wasn't sure what she might be thinking or feeling. It had been a few weeks, and hopefully she'd had time to absorb what happened. My gut said she'd want to see me again. I'd read that survivors were often driven to connect in ways which could be surprising. I never expected to experience such a thing with the wife of Char's murderer, but her signals had been so jumbled that there was room for optimism. My heart pounded and it wasn't from exertion.

The clock slow-motion ticked toward the time Sarah usually took her position and turned on the perpetually moving rubber sidewalk. I tried not to stare at the door, tried to breathe deep and slow my pulse as I waited. And then she was there.

She came in and gave a swift sweep of the room, coming to a halt when she saw me. Her face looked stony but beautiful, and my heart did a little dance again. She walked to her usual machine, and I began an internal pep talk about it taking time and the importance of patience. Sarah draped her towel around her neck and stepped up on the machine. She looked me in the eye without a smile, then turned on the motor and began her usual warm up jog. It made me irrationally happy that she wasn't ignoring me. At least not completely. My cheeks wanted to curve into a smile, but I forced them back to solemnity.

Though I'd started earlier than her, I keep trotting and sweating until she finished up, and even then, kept running. She dismounted, swabbed her face, then looked up at me. "Are you coming?" she asked, her face a challenge.

I nodded, hurrying to dismount while trying to not look overly eager. "Sure," I said, playing it super cool. Inside, I was crowing.

Sarah turned with military precision and marched out, not waiting to see if I'd follow. I hurried after her, feeling like an eager puppy bumbling after a ball. We took our positions on adjacent weight machines. "So. You decided to come back," she said.

"I did." My mind whirled, trying to figure out what to say.

"I'm glad." We were both staring straight ahead studiously, but I could see her out of the corner of my eye. Her face showed only exertion when she pressed against the tension of the machine. I couldn't read what was happening internally. "Obviously this is awkward, but we have a… connection." She struggled to find the word. "I'm not exactly happy you were going to kill me and I'm not thrilled you didn't actually do it." It seemed unlikely that the dude across the aisle could hear what Sarah was saying, but he looked over just then and I couldn't tell if his expression was quizzical or just permanently confused. "But I can't really blame you," Sarah said. "I kind of wanted to kill Chris after I found out what he'd done. I can only imagine how you must have felt. And I'm the next best thing." I hadn't expected it to go this well, but Sarah seemed like she was on a roll, so I didn't interrupt. "We're connected now, whether we want to be or not. It's like a spider web that we had nothing to do with creating, and here we are, wrapped up tight. Like stupid flies."

"*I* had something to do with it," I said.

"What do you mean?" Sarah finally looked over at me.

"I should have come with her. If I had, I could have stopped him."

Her face searched my own, and I kept moving, breathing the way she'd taught me as I pressed the weights. She took a minute to sit with what I'd said before answering. "Why didn't you come?"

Telling her felt super vulnerable, but there wasn't much choice but continue. "I have this fear of flying. It's ridiculous. I packed and was all ready to go, but at the airport, I almost passed out. I didn't get on the plane." Tears were threatening as I spoke, and I blinked furiously to stave them off.

Sarah waited a moment before she spoke. "I knew something was up when Chris told me he was taking the day off," Sarah said. "He wasn't acting right. He showered, for one thing, which he never does when he's hunting, and he only took a travel mug of coffee rather than the thermos. He thought I was stupid enough not to notice. Or maybe he didn't care." Sarah's gaze was focused inward, her face sorrowful. "I just thought he was having an affair, and pussy-drunk enough to be careless." I considered saying something, but figured she needed to talk it through. "Turns out it wasn't an affair."

It sure as fuck wasn't, I thought, but bit my tongue.

"When he didn't come home until the middle of the night it just seemed to confirm it. I was on the couch when he came in, because I had no interest in sleeping in the same bed whenever he showed up. I told him I didn't feel well, and he went upstairs. Relieved that I didn't grill him, no doubt. He took a shower again, which he doesn't do at night, and it seemed to take a long time. I just laid there, crying because the life we had together was over."

"What did you say to him the next day?" I asked.

"I left before he woke up because I didn't want to talk to him. I had a lot to figure out before I confronted him, and I wanted to try and gather some evidence because he'd probably try to wiggle out of it. When I got home after work, I just pretended everything was normal and he went right along with it. He seemed distracted and like he wanted to avoid me, which made me furious even though it was a relief. A few days went by like that, while I searched his dresser drawers and jacket pockets. I checked his phone in the middle of the night, but there was nothing. I couldn't understand how he'd be that careless the morning he claimed to be hunting, but cautious enough to not leave any sort of paper trail. Then I got the call, and it explained everything."

"You mean when he confessed?"

"Yes." Sarah was silent for a minute. "I had no idea. None whatsoever. I couldn't have seen it coming. I couldn't have stopped it. I've thought about it a million times, and there was absolutely nothing I could have done. But I still feel guilty." She looked me full in the face. "You couldn't have stopped it either."

I released the weights with a bang, and the guy across the aisle looked at me again, this time disapprovingly. "Our situations are not comparable," I said. "I could have done a *lot*. I could have gotten my ass on that plane or found some other way to get there. I knew how at risk trans women of color are. I even warned her to be careful." Anger at Sarah's innocence bubbled. I wanted her to be as guilty as I was. "I basically sat back and just let it all happen. Pretended that everything was just fine."

She was silent again, letting me breathe, letting me settle. "And I should have known that I married a psychopath," she said. "But I didn't. I have to live with that and keep telling myself it wasn't my fault. If you're smart, you'll start doing that too." Sarah picked up her towel and stepped away from the machine. "Ready for a smoothie?" I watched her for a beat, considering whether to tell her to shove the smoothie up her ass. "No special additions in mine today, okay?" One corner of her mouth turned up in a sly little grin.

I took a deep breath, and exhaled hard. "Sure. A smoothie would be good," I said.

She tipped her head toward the door. "Let's go."

She was making it really hard not to like her.

Chapter 54

That first day at the gym kicked off a new phase in our relationship. I didn't want to call it a friendship, given that I was still focused on vengeance, but I suppose most people would call it that. We fell right back into our old routine tougher, and I tried to figure out how to step it up to the next level. Turns out Sarah did that for me.

"Hey, would you want to hang out some time?" she asked. "Grab a burger or something?" She was slipping into her work heels and I'd just slung my bag over my shoulder, ready to leave. Sarah glanced at me out of the corner of her eye as she spoke, then shifted her gaze back down and away from me. All my years of evaluating and interpreting body language kicked in with a thud. The movement of her lashes reminded me of the arch of a soaring bird's wing, or the bent arm of a ballet dancer. The look made no sense, but I recognized it. It was the same look the teenage girls at my school used when they were assessing the boys they were interested in, though hers had an added layer of something smouldery. I was old enough now to understand bodily hunger, and hers shone thorough the tiny movements in ways which made those teenagers even more awkward and clumsy. She looked at me again, this time with a small, vulnerable smile which contained the longing I'd seen in the sweep of her lashes. It made no sense.

I knew Sarah's draw to me was fueled by poison that needed to be let out. I also knew it was going to be useful, and couldn't believe it had all happened that fast. Besides, who was I kidding? I was drawn too, though it made zero sense. Intellectually I had no interest in a relationship with

Sarah. Not that I didn't like her, she was a genuinely decent person. But there was a deep hunger in my soul, and a lesser, but still insistent hunger in my body. I thought I'd live forever with the cavern at my core, but apparently there's something in human nature which abhors a vacuum. I abhorred the chasm, but also cherished it, because it was the spot Char used to fill.

I couldn't be in a relationship with Sarah because I hated her, not only for being tangentially connected to the death of my wife, but also because the feelings she kindled threatened to put something into that space that didn't belong there. For one reason, it needed to remain empty forever, a monument to my guilt and love. For another reason, the space would be desecrated by being filled by *Sarah*. It would be farcical in every possible way.

The whole situation was bananas and pointed out that I needed to wrap things up quickly and cut her off before it got more complicated. Before she nestled deeper in places she didn't belong. I hadn't been able to kill her, or even take out her eyes, but I could at least use her. I could do to her what Jackson hadn't done to Char.

And worse; I could make her like it.

But first, I had to answer her question about going out for a burger. "Sure," I said, nodding and tucking my hair behind one ear in attempted nonchalance.

Sarah's smile transformed from questioning vulnerability to relief. "Great!" she said. "Tomorrow night, okay? I finish up about six."

"Sounds like a..." I almost said "date" but corrected myself at the last minute. "Plan," I concluded. "Just tell me where to meet you." Sarah prattled on for a few minutes about the redeeming qualities of varying restaurants as we walked to the parking lot. "You pick it," I said when we reached her truck.

"Let's go with the Kountry Kitchen," she replied. "It's got the best fries."

"Got it." I looked at the truck, wondering about it as I had for months. "Can I ask you a question?"

"Of course."

"Is this Chris's truck? The one he had when he took Char?" My voice had trouble forming the words, but they made it out, finally.

Sarah shook her head. "No. His truck was impounded at first, while they collected evidence. After that I told them I wanted nothing to do with it. I have no idea what happens with vehicles like that. Probably auctioned it off. I bought this from my brother when he upgraded."

"Good," I said, relieved that she hadn't been driving Chris's death machine all that time. "That's good."

"I wish you'd asked me sooner. That must have sucked to think about."

"It did."

"I'm sorry," she said, which I took to mean a whole lot more than the truck.

I shook my head dismissively, and shifted the subject. "Doesn't look like the vehicle an accountant would drive," I said.

"You don't look like someone who'd plan a murder. Turns out you can't judge by appearances."

I laughed and turned to go to my car. She was right. Appearances were deceiving. But judging people based on prior behavior was logical, yet here she was, still trusting me.

We met the next night as planned, and ate fries which were, in fact, spectacular. Over the next few weeks, we spent more time together, and her affection became more obvious. Meanwhile, my goal was to view the whole thing as a mission, and the mission was working because it didn't take long before we started talking about sex.

"I've never done it with a woman," Sarah said one day while we were drinking coffee at a diner after our workout.

"No?" The smell of waffles baking filled the air, and I was thinking about ordering them when she came out with her statement. I tried to hide my sudden alertness.

"Nope. I've always had two conflicting thoughts about what it would be like. Either it would be rough and sort of scary, S&M shit, or it would be fantastic because female bodies are so different from men's and women would know what to do with them."

"Everyone is different. There are good and bad female lovers just like some men are great and others suck."

"My experience is pretty limited. I married young."

You poor sap, I thought. Getting stuck with Jackson early on surely meant a sucky sex life. She deserved a moment of pleasure.

I told myself I didn't *want* to have sex with her. She wasn't the type I'd traditionally been attracted to. But falling in love with Char showed me body parts weren't key to lovemaking. When we made love, it was as if our souls were entwined. Our whole selves became erogenous zones. If the specifics of genitalia weren't necessary for lovemaking, they certainly weren't a requirement for sex. Which meant that particularities of breast volume, nipple size, and the dimensions of the excitable pleasure organ between a person's legs meant nothing when it came to vengeance sex.

I planned to make her scream, but not from the pain I'd previously planned. The pleasure she'd receive would be a form of taking on my part. An act of emotional carnage. A raping of her past concepts of sexuality. The pleasure I'd give her would be ruthless. Afterward, Jackson would get a finely worded letter from me, describing the whole thing, and I didn't want to have to exaggerate. It probably wouldn't be much of a challenge. Sarah and Jackson's sex life had to have been a nightmare, despite their intact genitalia. Most couples are blind despite eyes which are whole and sound.

Char and I weren't like that. I missed my wife with a terrible, burning need. But my memories of her, despite the dreams, were of her eyes beaming, our bodies wrapped together as we rested in sweet contentment after making love. I couldn't imagine Sarah and Jackson experiencing those things. How could you have them when at least one of the two souls was *that* broken?

I told myself I didn't *want* to have sex with her. But the more I thought about it, the louder my body screamed *yes*.

Chapter 55

The night finally came, faster than I'd expected. It was a few days after Christmas, during that in-between week when you aren't sure what to do with yourself. I'd ignored the holiday which was easy to do when you had no family nearby, no spouse, and worked virtually by yourself. Chip's take on the season was to offer mini-lectures about holiday music and the pagan roots of Christmas customs, so he wasn't a threat to my Scroogism. When Sarah invited herself to my apartment, ostensibly so I'd help eat the collection of cookies she'd amassed, the nervousness in her voice signaled her intention. I tried to keep the edgy anticipation out of my own.

The crunch of ice crackling beneath tires carried through the thin glass of the old windows when she pulled around the back of the museum. I'd left the side door open so she could come straight up.

"Brrr," she said with a whole-body shiver as she bounced through my door. She thrust a decorated tin toward me, then skimmed out of her coat.

"Temperature sure dropped," I said. "Can I get you something warm to drink? Cocoa? Mulled wine?" I pried the lid off the tin for a peek. It was half full of cookies. "Yum."

"Stronger would be good. I'll warm up in a minute."

"Tequila shots?"

Sarah gave me look of disbelief. "You've got tequila?" I'd mentioned before that my booze offerings were limited.

"I stocked up. But I also have whiskey, because you said you like it. Shot of that?"

"Are you trying to get me drunk?" she asked. I turned around quickly and headed to the kitchenette so she wouldn't see the guilt dancing across my face. I wouldn't be the first person to use alcohol to get what I wanted. "Rocks, please," she said.

The ice cubes clinked into the glass as she sat on the couch, rubbing her arms. The whiskey fumes reminded me of the scent of my father after we'd taken a rare trip into town. My own glass of red wine was half empty, so I topped it off, then joined her on the couch, trying to talk my body into quietness. She reached for her glass, sipped, then glanced at me and gulped down a mouthful.

"How 'bout that weather?" I said, joking into an awkwardness which didn't generally settle between us. We both knew where the evening was headed, and neither was sure how to waltz into it gracefully.

"Cold," she nodded.

"I didn't expect temperatures to go so low here. In Massachusetts it gets absolutely freezing, but I somehow expected winters in Missouri to be…" Sarah didn't wait to hear the end of my inanity. She slid close, leaned in, and kissed me. The desire I fought to quell burst into flame. "Well," I said once she'd pulled back. I didn't want to feel it. Sex with Sarah was supposed to be about revenge.

"Was that okay?" she asked.

"Welcome to my parlor said the spider to the fly," I thought. "Yes," I said instead, trying to look thoughtful, as if I was actually considering whether or not it was okay. I put my glass down, then took hers from her hand and set it next to it. My movements were slow, languid. I kept my eyes on hers, my expression shifting from thoughtfulness to something else. Sarah's expression showed she saw the shift. I moved so that one knee was on the couch, positioning myself slightly above her.

"Well," she said, echoing my response.

I placed my hands on her shoulders and pushed her back gently, assessing her resistance. There was none. She swung her legs up so she was fully reclining. I brushed my hand against her cheek, my eyes sweeping her face, increasing her anticipation of the first, real kiss. The other had been a trial run, an exploratory balloon she'd shot up nervously to see what would happen.

She was about to find out what was going to happen. We both were. My heart was pounding harder than if I'd been running.

I focused my gaze on her lips, then slowly, slowly, lowered my face so my mouth could meet them. Her breath caught. My kiss was soft, at first. Gentle. Lips on lips, hers thin, so much thinner than Char's, but I couldn't think about that now. I brushed my lips around the outline of hers, making her catch her breath again, and then gently sucked just her bottom lip into my mouth.

My fingers traced the flesh over Sarah's collar bones in the open neck of her button-down shirt, and her body arched. The seduction was going to be easier than I'd thought. She was a sitting duck, and for a moment, I felt guilty. "Are you sure you want to do this?" I asked, my own breath coming short. But this was what I'd been working for. And clearly she was digging it.

Her eyes had the dreamy quality which appears when someone begins drifting into desire. "I'm positive," she said. Then her eyes sobered up. "I'm lonely. You're lonely. Chris fucked us both, so fuck him."

I was surprised to hear that she was also thinking about Jackson in relation to what was happening, and I wasn't sure I liked it. This was supposed to be *my* revenge. But there wasn't much I could do about that. The mission had been launched. "Fuck him," I agreed with a nod. She closed her eyes again and lifted her face in invitation. Instead of going for her lips, I kissed her jawline, stopping to breathe for a moment just beneath her ear lobe, tasting the soft skin there. She smelled like too many perfumed body products. The berries were there, but buried. I couldn't smell *her* at all. Sarah's breathing picked up pace, and she suddenly moved her arms as if coming alive, reaching to tug at my sweater, the international signal for "take that off." I complied, and began unbuttoning her blouse, my lips following the trail opening up before them. She helped take off her bra, and then I was pressed against her warmth, my flesh meeting hers. Her palms glided over the bare skin of my back, and she pushed up with her pelvis, presenting her need. The demand of my own need pushed back.

But the softness of her breasts wasn't soft enough, they weren't large enough, and she didn't smell like Shimmy. The pressing against my groin didn't reach for me, it wasn't arching, it wasn't Char. A sob rose in my throat but I gulped it back down, knowing I had to get through this. I moved my hand down to the flat absence between her legs, pressing gently, wanting her to feel only a soft pressure. She reached down toward me in response, her touch more probing, more direct. Her need was so different from mine. Hers was so much simpler, even with all its complications. Hers was primarily the hunger that came from lack, coupled with curiosity and a touch of something darker. Mine was 100% dark, or close to it.

I hadn't considered that she'd try to satisfy me because my need wasn't satisfiable. But her touch made me realize it needed to be part of this. It was part of her own vindication, and while I would have preferred to just take her and be done, despite the raging of my body, I knew I had to let her.

I led Sarah to my bed. We helped each other remove the rest of our clothes, and I rolled to my back and took a position of invitation, hoping we could make it all happen quickly. Sarah didn't know what to do with me. I could read the discomfort on her face—a mixture of desire, curiosity, and dread—and I could tell she was afraid to use her mouth, which was fine with me. I let her off the hook by taking her hand and directing it down. The dread left her eyes, replaced first by relief and then by a soft concentration as she began to touch, exploring terrain that was similar but not the same.

"Try closing your eyes," I said. Her experience was too revealed, an intimacy I didn't think I should witness. I didn't want her touch but my body did, roaring into life, drowning out the sorrow my brain experienced at her differentness. I didn't want her to see all of that in my own eyes.

Sarah's good-girl training kicked in and she did as she was told, but the small muscles in her face still detailed the state of her thinking, with minute furrowing as she wandered and wondered, and lifting of her brows when she reached a sense of the familiar. I finally closed my own eyes in order to try and block her out. Her touch was tenuous and experimental, and my body wanted certainly. It would take me forever if I didn't focus, despite the ferocity of my desire, and her face was a distraction.

Shimmy's touch on my body had been a revelation, from the first time to the very last. My mind moved between those two moments with my beloved, remembering our first exploration and how her hands had moved with such smooth certainty. She was all elegance, and her love-making matched, fluid and drifting. The first time I thought she'd been showing off. Surely, she didn't always pay that much attention to a partner, couldn't pay that much attention, with all her concentration seemingly focused on the texture of my skin and the sensitivity of every bump. She kissed places that had never felt the touch of lips before: the arch of my foot, the soft skin near my armpit, the lower curve of my breast. The intensity of my arousal was similarly singular, and by the time she reached the center of me I was gasping. It turned out this attention wasn't merely a honeymoon performance, it was her norm for lovemaking. Not every sexual encounter was slow and measured, some were feverish. But even then, Shimmy brought a quality of attentiveness that made my flesh respond in a way it never had, nor, I expected, ever could again.

She and I existed inside a supernatural bubble. We left it each day to go and do our work but the memory of it carried into those moments of away-ness, carried me until I could get back home to her, home to that warm capsule of love and safety which we created together and which she represented.

My mind drifted to the last time we'd made love, an encounter rose-tinged with Char's joy because I'd agreed to go with her to St. Louis. She was playful and bore her excitement like a happy child, and we laughed a lot as we touched, before our touches changed and the laughter fell away as our breathing deepened. I remembered her lips on me, how beautiful her lovemaking was, and how quickly my desire blossomed.

I blasted my eyes open again to force away the thoughts, but memories of Shimmy had spiked my desire. My orgasm was a burst of frustration and satisfaction and left my most sensitive flesh still wanting, almost hurting. My heart felt even worse, but my mission was half accomplished.

Sarah smiled shyly as I caught my breath, perched next to me on her knees. I patted the bed in invitation and she lay down, her eyes showing nervousness and anticipation. So much of her vulnerability was exposed that it made me feel like an emotional peeping Tom. I took a few moments to simply look at her, knowing the power it would have in increasing her excitement. I noted the shape and color of her nipples, taking mental Polaroids so that I could describe them in future letters to Jackson. She bore a mole on one hip like a beauty mark on the cheek of a Georgian lady. I passed my lips over it, wondering if Jackson ever had, then urged her to lie on her stomach, tracing my lips down the center of her back, a valley scented too sweetly of raspberry and tropical flowers. I kissed the curving crease at the base of each buttock, and felt her shiver as if it was a delicious tickle.

She was soft at the hip, thigh, and the warm curve of her belly. Shimmy's body was hard nearly all over, the muscles lying close beneath her skin. Even her buttocks were nothing but muscle. The only soft parts were her breasts.

Sarah was obviously ready. When my tongue finally met her most sensitive flesh, I thought about the taste of Char's blood mixed with dirt and wood particles. Sarah tasted of sweetness and salt and utterly unlike Shimmy, and my spirit wept with shame and sorrow. Sarah's back arched and a short sound escaped her open lips, high-pitched and sweet like the perfumes she favored.

When my lips touched Char, she surged and her moans were throaty notes drifting through the air like smoke. The skin of her desire was smooth against my cheek. I missed the taste of that sensitive skin with a yearning so deep that I thought my heart would crack wide open. The thought of Jackson's lips on her penis suddenly intruded, transforming the longing to pure rage again, and I pulled myself away from Char and back to the act of vengeance, the act of taking, when I did to Sarah what Jackson would never do to Char.

I tuned back in to Sarah. Her sounds were as nuanced as her facial expressions. I heard surprise at my first taste, anticipation when I pulled back in a momentary tease, increasing urgency as I returned. Her body was familiar and strange and utterly wrong for me.

Her fingers dug into my hair. The muscles of her thighs were rigid against my cheeks. Her cries became urgent, a wordless begging, an urgent pant of yesses, and I stopped the game of tease I'd been playing and simply focused on finishing the horror and beauty of this thing we were doing. My mouth consumed her and she finally stiffened, all sound ceasing for a moment, her throat a column of white arching back so I couldn't see her face, could only imagine her mouth open, her eyes clenched shut, and then her sounds filled the room again, a haunting call of release that made my heart twist. I wanted to pull away then and run, leaving her there on my bed as I barreled outside, naked with bare feet pounding down the road and out to the highway. I wanted to run all the way home. I wanted to run all the way to wherever Char was.

Instead, I stayed there, with Sarah, the heat of her against my lips, judging her descent, easing my attentions as she returned, not wanting to overwhelm her with too much. Her breathing became a series of deep, sighing breaths. The arch of her back lowered to meet the sheets. I rested my face against her thigh, not wanting to move, not wanting to join her because this wordless moment would be transformed into something spoken. I let her rest, and breathe, still feeling the tingling of my scalp where her fists had curled, smelling her scent and missing Char so deeply it felt unsurvivable. I wanted to die then, right there, perhaps spontaneously combusting to burn the museum down and me along with it. But I didn't want Sarah to have to die too, so instead, I wished Medusa would appear in the doorway wearing her head full of snakes, and turn me into a stone figure of a person, stone to match my heart. Someone could ship me back to Massachusetts and I could be used as a marker for Char's grave, where I'd remain for a century or two, slowly being covered by lichen and regularly visited by adolescents who had no better place to party. But I wasn't consumed by flames and my heart of stone somehow managed to keep pumping blood in its damnable cycle of receive and release. There was no choice but to move up beside Sarah, which was what Emily Post's guide for sexual etiquette demanded. I knew she must be in her own state of crisis, but I couldn't summon compassion. I couldn't or wouldn't imagine her thoughts as they danced around the man she'd married, couldn't bear the thought of her considering him when she was with me. The idea was sickening and reignited the anger that simmered below every other thought and emotion. I brushed it away, and moved up, settling on the pillow a foot or so from her, giving her space. Giving us both space. She opened her eyes to look at me, and in them I saw sadness and wonder.

Oh, Christ, I thought. She rolled to face me.

"I'm kind of speechless," she said.

"You don't have to say anything. Really." I replied. *Please don't say anything.* I felt gross. Coupling with Shimmy had been so intimate, and so connected. The pleasure we gave and took was an extension of our connection, the fruit and the mulch of it, and this thing I'd just experienced was the opposite. It was vengeance fucking. Meant to harm rather than nourish.

Sarah tried again. "I'm not sure how I'm supposed to feel, but that was…" Her eyes turned soft and swimmy.

"Seriously. You don't need to say anything." She reached out to touch my cheek, and I knew I had to do something. Fast.

I decided joking was the best way out of this. "Best you ever had, no doubt," I said, sitting up and reaching for my underwear. She didn't move, just lay there gazing at me, her head beginning a slow, mesmerized nod. "Sex always makes me hungry," I said, which wasn't true. "Turkey sandwich okay with you?" I slid my legs over the side of the bed and slipped into my pants. Sarah still wasn't moving. "Hope you like mayonnaise, because it's either that or ketchup." I hustled to get my sweater from the floor near the couch, then went into the kitchen where I hoped I'd have a few minutes to think through my next move and try to get my heart to a state where it wasn't actively shattering. "You just relax," I tossed over my shoulder as I went. "I'll call you when it's ready." I sure as hell wasn't going to take food back to bed. The last thing I wanted was round two.

I heard her sigh, a deep sigh of satisfaction, and I couldn't blame her, in a way. She'd just climaxed, and was snuggled in the bed of someone who seemed to care while food was being prepared for her. The circumstances had every appearance of security and comfort.

There was barely enough turkey for two sandwiches. I threw on some provolone and a couple of outer leaves of iceberg for texture. It was far from gourmet fare, but that wasn't really the point. I didn't want to feed her crush any more than it was already fed. The thought made me consider adulterating her sandwich in some way to make it unpalatable, but realized I was being ridiculous. "You can come on out. Food's ready." Sarah sat up and stretched, tilting her head around in a slow full circle.

"Damn I feel good," she said. She stood up and stretched again, then reached for her underwear. Her naked back and the curve of her buttocks looked vulnerable, making me feel guilty for the rejection that was coming.

"It's chilly out here, so you'd better put some clothes on." I said, tossing her shirt and bra toward the bed. I wasn't sure if she planned to traipse out naked, but didn't want to take any chances. Sarah slipped on her shirt, but left the bra where it was, which didn't bode well. "Floor's cold. You might want your shoes," I said. Footwear seemed distancing, like she might be leaving any minute despite the braless-ness. She sat back down and put on her socks and shoes. I carried the food to the small dining table under the back window which overlooked the shed, then went for two glasses of water. By that time, she'd joined me, and sat down at the table. "Nothing special," I said. "But there you go." I gestured toward her plate, picked up my sandwich, and took a bite. My nerves were jangling so hard I was surprised the floor wasn't shaking. Meanwhile Sarah still hadn't said a word. Her expression was shifting though. It looked less dreamy, less filled with wonder, and was moving toward her usual look of calm practicality.

She tasted my offering. "Mmm," she said. "It's good." We chewed and swallowed, took drinks of water, and sat listening to the sounds our mouths and throats made as they worked their way through the food. "Thanks for not using ketchup."

I nodded back. "You're welcome."

We finished the sandwiches, and munched our way through most of the cookies, quiet again, awkward again. I could feel her need to speak simmering beneath her chewing, but she somehow, miraculously, refrained. When we were done eating, she sat back in her chair, looking across the table at me, appraising what she saw and waiting for my next move.

I debated about faking a yawn, but realized she was too smart, too observant for that kind of subterfuge. Instead, I went for honesty. "It's been a lot for one night," I said. "Maybe we should sleep on all this. Talk about it after some rest."

Sarah nodded slowly, as if not aware she was doing it, her gaze still seeking meaning behind my expression. I tried to keep my features friendly and cheerful. "Okay," she said, rising and pushing back the chair. She didn't seem angry, which was a relief. "I'll head home." She picked up her coat and slid her arms in.

"Don't forget your bra," I said, already moving to fetch it from the bedroom floor. "Here you go."

"Do I kiss you?" she asked.

"I think so," I said, because I couldn't see a way out. She kissed me, and when she pulled back, it was clear she recognized the kiss wasn't anything like earlier. Sarah turned and went down the stairs. "Good night," I called after her.

"'Night," she replied.

Much later, after Sarah drove away into the crystal darkness, I thought about how wrong the experience felt. I had no idea how I was going to get through the next stage of all this. I didn't have a single drop of emotional fuel left.

For the first time since her death, I started talking to Char out loud, demanding that she hear me. "Why couldn't you have just fucked him,

Shimmy? If you'd just fucked him, then maybe you'd still be alive." I meant it, and I didn't mean it, and I knew it wasn't the truth, and I didn't care.

I was so tired. So empty.

I changed the sheets, climbed in bed, and cried for a long, long time.

The words from the transcript kept running through my mind: where did you put her penis, Christopher?

Chapter 56

I called her the next day, asking her to meet me for lunch. It needed to be public, and performed with surgical precision. Just pluck the splinter in order to inflict the least amount of pain and prevent festering. We met at the Kountry Kitchen again, though this time I didn't think I'd be able to eat. Rehearsing all morning made me queasy.

Sarah knew it wasn't going to be good news from the moment she saw my face. She came to a halt beside the table, pausing for a second before pulling out the chair and sitting down. We made small talk and ordered food before I turned to the subject at hand.

"We need to talk about last night," I said.

"Do we?" she said, her gaze skeptical.

I tried not to roll my eyes. "Yes." She turned her face away then, her eyes blinking faster than normal. The muscles in her jaw and throat clenched repeatedly as she swallowed. "Sarah," I began.

"But I love you." Sarah interrupted. She looked like a confused child. "I know you felt it too. There are some things you can't fake."

I wanted to hate her, but couldn't. Sarah was broken like I was broken. Not as badly perhaps, but still fractured. She was right to say we'd been falling in love. And it wasn't just Sarah, it was me too. But real love wasn't possible. She was too small, too pale, too weak. Too many things that reminded me of me. We were both broken and frozen because of what Jackson did. Sarah was gutted because of her lack of awareness of who he was, deep down. I was shattered because of my lack of awareness of Char's mortality. "Look," I said, hoping she could cut through our lunatic emotions and acknowledge truth. "What we have isn't really love. It's the comfort of being understood. Or maybe something even weirder."

She looked away from me again. "What's wrong with comfort? What's wrong with being understood? I haven't felt either of those things in a very long time. Aren't they important in a relationship?"

They *were* important, but she was being deliberately obtuse, which meant I was going to have to dig the needle in a little bit deeper. "Yes, they're important," I said. "It's been a huge relief to know someone who understands even a tiny bit. But that can't be the basis of a relationship. Not a healthy one anyway."

"Listen," Sarah demanded. She was getting pissed. "Maybe that's all it was to you, comfort in being understood. But for me, there was more. I *like* you, Maddie."

I sighed from way down deep. "I like you too. But that isn't the point."

"What *is* the point?"

"The point is I tried to kill you, Sarah. I was going to steal your eyes. I had sex with you because…"

"Because why?"

"Never mind." I realized I'd gone too far, and I didn't want to hurt her any more than I already had.

"Say it, Maddie!"

"Your husband is always going to be between us. That's all. That's the bottom line. In every conversation, and every time we're in bed. I can't do it, and I won't. It's grotesque."

She stopped probing after that, just got quiet, and ate a French fry, which impressed me. I was so worked up I thought I might vomit. Finally, she spoke. "I haven't dated anyone since Chris was arrested. Want to know why?"

"Tell me," I said.

"After I found out what he did, I realized how stupid I must be about other people. I never guessed he'd do that. And if you don't know something that critical about your own husband, how can you ever know what's going on with someone else? I obviously couldn't trust my own judgment, so I didn't risk it." Sarah stood and tossed her crumpled napkin on her plate, the food barely touched. "Turns out I was totally right." She turned and left the restaurant. I sat for a few minutes, thinking about what she'd said, and what we'd done, and wondering what I should do next.

I'd accomplished what I set out to do, but now Sarah was even more wounded, and I didn't feel even a tiny bit better. It added a new level of pointlessness to the whole thing, from the time I couldn't get on the plane until that very minute.

Vengeance was much more complicated than I'd realized.

Chapter 57

Dealing with all the emotion of Sarah made me want to seek counsel from someone, but there was no one I could tell. I decided to call Maria just to say hello and be distracted for a few minutes.

"Ciao bella!" she said, when she realized it was me. "How wonderful it is to hear your voice!"

"It's good to hear yours too," I said. "How are you?"

"How I am is washing the front windows. The grim of winter has covered them, and they were still dirty from the fall." Maria's voice puffed out in curious bursts, and I could imagine her body moving in time with the motion of her arm, wiping the glass. "The customers, they walk by and can't see in to what I am featuring for spring hijacks."

"Could you mean hijinks?"

"Hijacks, high jinks, who knows what the turisti will get up to this year? But that is beside the point. Why aren't you here, helping me?"

She liked to ask questions I didn't want to answer. Or didn't know how to answer. My foolish plans for wreaking vengeance had officially wrapped up, but it still felt incomplete. "Are you trying to guilt me into coming home?" I finally offered in response.

"You are ready to talk about guilt, finally?" she said.

"What do you mean?" It felt like I'd walked straight into a trap.

"Again, you are acting like the stork dropped me on my head yesterday." Maria gave an exaggerated sigh. "You and guilt," she said. "You are like twins combined at the nose. And right now, you aren't even the pretty one."

I didn't know whether to laugh or be offended. "Okay!" I said. "So I feel guilty. You would too wouldn't you?"

But Maria barreled along as if she hadn't heard me. "Guilt is a thing, like a poison. I know it, this feeling. My life is long, and I've done things. We all do things." I wanted to ask what sorts of things, but it was unlikely she'd move away from her point. "I think it may be the most persnictive emotion, the guilt," Maria continued. "It never leaves you alone. It is all the time hiding, nibbling away like a mouse in the walls. Scratch, scratching on your soul."

I resonated with the incessancy she described, though an external scratching didn't match the ache of blackness in my chest.

"It never leaves you alone. But the biggest problema is that it is useless. You cannot go back and fix anything. You are stuck in the now and here. You can pray, of course, and Dio in his mercy can work miracles outside of time. But we are not content with prayer when we have done wrong. We want to do *something*, and the only something we have is to beat ourselves up."

She was right. Something had to be done, which was the whole point of my plans related to Sarah. Doing nothing was not survivable. Doing nothing meant certain death for me, and Char would be furious if I killed myself on top of everything else.

"Guilt becomes a hammer, and we keep banging our hearts with it over and over again," Maria continued.

I pictured my heart, and the black ache which surrounded it like an enormous bruise. "That seems true."

"It is a poisonous hammer, this thing we do. It can crush our whole life." Maria paused and she must have stopped moving, because her voice flowed more naturally again. "It is good you are finally willing to talk about it," she said.

I *wasn't* actually willing to talk about it, and I hadn't done much talking, which was typical. "I'm not sure what you want me to say."

"I want you to say 'Sì, oh saggia Maria!'"

"What does that mean?"

"It means that of course I am right, and that you know I am wise, and that you will stop with the hammering so you can give up on whatever nefertiti things you are doing down there and come home."

"I get what you're saying, but you just don't understand," I said.

Maria sighed again, but this time it wasn't for show. "Madelaina. You need to hear me. Do you have your ears on?"

"Yes. I'm listening."

"*Hear me*," she repeated, stretching both words out this time.

"All right! I'll try."

She didn't speak for a moment, and I could hear the small squeak of damp paper making circles on a distant window pain. "We are not able to know the future," Maria finally said. "We live our lives each minuto to the next, every time trying to simply do our best."

"But sometimes we don't really try. I should have tried harder."

"Were you able to get on the plane that day?"

"No. I thought I'd be able to, but I couldn't."

"So why do you blame yourself for not going?"

My heart began to pound as I forced myself to really consider the question. "For one thing, because I was relieved!" I finally blurted. My eyes burned. "Part of me knew I'd panic and not have to actually go. When she boarded, and I could breathe again and walked back to the car, I was just so relieved!" Tears ran down my cheeks. "On the drive home, I thought about what I'd watch that night because I wouldn't have to negotiate with her. I thought about eating junk she'd disapprove of." My throat caught. "I thought about sleeping in because she always got up early." The reality that I'd never feel her warmth next to me in the safe cocoon of our bed threatened to drown me. "I looked forward to all those things! I looked forward to her not being there! And now she's gone." The final words mixed messily with my weeping.

"Yes. She is gone."

"She's gone, forever." The tears overcame me, and I sat crying, alone but not alone, knowing Maria was there at the other end of the phone, with me though not with me. She let me cry it out, and I did, my sobs eventually slowing to sniffs and hitches.

256

"Take a few deep breaths, now, my Madelaina. In through the nose, out through the lips." I followed her instructions, and she listened to my breathing, as my body and spirit settled. "Okay. You were relieved that you didn't have to go because you have a terror of the airplanes. And you looked forward to the slight change in routine."

"Yes." I tried not to get caught back up in the storm of emotion.

"Does this make you a monster?" I thought about it for a minute. Of course, I knew it wasn't monstrous. And yet… "You aren't answering, which means you think it does. Could you have stopped her from going on the trip?"

"No. And I wouldn't have wanted to. She loved those events. And she was good at it. She deserved the award. Her work meant the world to her."

"So you couldn't go, and you couldn't have stopped her."

Maria had a point, but I wasn't ready to internalize it. "I could have gone early. Taken a train or something. Driven."

"But you didn't know you wouldn't be able to fly." I huffed a sound of sarcastic disagreement. "Did you know?"

I searched my memory to try to figure it out. Did I know? Was it all a set up to have her go without me? "I'm not sure."

"That is honest. But when you were there, at the airport, did you intend to get on the plane?"

"Yes." I knew that much to be true. I'd dreaded it, and hoped something would intervene. But when we sat down at the gate, I meant to get on the damned plane. "I wish she'd just dragged me on with her."

"You were not trying to deceive your beloved, and you meant to go with her."

"Yes. I guess."

"And you couldn't have stopped her."

"No."

"Then is it your fault? This thing that happened to her? This horrible thing?"

My heart wanted to scream yes, but couldn't. "No. It's not my fault." I felt a tiny lifting in my spirit as I spoke the words. "I just…"

"Yes, my bella Madelaina?"

"I wished I'd loved her more. Loved her better. While I had her." I began to cry again, my throat full and my heart breaking and breaking and breaking.

Maria gave me time to sit with the pain, then spoke. "We only love how we can. But the love you show me is so grand, so huge. She must have felt it. She must have known it. Your Charlotte could not be the person of sensibilità you have described without feeling it." I wanted to believe her. But the ache was going nowhere. "Guilt is the most persnictive emotion. Grief you can survive. But guilt... it is dangerous. I want you to promise you will try to let it go. Your knuckles they are white with tension, holding on to it. The grief will stay. Do not fear that you will be free from suffering. It will be here. But the guilt, it must go."

I wasn't sure how, or if I even wanted to attempt it. As usual, Maria read my mind.

"Promise me that you'll *try*," she said.

I didn't want to promise. Promises were real, and important.

"Madelaina?"

"Okay! I promise." The words felt like a betrayal, but I pushed the sensation away because the promise had been made.

"Grazie, amore mio."

We said our goodbyes and I clicked off the phone. The idea of letting go of the guilt felt like facing another loss.

Chapter 58

Life can take sudden shifts which change your understanding of the universe in a flash. Char's murder changed me on an atomic level. It was like what happens when chemicals are combined and suddenly a new thing exists, two liquids becoming a solid. I could earnestly *try* to stop banging my heart with the poisonous hammer Maria described, but I was a creature which hadn't existed before, and couldn't just magically go back to my previous incarnation.

Days passed while I processed it all. Museum visitors came and left, in small groups and couples. I wanted them to value each other, and their habitual disregard made me angry. I didn't bother pretending I was blind any more, just took their money and drifted around the place like a ghost when they weren't there. The knives went back to their cases, and I took to occupying empty chairs in the various tableaus, feeling myself becoming part of them, part of the sham history that was this place, part of the pattern of jealousy and vengeance to which the building paid tribute. I was so sick of it all, sick of the visitors who viewed Jesse James as a hero because he wasn't, and neither was I. His revenge didn't make anything better. It just made him a murderous thief.

Despite recognizing this, I still couldn't set my need for vengeance down.

A few weeks after my call to Maria, I watched Allister out the side window of the gift shop. He was there later than normal. The winter sky was dark as he trudged away from the Quickie Mart's fluorescent glare. He paused to light a cigarette on his walk up over the hill. The lighter flared bright in the darkness for a moment and then disappeared again, a small flash of brilliance against the dark barrenness of the slope. I hoped he'd be careful with the butt. It hadn't rained for weeks and the grass was crisp and brown. It was easy to imagine the hillside going up in a moving sheet of flame.

The image gave me an idea. I went to bed early to think it through.

The insurance policy was easy to find in the museum files the next day. It didn't take long to determine the Harrises wouldn't get screwed as long as I was smart. Next to review were books on the care and maintenance of wax figures. The process for their creation hadn't changed much since Madame Tassauds opened. The bodies began with a metal armature. Heads and hands were made of beeswax. Multiple layers of oil-based paints attempted to make the skin look realistic. Human hair was used for brows and lashes. The place was filled with human-shaped torches, but by some lunacy, the Harrises never installed a sprinkler system.

After a morning of contemplation, I finally settled on a plan and got busy with preparations.

The hours passed slowly as I waited for night to fall, and then for midnight to come, when the Quickie Mart would be closed and the highway mostly deserted. I carried an ancient space heater I'd found in the storeroom to the vignette in which the supposed Jesse James reclined in bed. The place smelled as it always did of dust, age, and fakery. My second trip to the storage room delivered rolls of paper towels and a bucket of aged solvent bottles, brushes, and rags. I wasn't sure how much of this stuff would survive the fire, but it needed to look realistic. Ether glugged stinkily into a spray bottle as a last-minute addition. I'd driven the rest of the ether jugs to a church dumpster over by the haunted hotel, using Jackson as inspiration. All that ether would have created a satisfying explosion once the fire hit the storeroom, but it would look too much like arson.

My eyes swept the place, conducting a final assessment as I turned on the space heater. Perhaps even saying an angry goodbye. I walked past the guns and the knives, wondering how many lives they'd destroyed. The eyes of each waxen face stared as if unafraid despite the destruction promised by the scent of dust burning on ancient heater coils. I wiped a solvent-soaked paper towel across each face and dropped the sodden towels nearby. In between, I scattered similar potential wicks, like bread-crumbs leading to the candy house where a witch put small children in an oven. When I'd made the rounds, I took a deep breath and returned to the deathbed scene. The elderly solvent splashed satisfactorily onto the blanket covering the imposter's feet, about a foot away from the heater. I scattered a few more rags between that space and the adjacent diorama, spritzing the area liberally with ether to give the fire extra incentive, then returned to do the same with the curtains and clothing of the figures gathered at the faux Jesse's bedside.

It turned out spraying ether wasn't my best decision. I started feeling woozy, and stumbled toward the chair, wondering what dying in a fire would be like.

And then I was gone.

Chapter 59

I dreamt I was being smothered by a pillow soaked in chloroform. "WAKE UP!" a female voice shrieked, and I tried to obey but it was a struggle. My head spun and nausea threatened to erupt. I blinked my eyes to try to wake up faster, but I couldn't shake the acrid smell, and my eyes were burning. I kept coughing, even though there wasn't really a pillow over my face.

Instead, it was smoke. Smoke everywhere. I was lying on the floor next to the armchair of the bedroom exhibit, and the museum was on fire. I pulled myself upright, trying to think straight and figure out what I should do. My head was filled with as much sludge as my lungs, but it finally remembered that I'd done this thing.

The bed was blazing; the figure in it covered in a blanket of fire. Flames hadn't yet engulfed his head, but the wax skin of his cheek dripped like a candle at some deranged Halloween party.

If I was a good person, I would have run to get the fire extinguisher near the cash register in the gift shop, but I didn't. It was probably too late for that anyway, the adjacent display was also blazing, along with one of the paper towels I'd created as a trail toward the other exhibits.

If I was a good person, I would have gone to call the fire department, but I didn't. The place was an emblem of what I'd become, and it had to be destroyed.

Instead, I grabbed the pearl-handled pocket knife from the table next to me, positioned near a wallet and some old coins, as if left there by a man who planned to put them back in his pocket the next morning. The knife was warm, but not too hot to hold, and the blade pulled loose from the case with surprising ease given its age. I stepped off the exhibit platform, and headed to my left, still coughing.

I headed toward Jesse. The real Jesse. It was finally time to get revenge.

Chapter 60

By the time I'd done what I'd taken the knife to do, the fire was consuming that display as well. The wood of the platform and backdrops were decades old and dry from years of heat, the antique furniture like kindling, the wax figures like fire starters. It may not have needed the ether spritzes I'd supplied. My lungs were on fire from all the smoke, and it was clearly time to get out of there. I hunched low and scrambled toward the exit. The bedroom display was like a furnace. I obviously didn't need to worry about the spray bottle, so I got out of there.

In the front, several smoke detectors were screaming. I barreled toward the front door, which was of course locked. I hadn't thought to leave it open. I ran toward the side door instead, fingers grabbing and fumbling the deadbolt and sliding chain that constituted security. The air outside was cool and crisp in my lungs, as delicious as cold water in August. I leaned against my car to catch my breath, watching the building for external signs of the fire. If things went well, the whole place would burn down, or even blow up as I'd worried the Quickie Mart gas pumps might. Optimally, the very land itself would be purged by the blaze.

When flames appeared in the storage room windows, I pulled out my phone, figuring it was safe to dial 911. With all the flammable junk in there the place would probably go up in just a few minutes. I reported the fire, then pulled my car away to safety.

A moment later, taps on the driver side window reverberated against my aching head. I'd leaned against its coolness, hoping to relieve the sick pounding brought on by ether fumes and smoke. I rolled down the window.

"Hey," Allister said. His eyes were on the museum, where flames blazed in the windows of my apartment upstairs.

"Hey," I replied. "You're out late."

"Had some people to see. Should we go try to do something about that?" He peered at me as he said it, as if gauging my reaction.

"It's pretty bad," I said. "Fire department's on the way."

"Shame. Museum's a fucking icon."

"You said a mouthful."

"See you later," Allister turned toward the hill he always disappeared over.

"Not going to wait around and watch the show?"

"Nah," he called back. "You've seen one fire, you've seen them all." With that, he was just motion in the decreasing darkness, a reflection of the increasing flames.

I sat and waited for the fire trucks to arrive, thinking about the prophets roaming among us, some of whom were dispensing pot and date rape drugs and an apparent shared desire to blow shit up. The wail of sirens approached shortly afterward, and I climbed back out to greet them, bone weary and feeling like crap. Two ladder trucks and an ambulance arrived with cops following them. I recited a few poems to stave off a panic attack. After confirming the museum was empty, the medics gave me an oxygen mask and told me to lie down, which was plenty okay. It gave me time to think through what I would report, and how.

I didn't feel much regret about torching the museum. The thing was monstrous and needed to go. A few pricks of guilt poked me about Gerry and Doris Harris, and I wasn't looking forward to breaking the news to them, but they'd already separated themselves and begun a new life, so they'd be okay. What I hadn't thought about until then was the potential danger for the firefighters. But from what I could see from the back of the ambulance, no one was going inside. Multiple hoses poured water on the flames which licked the starry blackness of the sky, but that was pretty much it. I later found out that it was what they called a "surround and drown," when there's nothing to do except try to flood the thing out. I was grateful for that.

Eventually the crew thought I was ready to talk, and the fire chief questioned me. I ran through my story:

It was cold. The heating in the museum sucked. I was cleaning the exhibits at night because I couldn't do it during the day with visitors popping in and out. I tripped stepping up on the platform and my bottle of benzene cleaning fluid splashed the heater and the bed which must have made the whole thing ignite. I banged my head when I fell and was out for a few minutes, and when I came to the world was ablaze.

"Lucky you woke up." The burly mustachioed fireman said, looking up from his notepad.

"I sure am. It's a miracle really." I meant it, too. The voice had saved me, and here I was to tell the tale. Or part of the tale, anyway.

"Place turned into an inferno. Unbelievable that there wasn't a sprinkler system."

"The owners are pretty old-school."

"We may have some follow up questions. Where will you be staying?"

"The Oaktree Inn, I guess." I hadn't given much thought to what came next, and hoped the place would have someone manning the front desk this late. I sure as heck wasn't going to call Sarah.

"All righty then. Here's my card." He handed me the white rectangle and I stuffed it in the pocket of my khakis.

I left after that, feeling no need to stick around and watch the final moments of the fire being tamed, and overcome with fatigue so deep it felt like I was wearing a lead cloak. The inn gave me a room, and though I showered for what seemed like an hour, the smell of smoke still penetrated my hair. The next morning, I put on the clean underwear I'd stowed in my car, and the sweaty gym clothes that were still in my gym bag from the last time I'd worked out with Sarah. I threw the smoky garments in the trashcan near the door of the lobby.

There was coffee and donuts near the front desk, and as I filled my belly it felt like my trip to Missouri was moving in reverse. I was in a cheap hotel again, wondering what was going to come next in life. But this time, I was mission-less.

Chapter 61

Fire investigations happen fast, at least they did in that corner of Missouri. The report came back that the evidence lined up with my story, though I wondered how much evidence was left to sift through.

With that bit of business wrapped up I knew it was time to return to Merrivliet. Time to stop being the person I'd tried to become and figure out who I actually was.

Before I did, I forced myself to read the rest of Jackson's transcript.

TRANSCRIPT

Young: Are you on any medications?

Jackson: Just my blood pressure meds. My wife makes me take vitamins. And Cialis. Once in a while.

Davis: No illegal drugs?

Jackson: I don't do drugs.

Young: Nothing else that could alter your perceptions? Make you see things? Hear things?

Jackson: Jesus Christ.

Young: Did you start hearing the voice before or after the wounds Ms. Mitchell inflicted became infected?

Jackson: I'm telling you, all the shit I saw and heard was real. I wasn't hallucinating. It stopped as soon as I turned myself in. And you can sure as hell see that my neck isn't better.

Davis: What did the voice sound like?

Jackson: It was the tranny. And she sounded…

<Pause>

Davis: Scary? Threatening?

Jackson: No. She sounded nice.

Young: Nice?

Jackson: Her voice was soft. Kind. Just like she'd sounded in the bar before I drugged her. Like she wanted to be helpful.

Young: You weren't scared, hearing her talking to you?

Jackson: No.

Davis: Then why'd you decide to turn yourself in?

Jackson: She just wouldn't stop. I couldn't sleep because she kept talking to me. It was exhausting.

Young: What did the voice say?

Jackson: For one thing, she wanted me to tell someone named Maddie that it wasn't her fault. I have no idea what that was all about.

Davis: Ms. Mitchell's wife is named Madelaine.

Jackson: So she was a lesbo on top of everything else? Jesus. The perversion.

Young: What else did the voice say?

Jackson: That I had to tell the truth. She said it was the only way.

Young: The only way for what?

Jackson: The only way I could have peace. Killing her was eating me up inside. It didn't help anything. The whole thing was just a fucking nightmare. I thought being with her would resolve something. Help me know who I was and wasn't. I thought I'd prove to myself that I wasn't gay, and she'd go back home to wherever the hell she came from, and that would be it. But none of it went the way I thought it would.

<Pause>

Jackson: I didn't plan to kill her. I told you that. I just sort of… flipped. I was excited and she wasn't and I heard my daddy's voice calling me a fag, and her dick turned me on. It did. I couldn't deny it and I didn't know how to make it stop and it just made me so fucking mad.

<Pause>

Jackson: And then I couldn't stop thinking about it. Even though she was a freak who was encouraging other people to be freaks. Even though she was going to rot in hell. I was probably doing the world a favor. But what I did was like a nightmare on replay every single night. And that voice. Day and night she kept whispering to me.

Young: The voice that told you to confess?

Jackson: Yes. She was right. I had no peace.

Davis: Do you have peace now?

Jackson: <Snorting sound> If that's what you call this.

Davis: Not exactly peaceful, I suppose.

Jackson: I'm going to prison. My wife is crushed. I'll probably lose her. My mom is a basket case. Thank God my dad is dead. But at least she stopped nagging me. At least I can be left alone in my own mind and try to figure out how to forget.

Young: How do you think she did it? Talking to you like that.

Jackson: I don't know, but I think that witch in the painting had something to do with it. That black Madonna. It's the only thing that makes sense. Fucking Catholics.

Davis: The Madonna icon at the shrine where you took Ms. Mitchell?

Jackson: Yes. I told you about those eyes. They were watching. She's supposed to be some version of Mary, but I don't know. Maybe she's a demon.

Davis: Is there anything else which might have impacted your decision-making or caused your perceptions to be altered during that period of time?

Jackson: God damn it! I'm telling you it was real! That Mitchell bitch was haunting me. Are you even listening?

Young: I think we can wrap up. You probably want some lunch?

Jackson: Whatever. It's not like I have a say in any of this.

Davis: Okay. I think we're done with this interview. But we'll let you know if we come up with any more questions.

Jackson: Does that mean I won't be seeing you two again?

Young: Probably not until court.

Jackson: Court. Fan-fucking-tastic.

Chapter 62

The Harrises were understandably freaked out that the museum was wrecked. I sent them a fat money order anonymously. Hopefully their insurance would cover the loss, but it was possible my story would mean their claim would be denied and I had to make some kind of reparation, even though their worship of the museum was a sickness needing cauterization. I felt a tiny bit sorry for the loss of the dream they'd had, but could feel no sorrow that the reality was destroyed.

Chip let me sleep on a cot in the Quickie Mart office for the few days it took to tie up loose ends. One of the things I decided to do after listening to the transcript was visit the shrine again to look for the signs I must have missed on my first trip.

Uncle Frank didn't greet me when I parked, and I went straight for the chapel. The little royal figure known as the infant of Prague stood in his Plexiglas cage, and I wondered about the kind of mind that could do what Jackson did in front of the child Jesus. A part of me must have always known I couldn't do that to Sarah, there, or anywhere else.

The transcript had filled in a lot of blanks. I felt a small shred of sympathy for the battle Jackson fought throughout his life simply because he was drawn to the same sex. I'd never faced that kind of internal struggle. Life as a lesbian had been pretty easy for me. I could sympathize with what it might do to your psyche to hate the reality of who you were, but that didn't excuse it in the slightest. Millions of gay and bi people lived through what he'd endured and more. His brokenness went much deeper than sexual orientation, and what he'd done could never, ever be justified by the things he'd suffered.

Anger and a familiar spinning hatred threatened to take control when I thought about Jackson for more than a minute or two, so I had to reel the thoughts back in, and remind myself that vengeance was a dark and slippery road which I'd decided to exit.

I looked at the scars on the Madonna's face in the icon, and remembered the legend of its warning against desecration. Her right hand was positioned near her heart, and for a minute she looked like Char, but I blinked and the resemblance was gone. I examined the faces of all the Madonnas and the child Jesuses on their laps, and at the odd enclosed case of the Infant of Prague. I saw all their eyes, though it didn't seem like they were watching me, as they'd watched Jackson. Perhaps he'd imagined the whole thing, driven by guilt at the atrocity he'd committed. Or perhaps the benevolent beings keeping watch over the place—Mary or the monk who'd built it—knew I meant no harm and didn't need to monitor me.

"Ahem." I never knew people actually said this, but apparently the caretaker did. "I'm about to close the gate."

"Sorry, Frank," I said. "Time got away from me." I got up and walked toward him.

"Do I know you?" he asked, squinting at my face in concentration. It looked like he hadn't registered much from our previous encounter. Thank God for hangovers.

"I know your niece, Sarah." We headed up the slow-sloping hill toward the graveled lot.

Frank shook his head, heavy features falling to make him look like a basset hound. "She's a good girl, Sarah. Helluva thing that happened."

"It sure was," I replied.

"Hope you had a nice visit." He extended his arm toward the parking area, obviously not wanting to take the conversation farther, and ready for me to depart.

"It's a lovely place. Thanks for taking care of it." He walked by my side until the path parted. I turned back to look for a minute, feeling a mixture of sorrow and relief knowing I'd never be back. "Hey!" I called to his retreating back. "Where were you, that night…" I let my words trail off, not sure what I was going to ask.

"What?" he said, lifting a hand to his ear.

I thought about interrogating him for not saving Shimmy, but the reasons he hadn't heard Jackson's truck didn't matter. The outcome wouldn't change, and it hadn't been his fault, just like it hadn't been Sarah's. "Never mind," I said. If he cared about the place at all, Char's murder must have been a horrible shock, and my asking about it wouldn't change anything. "Have a good night."

I pulled out slowly, and watched him lumber the rest of the way down to his caretaker's cottage and the liquor which waited to help him forget.

Chapter 63

"Remember we were talking about God a while back?" I asked Chip, wanting to debrief about everything that had happened, but sticking to the subject of the shrine.

"I do," he said. He plucked a rubber band stretched between two fingers, tilting his head back and forth like he heard music. The only thing I could hear was the news playing on the television, like it always did.

"What do you think about people who say they've had supernatural experiences? Do you think it's legit?"

"There are a variety of things which appear to be other than 'natural' yet which can be scientifically explained. Ball lightning. Poltergeists. Glowing swamp gases."

"I guess I'm talking about religious stuff."

Chip thought for a minute. "Occurrences of stigmata are documented, though the cause and mechanism for production is unclear."

"But do you think people can have real encounters with something outside themselves?"

"Human sensory and neural activity can malfunction and create many types of strange phenomena which feel real. That being said, if there is a god force or other intelligent energy forms we can't yet detect, it is possible they could try to communicate in some way. So while I deem it improbable, I don't rule it out completely. Each event would need to be thoroughly investigated." Chip pushed up his glasses, adding to the large smear on his lens.

"That makes sense. Thank you." His views were oddly satisfying.

Chip gave a small bow. "At your service," he said.

I stood by awkwardly for a moment. "I'm going to be leaving," I said.

Chip stopped plucking and flipped his shiny hair back out of his eyes to look at my face, though briefly. "I assume you are not referring to exiting the store."

"I am not."

"Where will you be going?" he asked. I heard the faint pinging of the stretched rubber as he resumed plucking. I wondered if it was some sort of tick.

"Home."

"Back to Massachusetts."

"Yes."

"Your announcement doesn't come as a surprise. You're without a job, and something's always been off about why you were here at all."

I nodded, not bothering to try and hide that he was right. "All true."

"I have enjoyed our friendship, and I suppose I will miss you."

"I've enjoyed it too," I said, watching as he pulled his latest textbook out from beneath the counter.

"How soon will this come to pass?" he asked.

"As soon as I get the gas tank filled."

Chip nodded, and looked down at his book.

"If you ever come to New England, be sure to look me up. Here's my number and address." I slid a scrap of paper across the counter toward him.

"I don't really travel."

"Well, you never know. That could change."

"It's very unlikely to change."

"Still. Put my info in your phone, just in case. You *do* have a phone, don't you?"

"Of course."

"Good. Then do it." Chip sighed and pulled out his phone to comply. I didn't think it would make a difference. It was super unlikely he'd ever show up, but I'd grown to care for the guy. He was the one good thing about the place, and he was kind of like the big goofy brother I never had. My throat swelled as I thought about it. I cleared it before speaking again. "Thanks for everything," I said.

"There is exceedingly little to thank me for."

"You've been my only real friend here. Plus, you vouched for me with Allister."

"I take it you enjoyed the marijuana?"

"Not as much as I expected."

"Your information has been added to my contact list," he said, slipping the phone back into his rear pocket. "As instructed."

"I know how to reach *you*, of course," I said. "I can just call here."

He tipped his head in acknowledgement, then pushed his glasses up. "Indeed."

"Do you hug?" I asked, extending my arms.

Chip sighed again, but came around to where I stood. I put my arms around him, my head resting a little lower than his heart. I could hear it beating against my temple. His hands moved up to my back, and the right one patted me the way you'd soothe a crying toddler if you didn't know how to soothe a crying toddler. He was really bad at this. I released him to let him off the hook.

"Okay then. Guess I'm off."

"Fare thee well." He went back behind the counter, sat down on his stool, and picked up his book again. "Be careful on 55 north of the city. It's under construction."

"Good to know," I said, and walked to the door. "Bye." Chip raised a hand in response, but his eyes were glued to the pages in front of him.

I drove away from the place which had been my home for nearly a year, feeling excited and sad. I wondered if emotion rumbled behind Chip's smooth façade, and if not, I was sort of jealous. Chip's life wasn't conventional given how his brain worked, but if he really was as reason-based as he acted, and so little influenced by emotion, how much less painful would life be? Or was all the emotion still there, just hidden, like the rivers which ran underground throughout Missouri, rushing through caverns and taking centuries to carve out paths through rock? My own emotion was right on top, a desert creek bed that raged in the aftermath of the storm of Char's murder. It was all right there, visible and dangerous, ready to take out anyone or anything that got in its path. I knew I needed to work on that, though I wasn't sure how.

In the meantime, I was heading home. Just one night in a hotel somewhere around Cleveland, and I'd be home.

Chapter 64

I didn't tell Maria I was back, instead, I just showed up at Good Good's the day after I arrived. She was sitting at her usual spot behind the counter, a position I understood better after months manning the stool at what *had* been the Wild West Wax Museum. "Benvenuto," she called, without looking up. "Please let me know if you need assisting."

"I quite definitely need assisting," I replied.

Maria's head whipped up and her eyes grew large and round behind her thick lenses. She pushed off the counter to a stand, and rushed around to greet me in her odd, rolling gait. Her plump arms wrapped tight, pulling me into a cloud of warmth and the scent of cinnamon. "Madelaina!" she said. "Grazie Dio, you came back! I knew you were coming, but I did not know the little bundle of miracle would arrive today!"

"I did come back," I said, staying right where I was in the warm pudding of her arms. "What have you been cooking? You smell delicious."

"What have I been cooking, she asks, like this is a nothing when she walks in the door after months of lunaticking." She pushed me back and examined my face closely. "I was in the mood to make something spicy and sweet, so there are cookies. If you are lucky, I may offer you one." Maria pulled me in again.

"I'm sorry I worried you," I said. Hugging her was like a little bit of heaven.

"Worried is an understating. You have been up to things you should never be up to. I've been sick from all the stress you caused me. I could barely eat."

I pulled away this time, looking her up and down to assess the claim. She was as perfectly padded as she'd been before I left. "You don't look like you've been on a hunger strike."

She waved a hand to dismiss me. "Come. Make a full confessione and I will absolve you with a taste of the biscotti." She wobbled her way toward the workroom door. I followed and sat watching while she poured coffee and set out a battered tin. "Tell me all the things. What have you done, and will you get in trouble?"

Maria's strong coffee and delicious cookies acted as a truth serum, and I decided to tell her what happened. She listened closely while I talked, and weirdly, never looked shocked.

"I avenged Char sort of, by doing away with that horrible place, which obviously wasn't a very nice thing to do. And now I feel guilty about Sarah, and guilty about burning the place down, though not very much, and it's still a struggle not to feel guilty about leaving Char to face her death alone."

"We discussed this thing already."

"We did. And I'm trying. But it's a lot."

Maria was silent for a moment. "Do you know the story of St. Paulo?" she asked.

"Paul from the Bible? The one who got knocked off the horse and wrote all the letters?"

"Sì. Poor Paulo. He thought his job was to collect all the worshipers of this crazy Gesù and put them to death so they could not go on telling stories and making new discepoli. He thought this was his mission, his important task. You understand this feeling, no?"

"I do."

"Well, God spoke to him and told him to stop torturing him. Paulo went to the desert to think and pray and be with God, and then he became the hero who created new believers in cities all around."

"Right?" I said, tipping the end of the word up like a question because I wasn't following what she was trying to tell me.

"Paulo became a great saint, a hero. But do not think he forgot all he'd done. The people who were killed with stones filled his memories and his dreams."

I thought about the things which filled my memories. "I'll bet they did," I said.

"You still must work on letting go of your guilt about your Shimmy's trip to Missouri. But you've added on some wrong things which were intenzionale."

"I sure did."

"There is no undoing in life. There is no shrugging away. Not everything can be fixed. Sometimes we must simply exist with guilt and regret, and learn to be happy even with them there, pooping on your shoulder."

I knew I'd never stop regretting not going with Char. Life without her was a hair shirt of loneliness. My actions in Missouri felt embarrassing the way a decades-old photo of a bad fashion moment was embarrassing, though a lot worse. But she was right. I was just going to have to exist with both. I took a deep breath and let it out again. "Okay," I said. My tummy was full and my heart was warm with gratitude at simply being in Maria's presence, the sensation a luxury I hadn't been certain I'd ever enjoy again. "I will learn to coexist."

"Bene," she said. "One more biscotto before I put these away?"

"I'm stuffed. But thank you."

"I knew I was making these for a reason, but who could have guessed the reason would be you. You take these home," she said, thrusting the tin toward me. "I have more upstairs."

"Thank you," I said, knowing she'd win any argument I offered. "I sure missed you."

"And I missed you, cara mia," she said. "Now I must get back to work. You think I have all day to sit around getting sentimotional?"

I left, smiling and feeling better than I had in months. Years really. Since before Char died.

Chapter 65

Clyde's fur was silky and warm from the sun puddle he was lying in when I arrived at Good Goods. "He is like me. Glad you have returned to us," Maria called by way of greeting.

"I'm glad too."

"My osso bucco will be ready in twenty minutes. You must share it with me."

"I'd love that. It smells fantastic." The rich scent of meat and tomatoes made my stomach growl. "I'm also here to shop," I said, making my way to the corner of the store where Maria clustered religious items, and began selecting crucifixes.

"This batch is so delizioso you may find yourself fainting from pleasure," she said. "Clyde suggested that it needed herbs, but that is not how my madre made it, and I am not going to change things for a bossy cat."

I giggled. "Did he suggest catnip?"

"Origano. Which is proof he knows nothing. Origano is too aggressive for veal. He has more opinions than common senses."

"I'm glad he isn't the one cooking." I selected a total of five crucifixes, and carried them to the jewelry counter. I wanted to find a few rosaries, but the sacramentals weren't the only reason I'd come to the store. "I need to talk to you about something," I said.

"Do not tell me you are going away on some new mad hat journey. You've only been home two weeks."

"No, I'm staying put. It's this dream I keep having." The memory of the nightmare which had come again pushed at my heart and made it pound. I ignored it as best I could and explained to Maria how it went from beauty to horror. I left out the part about my orgasm. "It's so awful, and I don't know what to do about it," I concluded. "Is there a way to make them stop?"

Maria's face was somber as she listened which was in itself comforting. "We cannot control our dreams, though you should try praying for protection over your mind before you sleep," she said. I'd known deep down there wasn't anything she could do to make the dreams go away, but still felt disappointed. "You may not be able to make them stop. But you can control what happens afterward," Maria said. "Each time, as soon as you wake up, remember her as she really is."

"Was."

"*Is,* Maddie. She still *is,* and she is whole again."

I wanted to believe her, and there'd certainly been enough of the miraculous to make me lean toward optimism. "You think that when we die, we somehow remain… ourselves?"

"Of course! You will be you and I will be me, but I will be me much sooner than you. And I will greet your Char Shimmy and hug her and we will come and watch over you and pray together until you come to join us."

The image made me smile. "Char would *love* you."

"How can she not love this?" Maria pulled herself into a regal stance, and swept her hand from above her head down the length of her body, like a matador preening before a crowd.

"You *are* irresistible," I admitted. "And if the energy that made up her matter is somehow still hanging together, I'm sure she does."

"It is not just what she mattered, my little Madelaina, it is also her spirit. Her soul. It's her whole persona. She is still the same persona," Maria said. "She is more whole, even, then when she was walking around with you here in Merrivliet, or talking to us on the television."

"More whole?"

"Si. More of all the things which make her beautiful and kind and smart and made of fire like you told me. Much more your Char Shimmy than you even knew."

I tried to imagine an intensified Shimmy, but she was so saturated with depth and beauty already that it was hard.

"Are you envisioning this Char, Maggita?"

"I'm trying."

"That is what you do. Each time you have that disgustoso memory. You think of her as she is *now*. So beautiful and shining with love for you."

The image of Char from the dream and the morgue tried to come back, but I did as I was told. I focused on the Shimmy smiling up at me from a tub filled with bubbles, her inner glow beaming and happy, gesturing for me to climb in and sliding sideways to make room. The warmth of her eyes as she yawned thank you for bringing her coffee in bed. The twinkle I saw each time she signed off from her newscast, twinkling out just for me, carried magically across the airwaves, and now, maybe, carried magically across time and space and the separation of physical matter.

I realized I'd been silent for a long time, and shook myself loose from the images. "Sorry about that," I said.

"Did you have a good visit with her?" Maria answered.

"I did. Thank you."

"It is always my pleasure, il mio Madelaina, to talk with you about any and all of the things. And most extra specially to talk with you about love."

I paid for my purchases, Maria closed the store, and we went upstairs to eat the gorgeous osso bucco.

Back home, it didn't take long to hang the crucifixes on the nails which were still in place from where Char's had been. The last one to go up was in the bathroom, and I knew she'd be happy knowing Jesus would once again watch over me as I sat on the toilet.

I spent the rest of the evening tucking this experience of Char away in my mind like a treasure to be taken out periodically and examined. Grateful to finally have a defense when haunting images were brought before me by the darkness.

Chapter 66

Char's demand that I create some sort of foundation with the money she'd left me still pissed me off. I considered starting some sort of anti-hate program to try and prevent trans people from being murdered, but Jackson killed Shimmy out of homophobia-fueled self-loathing. Each murderer had their own disgusting motives, and in order to do any kind of effective job I'd have to study hundreds of broken minds. I'd barely made it out of Char's death alive, and I didn't think I could handle probing the depths of all that sickness. It was too personal. Too painful. Too likely to drive me into darkness.

Instead, I launched the Charlotte Mitchell Scholarship Program for Transgender Students. Each award was made in the name of a person who'd been murdered in the US. Given the numbers of murder victims, the dollar amounts weren't jaw-dropping, but they made a difference to the students, and acted as a way to immortalize lost loved ones for families and friends. There was a ton of other work that needed to be done to help stop the ignorance and hate from propagating, but the scholarship was what I could offer without destroying myself. That had to be enough.

Meanwhile, there was Jackson to deal with.

While I'd spent significant amounts of time fantasizing about writing him a detailed account of Sarah's moles and the sounds she made when she climaxed, I realized I wasn't going to actually do it. I didn't want Sarah to have to deal with the blowback. Regardless of how much I still wanted to hurt him, it wasn't Sarah's fault.

Maria's relentless optimism and focus on the otherworldly inspired me to something more useful. I ordered a whole bunch of books on sexuality, gender, and Christian inclusion of LGBTQI+ people. I also ordered a bunch of Mamma Schiavona prayer cards. When the whole batch came, I created a schedule. Each month one of the books would be mailed to Christopher, with a prayer card tucked inside.

I never found out what happened to the books; whether he read them or threw them away. But the packages weren't returned, and it was comforting to think they were making a difference just by being sent out into the world as a gesture of belief that the arc of the moral universe bends toward justice.

Chapter 67

The lock of hair was the same size Char's grandmother's had been. I'd used the memory of Nokmes' silver strands as a model when I cut the section from above Shimmy's shoulder once they'd sent her remains home from Missouri. The slip of hair had waited in an envelope in my bedside table ever since.

Now it was assembled with the other items I'd collected on the kitchen table where Char had worked, and I tried to follow the steps she'd performed, lifting my heart to hers and to all the people who'd created sacred bundles throughout the centuries.

Char had cut a rectangle of fabric from Nokmes' well-worn flannel nightgown. I hated desecrating Shimmy's satin robe, but we slept naked so the few nightgowns she owned had no real connection to her. The robe was the nearest approximation. I cut a section from the bottom and spread the rectangle on the table, assessing the collection of jars behind it. Jars of blood-soaked wood shavings, and hairbrush cleanings. They were too big to fit in the bundle, so I transferred some of the contents into the jewelry pouches I'd gotten from Good Goods for the purpose. Other objects followed. An old tube of mascara. A set of interview notes from a news story she'd prepped a few weeks before her murder. A flask of perfume. Her press badge. The rosary hanging from the lamp on her bedside table. The certificate ordaining her name change. A string-tied bunch of sage I'd purchased from a Potawatomi shop online.

I talked to Shimmy as I did all of it, thanking her for being the person she'd been, for letting me share her life, for making me feel like I was so much more than reality demonstrated. I thanked her, and I cried, though not as much as I'd expected.

The last item to go in was the Mamma Schiavona card from my pocket. It bore white creases and worn spots from having spent so much time against my hip. I'd debated about whether to include it in the bundle, and knew I'd miss its presence. But the saint was so central to the whole story, to Char's story and Jackson's and mine, that I knew the card needed to go in.

I rolled the bundle up the way Char had, then tied it shut with her favorite scarf. Nokmes' bundle had looked worn and comfortable, a reflection of the woman it represented. Shimmy's was glamorous and shining, just as she had been.

I placed it on top of my dresser, where I could see its image each night before I fell asleep, and each morning when I woke. At first it was kind of painful. But it got better.

Chapter 68

"We're going to have to do something about the smell," I said. I'd just finished hanging the final pinafore in a display wall full of aprons.

Lee looked over her shoulder at me, her shining copper ponytail swinging as she did. "Now we know what a century's worth of cooking smells like," she said with a wry smile. "Or it could just be me. I walk around smelling like onion rings and meatloaf when I get out of work." She turned back to continue organizing a shelf of cookbooks. It wasn't her, of course. She smelled like soap and sunshine.

"Maybe it's because there's so much kitchenalia packed into a small space? It never smells like this at Good Goods."

"No, it doesn't," Lee agreed. "Maria's store smells like a church that does catering." She'd captured perfectly the mixed scents of incense and delicious food which filled the junk shop.

"My place *is* a kind of church," Maria said. "People come to give things, and to get things. I pray for them and send them away, hopefully more happy than when in they came waltzing."

"You feed their souls. Just like you feed ours," Lee said.

"Speaking of which, are we ready for lunch? I'm starving," I said. "I made sandwiches. They won't be as good as Maria's, but they're edible."

I broke out the food and we munched as we looked around at our progress. The large room was divided into six sections, progressing from the 1920s to the 1970s. Each section was set up like a kitchen from the era, complete with appliances, a table set with linens, dishes and flatware, and shelves of the convenience gadgets of the day.

"Thanks for helping me get this stuff organized. It would take forever if I did it by myself." Sending Jackson the books on sexuality and gender felt good, and starting the foundation had been a requirement given Shimmy's wishes. But settling back into a house filled with old cookbooks made me realize there was something else I could do.

"I'm happy to help. It's fun," Lee said. Her face was open and pure in a way that was rare. I liked her a lot.

"I am happy also," Maria said. "You are right here where I can keep my eyeballs on you in case you get more big ideas about espadrilles."

When the space next to Good Goods had opened up, it seemed like a sign. It was the perfect location for my new mini museum, which I hoped would offer the sense of comfort and peace I got from reading vintage cookbooks. Being right next door to Maria meant we could spend coffee breaks together, and she could let me know when objects came in that I might want for the exhibits. It felt good to be close by, in case Maria ever needed a hand. "Do you mean escapades? Espadrilles are shoes," I said.

"Speaking of shoes, the ones you are wearing look like they are nothing but strings."

I looked down at my running shoes, and saw she had a point. But Maria had moved on by then. She balled up her napkin and rose from her chair with a groan. "I must get back to my shop," she said. "Clyde will be grumpity, and some new things came in which must be blessed." Lee helped her slip into her coat. "We should make a hole in this wall, so we don't have to walk outside and back in again," Maria said.

"That's brilliant! Let's do it," I replied.

Lee and I worked for a few more hours, stopped in to say good night to Maria, and went our separate ways.

In the months which followed, I puttered among the displays, swapping out objects, dusting, and rearranging books in the cookbook store which functioned as the museum's gift shop. I loved sending each visitor off with the feeling that they'd stepped back in time and returned with a little bit of something simpler and purer, even if life in the past wasn't really any of those things. I loved that the nostalgia my museum delivered was built on warmth, love, and family rather than violence and revenge. I grew to love my new life even though Char was no longer in it.

And I never once pretended I was blind.

Chapter 69

Maria pulled to the curb at the departure gates and dropped me off. "Madelaina," she said, after hoisting herself out to hug me, despite my protests that she didn't need to, "I am so proud of you." Her eyes were warm and teary through the magnification of her lenses. "I know you can do this thing. The strength, it is there."

"And the Valium is too," I joked, my throat closing in response to her encouragement. Her face turned disapproving. "Just kidding," I said. "I believe I can do it. I have to, really." Making the trip wouldn't change the reality that I hadn't been able to fly with Char, but it was something. It felt necessary. I pulled out the handle of my suitcase.

"My prayers, they travel with you. And my love. Vai con Dio, little one." I nodded and turned away, needing to step out of the emotion and move into what needed to be done.

I made it through security, and then to the gate, where I popped my second Valium in an attempt to ward off the panic which threatened. Noise cancelling headphones, an audio book, and closed eyes kept me from freaking out until it was time to board. *This is for Char, this is for Char, this is for Char* ran through my head as I trembled my way through the tunnel to the plane. But I made it.

The rest was easy. Once we were up in the air I was trapped, which weirdly, made me relax. I knew I'd have to go through the whole ordeal again on my way home, but that could be faced when the day came. We landed in Naples, where I stopped for the night to prepare for my pilgrimage, getting my first taste of Italy.

I made it to Mama Schiavona's shrine on third anniversary of Char's death. The church was perched on the side of a mountain, and the air was clear and cold on the steep funicular ride to reach it, which somehow didn't terrify me. A group of the femminiello Maria had described so long ago accompanied me on the ride, their mood alternately festive and somber as they traveled to honor the Transgender Day of Remembrance. I understood the conflicting feelings. The trip up the mountain was simultaneously terrifying and joy generating, and none of us seemed to know what to do with our emotion. We tumbled out at the culmination of the climb, and I made my way to the main entrance.

The place was much larger than I'd envisioned, like a small city, and the church itself was a basilica built over the remains of a previous sanctuary on the grounds of an ancient goddess's temple. The ceiling soared overhead, held up by tapering columns and panels of paintings and mosaic work which reminded me of the open chapel in Missouri. The space was silent except for the hushed sounds of those gathered to pay homage or remember, and the air smelled faintly of incense with a touch of honey from the beeswax candles.

I wondered if I should find a caretaker priest and warn him about wax worms.

Mama's Schiavona's icon towered behind the altar, the position commanding attention from all who entered. She and the child were less gloriously arrayed than they had been in the Missouri shrine. Their crowns were simplified, and the position of the lady's head and hand were slightly different, tipped more toward the child. But her gaze was just as steady, just as filled with peace and subtle sorrow.

I made my way to the front, and stood beneath her, this mother of Jesus known as the slave because of her black skin, mother of those whose gender doesn't match up to society's expectations. She gazed out into the sanctuary filled with people gathered to mourn and hope for change, and she looked down at me, her eyes able to do both, to capture both, to uphold us all. I fell to my knees at the ornate rail and prayed to the God she mothered, who Maria worshipped, and who Char believed in.

I didn't know where the prayers went but I could feel them joining with the prayers of all those gathered there with me, and all those who'd come throughout the centuries.

I cried with sorrow intermixed with a strange joy which I could not understand, and as I looked up at her face, full of stillness and peace, it looked like she was bending toward me. The color of her skin shifted, darkened, the lips filling in and widening, the eyes growing and changing from placidity to warmth and love, transforming into Shimmy's eyes, and it looked as if her hand was extending to me, reaching toward me, reaching to cup my cheek the way Char did when she needed to tell me something important, like that she loved me or that I needed to write my parents a letter. I closed my eyes and could almost feel her touch on my skin, if perhaps I tried harder, or leaned against it. My heart pounded with a fierce and particular joy, and with sorrow, and with gratitude, and I stayed there until my knees started to shriek and I could no longer sense her presence.

When I opened my eyes, the icon looked as she had when I got there. Calm, placid, small-mouthed and long-nosed, with her thin fingers extending toward Jesus.

I wiped my eyes on my sleeve, feeling stupid for not having thought to bring tissues or a hanky like the ones Maria kept tucked in her bra.

There was one last thing to do.

The pint canning jar containing Jesse's eyeballs had made it safe on the trip, wrapped carefully in a tee shirt and then rolled in a pair of pants. I pulled them out of my backpack to take a final look. If Jesse had had a penis, I probably would have taken that too, but of course he didn't. Maybe if there *had* been a penis, I would have left it out of some last shred of respect, so it would be consumed by fire with the rest of him, all at once, all together. Maybe I would have been big enough to do that.

The basilica map showed a hall of blessings, where people could leave behind objects to offer thanks to the Madonna. I made my way to that room and was happy to find myself alone. Looking around I saw photos, lockets engraved with names, and even a lock of black hair, which made me feel at one with the person who'd left it. I'd somehow pictured the place as being hewn out of rock, the way the Missouri shrine had been, full of nooks and crannies into which I could tuck the eyeballs where they'd remain down the centuries unless some other thief took them, carrying on the tradition of me and the person who stole Jesus' foreskin from beneath the priest's bed. But it wasn't like that. It was too clean, too tidy. Too public. It was nothing like I'd imagined, but I'd come here with a purpose, and I wasn't about to take the relics back home with me.

I found a place for the jar, hidden from sight because I didn't want to freak people out, or scare children, or anything like that. There was a good chance some Italian version of Uncle Frank would come along and dispose of them, thinking they didn't belong in this sacred space. But that wouldn't be my problem. My task was to bring them to Mama Schiavona and leave them there. It was a final act of relinquishment and closure, a final goodbye to the idea of vengeance.

So that's what I did.

I left the basilica feeling lighter than I had in years, resolved to walk back down that mountain, following the path of the pilgrims who'd trod there for centuries, many barefoot. I took off my threadbare sneakers so I could merge with them further. But it didn't last long. The ground was rough and frozen, and I realized I didn't need to punish myself.

I'd suffered enough.

Acknowledgments

Novels are intricate webs of words woven from strands contributed by many people in multiple ways. It's hard to remember every individual who played a role in getting *The Language of Bodies* into your hands, but this is a start:

To the Newburyport Writers Group and Pen Friends critique group. Thank you for showing me the power and importance of writing communities.

To Dori Hale; long-time friend, first recipient of our coming-out story, and sophisticated early reader. Thank you for seeing past the awkward clunk of my previous draft novels and encouraging me to keep going.

To Brittney Bender, Joshua Nelson, and Kiera Topping. Thank you for in-depth storyline discussion while hanging out in a log cabin in Western New York. And for being super-cool, super-smart humans. We love you.

To the Strachan Literary Agency, and Woodhall Press. Thank you for believing in the power of this odd, dark story.

To C.B. Bernard. Thank you for introductions, pep talks, and score trading. It was good to share the suffering and joy with someone who traveled in parallel.

To the transgender community. Thank you for showing the world that gender can and should be something other than what we're programmed to believe. Your bravery is astonishing. Your spirits are magnificent. Your lives are worthy of celebration. I see you, honor you, and stand by you. Always.

To Ally Steinfeld, a young transwoman from Missouri whose gruesome murder was the catalyst for this story, and to all the trans people who suffer violence at the hands of those who can't or won't understand. In the words of Charlotte Mitchell: rest in power, children of God; now that you are free to be.

Lastly, to my beloved Declan, without whom this novel would never have existed. Thank you for…everything. You believed in me before I did. You wept your way through early iterations of the tale, offered feedback which made it better, shared the highs and lows of the publishing process, and held my heart through every phase. My love for you, and yours for me, were inspiration for Maddie's passion. I wish every writer had a Declan in their life. You are the very pulse of mine.

About the Author

Suzanne DeWitt Hall is the author of *Reaching for Hope: Strategies and Support for the Partners of Transgender People,* the acclaimed *Where True Love Is* series, and the *Rumplepimple* adventures. She is mildly obsessed with vintage cookbooks and the intersection of sexuality and theology. Her work is designed to shine the light of love into hearts darkened by discrimination and fear. Learn more at: www.sdewitthall.com